The Social Media Bride

KRISTI ELLIOT

CHAMPAGNE BOOK GROUP

The Social Media Bride

Published by Champagne Book Group
2373 NE Evergreen Avenue, Albany OR 97321 U.S.A.

~ ~ ~

First Edition 2021

pISBN: 978-1-77155-412-1

Cover Art by Robyn Hart

www.champagnebooks.com

Version_1

For Stephanie and Cindi

Chapter One

Nervousness and excitement thrummed through Kate Miller's chest. In less than an hour, she'd recite her vows and take her first steps as a newlywed with Matt.

She squirmed in the lobby, too jittery and impatient to sit. Her shoes lay abandoned near her chair, one resting on its side while the other remained upright on its three-inch heel. Pacing, she studied the pink acrylic nails her sister had talked her into getting yesterday. Was that a chip on her ring finger?

Deep breath. It's your wedding day. Everything will be fine. It has to be.

A giggle drew her attention to the doors leading to the nave of the church. Three bridesmaids—two cousins and her sister, Maddie, didn't appear nearly as nervous as they huddled together in whispers and squeals. Why would they? They weren't the ones praying for everything to go without a hitch. All they had to do was stand at the altar and be pretty.

Maddie stopped mid-sentence and met Kate's gaze with familiar disapproval. It was no secret she distrusted Matt, something that had soured the wedding preparations on and off, but Kate was determined not to let her sister's opinion ruin her wedding.

"Can you help with my veil?" she asked in a honeyed tone, not wanting to bring more attention to their ongoing feud.

With a tight smile at the bridesmaids, Maddie excused herself and ambled to Kate's side. "What's on your mind?"

"Nothing," she said, smoothing an invisible wrinkle in her dress. "Restless, I guess. Is my veil straight?"

Maddie's chocolate gaze softened a fraction as she adjusted the lace in front of Kate's face. "You look wonderful."

She sighed, and Kate heard a hint of doubt. She wanted to join in with a loud groan.

"But?" she asked.

Maddie wrinkled her nose and glanced over her shoulder before dropping her voice to a whisper. "I can't help wondering if this is a good idea. Are you sure you're making the right decision? It's not too late to call off the wedding."

It was shocking for a woman who flirted with nearly every man in sight to see her treat Matt with such disdain. It was a wonder she had ever agreed to be the Maid of Honor and shown up this morning with a smile on her face.

Kate worried her real mistake was allowing her family to be so involved. Between Mom's overbearing nature in managing the wedding preparations and Maddie making one barb after another, Kate was emotionally and mentally exhausted.

She hoped this wasn't an omen of bad luck.

Forcing herself to remain calm, she said, "Yes, Maddie. We've discussed this a million times, and I'm not changing my mind at the last second. I'm marrying Matt."

"He's too smooth." Maddie waved her arms with enough force one of her bracelets flew off her wrist. "He talks like a sleazy car salesman. Seriously, it's not too late to run."

Kate pinched the bridge of her nose and counted to five. This day was not going to become her personal version of *The Runaway Bride.*

"Fine," Maddie muttered, snatching her bracelet and lifting her skirts like a Disney Princess.

She joined the other bridesmaids. They smoothed their skirts and fluffed their hair, rolling back their shoulders as Mom prepared to start the procession.

She locked gazes with Kate and smiled, perhaps for the first time in her adult life. "I'm proud of you," she mouthed.

Kate acknowledged her mom with a jerky bob before retrieving her shoes. She probably should have returned the gesture or said something, but she didn't like formal processions and being in the spotlight.

The best part would come later when she and Matt made their exit from the party and began the next chapter of their lives in the privacy of their ship cabin off the coast of Cuba.

The door opened, and music filtered in, signaling the start of the wedding. The women filed through, beginning with Mom and ending with Maddie.

Watching her go, Kate took in her sister's dress. Maddie had insisted on a vintage pink form-fitting bodice with too much cleavage threatening to escape. Nobody chastised her for it, nor did they mention a bridesmaid should never tower above the bride.

Her pink stilettos were another reminder of how Kate was forced to wear heels too high for comfort. She prayed she wouldn't trip over her feet. The notion of wearing these torture devices for the duration of her wedding and reception made her shudder.

Clutching her flowers close, Kate took a deep, cleansing breath, releasing it to a beat of eight.

Happy thoughts.

She was getting married, surrounded by family and friends. The service was held in a church filled with pearls, pink curtains, and flowers covering every inch of the building. Her mother had spared no expense for the daughter she believed would never find a man after hitting thirty.

Instead of being Kate Miller, the perpetual bachelorette and Plain Jane, she would become Mrs. Lawson, joined with her lifelong partner.

The wedding march began, prompting everyone to stand and admire all her bridal glory. Matt waited at the end of the aisle beneath an arch swallowed by ivy, more flowers, and pink tulle. When his gaze landed on her, his smile widened like the prince in a fairytale.

Her lips curved upward in return. Jordon, the best man, along with groomsmen and waiting bridesmaids, faded away. Kate couldn't ask for a more perfect setting.

Her father appeared by her side and tucked her arm into the crook of his elbow, observing her with glowing eyes and pink cheeks. For the first time in years, his hair didn't seem as gray, and there was no stress lining his brow. It was as if he was in his early fifties instead of his sixties. His chest puffed out, and he held on until her arm went numb. The excitement radiated from him in waves, and Kate would have sworn *he* was the one getting married instead of her.

"Are you nervous?" he asked.

Bouncing on her toes, she shook her head. "Nope."

"That's my girl."

Gripping his arm more for balance than the need to skip across the aisle, she paced in rhythm to the melody. With each step forward, her heart raced faster until she felt like it would explode. Her feet screamed every time the shoes pressed into her arches, but she tried to ignore the pain.

On her way to the altar, she resisted the urge to scratch the bobby pins stabbing her scalp. If she touched it now, she'd ruin hours of hairspray and flowers that went into the masterpiece. She could be uncomfortable for a day if it meant spending her life with the man of her dreams.

Thirty feet left—so far, so good. Twenty—a slight stumble. No big deal. Ten—she thanked the gods for her good fortune at making it across the room in one piece.

Stopping before the altar, Kate faced her father, where he lifted the veil and planted a kiss on her cheek. Unshed tears brimmed in his eyes, and his jaw twitched. He lingered for a moment, seemingly unwilling to let her go.

"I love you," he whispered. "Make sure he treats you well."

She squeezed him again, the same way she did when she was a little girl. In a way, this marked the last severance to childhood, leaving the nest for good, no longer dependent on her parents. It was scary yet thrilling.

Swiping her cheeks to ensure she wasn't crying, she watched him take his place in the front. Mom sat next to him, dabbing at her tears with a frilly handkerchief.

Passing her flowers to Maddie, Kate took her fiancé's hands into hers, admiring his sharp gray suit. Despite the pink cummerbund and tie, he made it work.

She wiggled in excitement with a squeak, shaking her limbs until Matt laughed. He'd always called her nervous energy adorable, often one-upping her antics until they drove her mother insane. With him, there was no need to conceal her quirks. Kate was free to be herself.

Inhaling slowly through her nose, she ignored the butterflies in her stomach as they faced the pastor. He fixed them with crinkled eyes and upcurved lips beneath a salt-flecked beard.

"Dearly beloved," he began. "We are gathered here today—"

"I object." Jordon's words echoed through the church like a cannon signaling battle.

His gaze dropped to his feet as a collective gasp filled the space. He shifted and curled his fists at his sides, and his chest heaved under the weight of everyone's stare.

Kate steadied herself, dropping Matt's hands as shock surged through her body. There were rules about weddings. The biggest being, never *ever* object or interrupt the ceremony.

"I'm sorry?" she breathed.

Red colored his cheeks as he bit his lip. In an uneven voice, he repeated, "I object."

"Okay…I heard you the first time, but why?"

With dozens of guests leaning forward to catch the exchange, Kate's head swam. This was worse than that dream of going to a presentation in her underwear.

Matt tugged at the collar of his shirt, swallowing hard before wordlessly lifting his head.

She wanted to punch him. He always refused to blink when he was feeling guilty about something or preparing to lie. She looked past him to Jordon, waiting for his response.

He cleared his throat, still refusing to meet her eyes. "You can't go through with this." The words tumbled from his mouth in a rush. Then he hesitated a beat before blurting out the rest. "Matt slept with someone at the bachelor party."

It was like he'd kicked her in the ribs, and she wobbled on her feet. "Is this true?"

Matt glared at Jordon with betrayal flashing over his face.

Kate yanked the lapels of Matt's suit when he clamped his mouth shut and tried to retreat. "Who was she?" she demanded in a shuddering whisper.

Pursing his lips, he took a step back, trying to break free.

Her temper reaching a boiling point, she slapped him with a loud, ringing crack. Someone in the crowd whooped, a man laughed, and women murmured to each other.

Blood pounded through her ears. This was probably the best entertainment they'd witnessed all year. The only thing missing was popcorn.

Who?" she insisted again, wiping tears from her blurring vision.

"Does it matter?" Matt asked in a small voice, rubbing his swelling cheek. "It was a bachelor party, and I had a lot to drink. I made a mistake."

"Oh, so your penis accidentally slipped into another woman's vagina?" The audience gasped, and the pastor cleared his throat. Kate whirled on the crowd and snarled, "Oh, grow up!"

Several of the guests lifted their phones, recording the spectacle. Others wore expressions ranging between mortification and horror. Her friend and boss, Carlos, grimaced and covered his face. A few of her friends and colleagues stared with gaping mouths as if unable to tear their gazes away from the train wreck before them.

What had promised to be the happiest day of her life was morphing into her worst nightmare.

The walls of the church closed around her. The pressure inside her lungs constricted until she struggled to breathe. She needed an escape, a place to fall apart in peace without her family and friends hovering.

She moved to the stairs, but Matt grabbed her arm. "Kate, please," he begged. "We can talk about this. I swear I'd never jeopardize our marriage."

She jerked her arm out of his grasp and shoved him backward. He lost his footing and fell onto the pastor, sending them both crashing into the podium. The groomsmen rushed into the tangle of arms and legs to help the men to their feet as bridesmaids screamed.

The rational side of her wanted to apologize and help them, but she was beyond reason. Heat scorched her cheeks as people raised their phones higher and craned their necks as if to get a better view.

They could go to hell as far as she was concerned. After everything she put herself through to make this day work, something inside of her snapped.

"Oh, do you want a show?" she shrieked, snatching her bouquet off the floor.

As Matt stumbled to his knees, she whacked him with the flowers, sending them everywhere like feathers in a pillow fight. He raised his arm to block the attack as she wailed on him until only the stems remained.

She knew better; she really did, but her rage escalated until red clouded her sight. Reaching to remove her shoes and chuck them into the crowd, she tripped and faceplanted onto the steps, tearing the fabric with a loud rent.

As she picked herself up, her foot got caught in her skirts, separating the dress from the waist, exposing her bright red panties. Laughter erupted throughout the church. Kate gathered the torn bits of lace, trying to cover herself.

David, her older brother, jumped from his seat and ripped off his suit jacket. Covering her shoulders with it, he gathered her into his arms and guided her against the swarm of bridesmaids. Maddie and their mother joined them, forming a cocoon around her.

On their way through the nave, her dad yelled at the crowd, "For the love of God, put your devices away! What is wrong with you people!"

This would be the story of the decade. The one family laughed at every Thanksgiving and Christmas after too many drinks.

Ignoring the cacophony of shouts, crying, and laughter, she fled, burning in humiliation. She stopped by the dressing room long enough to swipe her white clutch before tearing away from everyone and sprinting out of the church with the speed of an Olympic runner.

People passing by on their morning walks stopped to gawk. Tires screeched, followed by the sound of metal crunching on metal in a fender-bender. Looking down, she noticed her brother's jacket was no longer wrapped around her. She was exposing everyone to her wardrobe malfunction.

So much for a clean exit.

Her family followed her outside, calling for her to wait. A limo sat parked across the sprawling lot, with the driver leaning against it as he smoked and talked on his phone. Before he could extinguish his cigarette, Kate pried the door open and slid into the back seat.

The driver jumped inside, sending tobacco and cheap cologne wafting into the back. Toggling the ignition, he glanced at her in the rearview mirror with a raised brow. "Miss?"

Tears flowing freely, she squeaked, "Just drive."

Chapter Two

A loud click rang through Kate's apartment when she bolted the door. She didn't bother flipping on the lights before sinking onto her couch.

The apartment was quiet and lonely without her cat, Dodger. He was at a kennel because she was supposed to be on her honeymoon in the tropics, sipping frilly drinks and making new memories with her husband.

How had today gone so wrong?

A sob escaped her throat, and tears trickled down her cheeks, splashing onto her torn dress. Now alone, she gave in to her emotions and bawled, trying to wash away the humiliation of the morning.

Soon, the onslaught of wedding guests arrived, ringing her doorbell with abandon. She stifled her wails and curled into a ball, refusing to acknowledge anyone. If she wrapped her arms around herself tight enough, she could almost believe the couch would swallow her.

Soon, banging followed the bell. Kate covered her ears and ignored it. Noise filtered through, prompting her to shove both of her accent pillows against her head and bury her face into the cushions.

She was suddenly thankful she hadn't given her parents a key. Everyone needed to get a clue and leave her the hell alone.

Five minutes became ten. After fifteen torturous minutes of unbearable banging and shouts, the noise subsided. Kate didn't dare move to peek through her window. Anyone could be waiting.

In the dark room, she stood and silently made her way into the bedroom, undressing without a care for her dress. In fact, she couldn't wait to burn what was left of the damn thing. It could be one of those special rituals brides went through after a failed wedding.

Padding into the bathroom, she started the shower, washing off her makeup and letting the water cleanse away the toils of her day. Long after the water turned cold, she remained completely numb.

Why couldn't she be a newlywed on her honeymoon, tanning on the deck of an extravagant ship and sipping frilly drinks with her husband? Why couldn't she have someone in her life who actually gave a shit?

She was a fool for believing in happiness. Maddie didn't seem to understand the meaning of commitment, and their parents hadn't taught them what a healthy union looked like; they hated each other.

All she could fathom for Mom and Dad's depressing continuation was that divorce was expensive, and her mother loved to put on a front. If anything, growing up around her parents' misery was reason enough for her never to get married.

However, after seeing her brother's successful marriage, Kate had hoped for the same.

She stepped out of the water and dried off. *Life isn't fair.* She would have to accept that she wasn't meant to find love. She'd be one of those clichéd, stereotypical science professors doomed to be a terminal bachelorette.

Wrapped in her towel, she crawled into bed and instantly fell asleep.

After what felt like a few minutes, her phone rang. She groped for it, checking the time and caller ID. Work. *What the hell?*

Why was her job calling her this early on a Saturday?

"Hello?" she answered through a loud yawn.

"It's Carlos. Do you have a minute?"

If her friend, head of the Geology department at ASU, called from a working number at this ungodly hour, something was wrong. Especially given he was at yesterday's disastrous wedding.

She groaned. "It's six-thirty in the morning! Call me back later." She rolled to her side, squishing the phone between her cheek and pillow.

"I know," he said in a serious tone, "but I need you to come in today. We need to discuss the video that was posted last night."

~ * ~

"Let me get this straight." Kate sat across from Carlos in his office, slumped in defeat. "You're firing me because someone posted a video of me from my wedding on YouTube? Something showing me having an honest reaction to my ex-fiancé being an unfaithful douchebag?"

He shifted in his chair and cleared his throat, clearly uncomfortable. Not that she blamed him. He probably had secondhand embarrassment from it all. God knows she would have if their positions had been reversed.

She hadn't known the video existed until he'd showed her.

Despite the fact she'd lashed out and dared everyone to enjoy the show, it never occurred to her someone would post it online.

Just thinking about it made her cringe. Although watching herself behave like a child was a million times worse.

The one time she abandoned her good-girl persona, someone had posted her tantrum for the world to see. In less than twenty-four hours, it had gone viral, and people laughed at her expense.

At first, she sat with her mouth gaping as it played. It was easy to see how it had gained popularity. Under normal circumstances, she'd find it funny too. However, this was happening to her and not some random stranger.

To top it off, the university was asking her to resign because of it, even though it would be forgotten when the next big scandal hit.

How had her life come to this in less than a day?

She let her gaze wander to Carlos's collection of rocks on display to her left. Every time she walked into his office, he added something new to his stand. They were either from class trips or his time in Mexico with family.

The man had been around the world while Kate confined herself to her classroom. Visiting his office was often like going on a field trip, but today it reminded her of her current troubles.

They'd worked closely together for five years. He'd been a senior professor when she'd been hired, and they'd spent countless hours having grading parties, debating research and theories, and ordering Mexican food from Filiberto's. They'd always been honest and shared every aspect of their professional lives together, and until now, neither had ever been in a position to deliver bad news to the other.

Carlos leaned forward and sighed, looking like he'd rather be anyone else. The corners of his eyes crinkled, and his forehead creased as he frowned. He reached for her hands across his desk and rubbed her knuckles with the pads of his thumbs.

Pencils and halved geodes sitting on neatly stacked papers almost tumbled off the surface when she tried to move away and curl into herself.

"Kate," he said, dropping formalities. "I can imagine how difficult this must be for you, but you have to understand my position. The moment the video went viral, calls flooded into the president's office. It doesn't matter that your career has been exemplary. People can be short-sighted when it comes to things like this. They don't know you like I do. All they saw was what you did, and that was enough for your character to come into question."

Kate could read between the lines. No one wanted the crazy

YouTube bride teaching and shaping their children's future. Never mind the parties, wild sex, and the pot smoked at the 'A,' the mountain right behind the college where students gathered for their daily debauchery.

Tears burned, and her nose twitched with the urge to sniffle. With a shaking breath, she said, "So, I have a justified tantrum and I get fired. You see people posting racist shit on Twitter and they're allowed to keep their jobs? How does that work?"

"If you're referring to the incident in California, there was a huge outpouring of hate and negative responses. However, that was a unique situation where the university was forced to keep the professor due to tenure. Which is something you don't have yet."

Kate rested her elbows on the desk, cradling her head. It didn't matter what she said. The president, Mr. Walsh, had hated her from the start because she was a woman in a man's field. This finally gave him an excuse to fire her without a discrimination lawsuit.

She had nobody to blame but herself.

"It's not fair," she mumbled.

Everyone from her mother to colleagues had told her never to cry in public. It was undignified. Yet, she was unable to stand strong as her life unraveled.

"I'm sorry. I tried to make him reconsider." Carlos probably meant to be consoling but talking made it worse. "He said if this is how you react when upset, there's no way to tell how you'll behave with challenging students. I know you aren't a loose cannon, he and everyone else don't. That's just the way of the internet. They see what's in the clip and make their judgments based on it."

His words pierced her to the core, freezing her as if he'd thrown a bucket of frigid water at her.

Kate needed to get the hell out of there and have her pity-party in private. She jumped to her feet, choking on her words. She cleared her throat twice before she could manage to say anything coherent. "I need to go. I have some errands I need to run."

"Wait."

She shook her head. "I'm not in the right frame of mind to deal with this. I need to be alone."

Carlos made his way around the desk, wrapping her in a tight hug. "I'm sorry this happened to you. As your friend, please call me if you need anything. You're strong, and I know you'll get through it."

That did it. His small act of kindness dissolved the dam she'd been repressing, and her heart shattered into a thousand more pieces as she sobbed. To the man's credit, he remained silent while she ugly cried into his shirt.

Kate wondered what it would have been like if he wasn't her boss and if he'd asked her on a date instead of Matt. Carlos was tall, athletic, and adorably nerdy. He wasn't much older than her, and he displayed the qualities a woman wanted in a man: hard-working, loyal, and empathetic.

Why couldn't Matt be like her friend? Why hadn't Carlos warned her away from him when the two met at last year's Christmas party? Unlike Maddie, Kate trusted him and would have respected his opinion enough to consider it.

Life's not fair, remember. Some people got lucky, and others struggled to survive.

When the tears finally stopped, she released him. She laughed nervously at the state of his clothes and gave him a frail smile. "Thanks."

He squeezed her shoulders. "Anytime."

The moment they parted, Kate ran to her car. There weren't many people on campus with it being summer, but she didn't want to risk sniveling in front of the few colleagues who weren't on vacation. Plus, Carlos hadn't been the sole co-worker at her wedding. Nearly the entire Geology department had witnessed her self-destruct. She didn't want anyone's sympathy or pity.

The moment she sat inside her vehicle, she slammed the door and slumped. She banged her hands against the steering wheel and wept, recalling the video. It was bad enough being humiliated at the altar, but in front of the whole world too was a new level of shame.

When she thought she could drive again, she wiped the tears from her face and stopped by Fry's Food and Drug Store on the way home. Her cupboards were bare because she was supposed to be on her honeymoon. Her freezer looked like Antarctica, empty and covered in blocks of ice. Unfortunately, she couldn't survive on ice cubes filled with germs and bacteria.

Now that she knew about the video, she felt eyes on her everywhere. A teenager with earbuds removed them when she walked inside the grocery market, staring with his head tilted to the side.

Ignoring him, she snatched anything she could heat in the microwave, along with a large tub of ice cream, before making her way to the self-checkout line.

The kid she'd seen lurking earlier hovered nearby, still watching her like a damn creep.

She glared at him. "Why do you keep staring at me?"

He blushed a bright red and cleared his throat, wrapping the wire from his earbuds around his fingers. "Um, sorry, you remind me of someone I saw in a video."

Oh, Lord. "Maybe you should do something more constructive with your time instead of harassing strangers," she said in a cold tone.

"Sorry," he muttered, hastily shuffling away.

Kate grabbed her bags and hurried to her car. This was the last thing she needed. Wasn't Phoenix supposed to give her anonymity? Who had time to gawk at a nobody?

When she pulled into her parking space, she reconsidered her last thought. A news van waited in front of her apartment with a crew outside, ready for an ambush.

At the sight of her car, they scrambled to her, blocking her path to the building. She smacked her head on the steering wheel with a loud groan. *Goddamnit.*

"Kate! What's it like having your disastrous wedding posted online?" called a reporter.

"Will you give us a statement? ASU isn't answering questions regarding your termination."

Oh my God, did people really ask this kind of shit?

Whatever happened to decency, of letting someone suffer privately? She didn't deserve this harassment.

She could already see this confrontation flashing across the evening news and media outlets. And for what? People got angry all the time. What made her special?

"Is the pastor okay?" a journalist shouted.

"Has anyone pressed charges?" called another.

Shit. She needed to apologize and check on the pastor.

She grabbed her things and pushed through the crowd, ducking beneath cameras and shoving microphones away from her face. She made it from the carport to her first-floor apartment. Once inside, she slammed the door and bolted the lock.

When she refused to answer, they banged on her window. She couldn't see how this crap was legal. This must be what it felt like to be a celebrity. Always followed and never given a moment's peace. She'd never considered their lives before hers spiraled out of control. Tinsel Town was Maddie's thing, but Kate suddenly empathized as the crew continued to harass her.

Resisting the urge to flip the media off through the window, she unlocked her phone and called the police.

The moment a squad car drove through the complex, the reporters scattered faster than roaches under a light. Once they left, Kate walked into her room and packed before realizing she had no destination.

As she considered places, she logged into Facebook to delete Matt. The sooner she erased him from her life, the better. When the page loaded, she paused, staring at the screen with a gaping mouth. At the top of the feed were pictures of the asshole on their fucking cruise.

While she was being hounded by local news crews, this bastard was on *their* honeymoon. Dozens of images showed him drinking and surrounded by smiling people. Beneath the caption were the hashtags #singlelife, #carribeancruise, and #summerlife, among others.

She forced herself not to hurl her computer across the room. Instead, she promptly deleted him.

More than anything, she wanted to leave Phoenix. What she needed was a hole in the ground or a deserted island. Anything was better than facing everyone she knew and having them mention yesterday's incident.

Every time she replayed the events, her chest tightened, and her stomach churned, forcing her to run to the bathroom. She needed time to think and pick up the pieces of her life.

She wasn't one to overindulge in drinking, placing her career first. She'd spent more nights sucking down coffee for research and grading than she ever did consuming alcohol. However, unable to function properly, she made yet another bad choice; to get drunk on a bottle of whiskey Matt left behind.

Running into the kitchen, she located a stool and stood on her toes, barely able to reach the liquor on the top shelf far above her head. When her fingers brushed the bottle, she stretched higher. It wobbled and fell into her grasp before it could shatter on the tiled floor.

She squealed in victory, twisting the cap and taking a mouthful of the burning liquid.

A quarter of the way through, her phone buzzed on the bed. Fumbling for it, she plopped onto the mattress and pressed accept. "Hi, Mom."

"Hey, sweetie. How are you holding up?"

"Terrible." Kate pressed her phone into her shoulder and gently massaged her temples.

Why was hard liquor so gross? She stared at the label, but the words refused to make sense. Whatever it was, it was cheap, settling into her stomach like a rock. And now, she had to deal with her mother too.

"I know the wedding was a tough blow, but it will get better. Maybe you'll feel different when you hear his side."

Kate sucked in a sharp breath. "Excuse me? You did *not* just defend him."

A sigh came across the receiver, signifying Mom was preparing a speech only a lawyer could deliver. "Unlike you, your father and I *listened* to what he had to say. I'm not saying I condone his behavior, but he was very upset. He's not the first person to be unfaithful, and he won't be the last. He wants to talk to you."

Blood rushed through her ears, and red clouded her vision. Several minutes of silence passed before she could speak. When she found her voice, it trembled with unconcealed rage. "You're out of line. Instead of taking his side, you should be supporting *me*."

"All I'm saying is the world isn't perfect. Your father and I have been married for nearly forty years. Do you think we haven't run into setbacks?"

With clenched fists, Kate swallowed a scathing remark. Her parents had been fighting for longer than she could remember, and she doubted anything changed after she left home. "A setback is blowing your money in Vegas. It doesn't involve cheating!"

"Honey—"

"Don't. His pants didn't accidentally slip down while he fell between some bitch's legs."

Saying the words made her wonder what the woman looked like and if she'd been worth it and most importantly if she was anyone Kate knew.

"Language," Mom huffed, then continued as if they were conversing about the weather, "Matt and his family are refunding half of the wedding costs. They're as mortified as we are, and they agree this can be resolved if you talk to him."

Of course, his family threw money at her. The Lawsons had almost as much money as her parents and were old friends. If anything went wrong, both families wrote a check and moved on.

Matt was the same way. He earned a decent wage from his accounting firm, and it had led him to indulge in a materialistic lifestyle, desiring fancy labels rather than quality.

"Not happening. Maybe you're the forgiving type, but I'm not. He went on the honeymoon *without* me. He's made no effort to contact me since yesterday, and he can fall off that damn boat for all I care. And before you go on, you should know the university fired me this morning."

Mom's voice rose half an octave. "What?"

"Oh, you know, someone uploaded a video of me going on a rampage at the wedding. The university said it didn't reflect well upon them."

"That's outrageous! You need to fight for your job. You need to—"

"File a lawsuit?" Kate finished for her. "Yeah, no thanks. That's what you would do. I don't need to be in the news as the Bridezilla who sued the university and caused more problems. Everyone is already going to think I can't control my temper. Besides, this is a right to work state, remember? The university doesn't need a reason to fire me."

"Yes, dear, but there are always loopholes."

That was where the two of them differed. Her mother was a lawyer and a fighter. She planted seeds of doubt in people's minds, arguing until the other party fell to their knees. Kate preferred to keep to herself and move on.

When she insisted on different wedding colors, Mom and Maddie disagreed, and she'd given in. When Carlos fired her, Kate accepted it without contesting it.

The truth was that she wasn't as strong as her mother.

Before the argument could continue, Kate said, "I need to leave."

"Why would you do that? I didn't teach you to run from your problems. And where would you go?"

"I don't know. Anywhere is better than here where people stare and news crews harass me. Don't you have a beach house in Florida somewhere I can go to?"

"I'm not letting you hide," Mom said firmly. "You need to be with your family and people who love you."

Kate burst into loud laughter. "You're joking, right? You told me to get back together with Matt, you won't let me lick my wounds quietly, and you want me to be around you guys? You know what happens when our family gets together. We're a fucking train wreck. No thank you."

It was a wonder her family didn't have a reality show or hadn't at least appeared on Doctor Phil. They'd be the laughingstock of America.

She hiccupped, eyeing the cheap whiskey.

"Are you drinking?" Mom's tone hardened. "That isn't healthy. We can help you."

"You don't get to tell me what's not healthy. You push everyone's buttons until they explode. Dad drinks himself numb, and Maddie and David both have to hide when you tell us how superior you are."

Her mother and sister would talk about the wedding disaster every chance they got. Mom would make herself the victim, asking anyone who'd listen where she'd gone wrong with her oldest daughter. Maddie would trill, "I told you so," and wear a smug expression that said she was right and Kate was wrong.

"Fine," her mother seethed. "But don't expect to travel on my dime. If you want to leave and make a fool of yourself, that's on you.

When you're ready to act like an adult, you have my number."

The call ended, and Kate stared at her phone. Mom was difficult at best, but she didn't hang up on people. She was too poised.

Tossing her cell onto the bed, Kate stared at the whiskey bottle clutched to her chest and set it aside too. She wouldn't admit it to her mom, but drinking was a bad idea.

She sank into her pillow and propped her computer on her lap. The thought of getting away for the summer was tempting. Pristine beaches flashed across the screen as she googled popular destinations. Anything with water would make her happy, whether she rented a cabin by a lake or woke to the sound of waves washing over a coastal shore.

During her last trip to Seattle with Matt, they'd gone to various lakes where she spent hours watching the surface ripple across the smooth rocks. Then she'd dipped her feet into the water and examined the stones, determining their composition and age as Matt fished.

Back then, it hadn't bothered her. He had his hobbies, and she had hers. When finished, they had dinner at the Space Needle. It never occurred to her they were horribly mismatched. Perhaps Matt hadn't ever been happy, and his cheating was his way of coping.

Dwelling on the what-ifs wouldn't help. Their relationship was destroyed, and there was no returning to the illusion they'd maintained. She needed to accept it and carry on alone.

With no job and barely enough savings to last a few months, she wasn't going anywhere. Not to mention, she couldn't afford another hefty boarding fee for Dodger.

Crap. She needed to get her cat from the kennel.

Sighing, she had to accept that Matt would have his fun. Meanwhile, she was stuck at home, trying to find a way to bounce back while living on microwave meals and ramen.

Staring at her phone, she chewed her lip, building the courage to text David. She would have asked Mom but had forgotten about Dodger until now.

'*Can you please pick up my cat from the daycare? I lost my job this morning, and I don't know if I can afford the fees and have money left over to cover my other bills. I promise to pay you back.*' She hit send.

A few seconds later, her brother answered. '*I'm sorry about your job. Don't worry about your cat. I'll get him first thing in the morning.*'

'*You're the best.*'

'*Yeah, yeah,*' he replied. '*Take care of yourself and don't worry about the money. Love you, sis.*'

'*Love you too.*'

She closed her laptop with a loud sigh. Her open suitcase rested on the edge of the bed, and she kicked it.

While she was grateful for David's help, Kate's loneliness was a hole in her heart. She was so alone.

No matter what Mom said, there was no support from her. Unless Kate's views aligned with her mother's, she was on her own. The only friend she had fired her. Her relationship with Maddie was tenuous. David had a family of his own to worry about, making it difficult to run to him with all her problems.

More isolated than ever, she cried herself to sleep.

Chapter Three

Four days later, Kate sat in a trendy nightclub in Scottsdale, downing tequila shots with Carlos as she listened to musicians attempt to sing at open mic night. Most of them were mediocre at best, though a few showed exceptional talent.

Couples danced behind her, sometimes bumping into her chair on their way to order more drinks. Between the off-key music and chatter, Kate could barely hear herself shout.

Carlos nudged her. "Can you at least try to look like you're enjoying yourself?"

She glared at him. "Seriously? *I* wanted to stay home and avoid this."

"Yeah, well, being alone won't make Friday night go away or make you any less single."

"Thanks, asshole. As if I needed the reminder."

She couldn't remember the last time she'd been to a bar, but Carlos had insisted. Plus, he was right. If they hadn't gone, she'd be drinking by herself again, wallowing in another pity party.

Despite being older than half the twenty-somethings in the crowd, the bar wasn't bad. Like many of Phoenix's suburbs, Scottsdale was busy every night of the week, drawing in tourists and college kids.

The historic district, with its Wild West culture, appealed to snowbirds and families. In contrast, the nightclubs attracted women in short dresses with too much makeup and equally pretty men.

It wasn't a place she would have chosen to visit. However, the club Carlos picked had decent lighting, good food, and the overpriced alcohol drowned her sorrows. Being with her friend was a bonus.

He was the only person who didn't treat her like a ticking time bomb. Carlos was blunt to a fault and refused to let her hide.

When he knocked at five in the evening, she'd been in her sleep shorts. He was her opposite, dressed in jeans and an ironed black button-up over a gray fitted tee.

Glancing at the tub of ice cream tucked beneath her arm, he dragged her into her bedroom, demanding she change and get off her ass.

So there she was, in her sister's sequined shirt with more skin showing than fabric and tight jeans she hadn't worn since her college days.

After downing a large gulp of dark beer, he set the glass on the bar and leaned close to her ear. "Forget about your problems for a night and have fun."

He propped his elbow on the bar, meeting her gaze full-on and silently daring her to tell him otherwise.

She held her glare until one corner of her mouth twitched, and then the other. Soon, she was fighting the urge to simultaneously giggle and cry, grateful for the lengths he went to make her feel better and appreciated.

If they sat like this for much longer, she might throw herself at him. Unwilling to open the proverbial bottle of tequila worms, she shoved his elbow, making him slip and almost topple his drink.

"Hey," he yelped.

She stuck her tongue out before draining her shot, shivering as the burning liquor stung her throat.

His hand settled onto her thigh, and she stared at it, feeling like she'd suddenly swallowed a glass of butterflies. It wasn't that she didn't find him attractive. Muscles bulged in his loose sleeves, and his T-shirt clung to his tight abs.

The problem was that before tonight, he'd been her superior and friend. Adding alcohol and a recent breakup might lead her down a rabbit-hole of regret the next morning.

Not wanting to make things awkward, she shifted her leg and hoped it didn't seem like she was outright rejecting him. It was possible he was tipsy and didn't realize what he was doing.

Instead of taking the hint, he slid off his stool and took her with him, grinning like a fool. Kate tripped and fell into his chest, where his arms easily went around her waist.

"What are you doing?" she asked as he tugged her toward the dance floor, maneuvering through a thick crowd of dancers.

He twirled her and watched her with gleaming eyes. "I'm showing you a good time."

Who was this man, and what had he done with her old boss?

"You do realize I have two left feet," she said with a laugh.

Right on cue, she stepped on him, causing them both to lose their balance. He recovered first, shaking his ass like nothing happened.

"This is what normal people do. They spend time together, have fun, and do it again." His breath tickled her ear as he swayed his hips and dipped her backward, making her squeal.

"They also kiss after too many drinks and wake up together the next day," she said, cackling. Several heads swiveled in their direction, and she ignored them, not giving a damn what anyone thought.

He shrugged and moved behind her, settling his hands on her hips, moving in rhythm with the music. "You couldn't handle me. Now follow my lead and let me show you how to dance."

No matter how hard he tried to guide her through the most basic steps, she kept falling or tripping, chortling every time he caught her before she face-planted. After the eighth stumble, he led her back to the bar, where he signaled the bartender for more drinks.

She'd never known this fun side of Carlos. He had wanted to see her more, but Matt didn't like him, and the feeling was mutual. Thus, most of their interactions outside of school were limited to grading parties and occasional drinks with colleagues.

If she'd met him before taking the job at ASU, she'd have jumped at the opportunity to date him. Instead, they were two friends dancing, and nothing more.

Waiting for her next shot, she noticed the man singing on stage. Some musicians throughout the night had been good, but *he* was mesmerizing.

His dark rumpled hair and his five o'clock shadow gave a sexy appeal to his otherwise perfect appearance. He looked like he worked in an office with his creased black slacks and crisp, deep blue shirt, unbuttoned at the collar.

His tenor voice rang throughout the room as he strummed his guitar. She couldn't help her wide-eyed stare, and she wasn't alone. Nearly every woman in the bar kept their eyes glued to him, ignoring their scowling partners.

The man was gorgeous. His legs stretched for miles, forcing him to sit on a barstool instead of the chair set out for the other musicians. She couldn't imagine what his girlfriend must think of all these women staring at him with lust-filled gazes, herself included.

For a split second, he made eye contact. She couldn't see the color, but they spoke of a man with deep secrets and a past. The intensity of his smoldering gaze sent a shock through her. The sensation stirred an emotion she couldn't name. If she had to describe it, she'd go with intrigue mixed with desire. She decided to blame her raging hormones and sex deprivation on the tequila.

Then she realized she couldn't recall the last time she and Matt had sex. The wedding preparations and class plans often left her too tired. She'd been saving the fun stuff for after the wedding.

The musician tilted his head again and winked, smirking between singing. If she didn't know any better, she'd say he was flirting with her.

Was she drooling? She pressed her lips firmly together and swallowed hard.

Someone brushed her shoulder, and she jumped, spilling the drink beside her. Tearing her focus away from the hot mystery man and spinning in her stool, she faced Carlos.

"Shit, you scared me," she said, bringing her palm to her chest, where her heart raced steadily beneath her rib cage.

Dark clouds seemed to pass through his eyes, and his easy smile had tightened as if he was pretending to be happy. "Well, it didn't take much time for you to move on."

His behavior was confusing.

He'd never shown interest in her. However, tonight he was treating her like a date. If that was what this was, she missed the memo.

Besides, attractive or not, she needed a friend, not a lover.

Kate scratched her neck. "It's not like that. It hasn't even been a week since the wedding. He's an attractive man with a nice voice." She looked at the spilled drink then fixed him with a pointed stare. "You owe me a new shot, by the way."

Carlos signaled the bartender again, and another tequila materialized. "You might wanna take it easy on those. You're gonna hate yourself tomorrow morning."

"Too late," she said, swallowing her drink in a single gulp. "I've been hating myself since last week."

He plucked the glass from her hand and set it aside. "Okay, we're done with these. I wouldn't be a good friend if I didn't cut you off."

She pouted, but he stood firm, and she switched to water as a hint of a migraine took root in her temples, making her stomach churn. She opened her mouth to thank him for having her back when the handsome stranger finished his song and left the stage, walking toward them. Kate's attention turned immediately to him, and the words never left her lips.

The man stopped in front of Carlos, and they fist-bumped.

She pursed her lips and raised an eyebrow. "You could have told me you're friends."

Carlos shrugged and had the decency to appear ashamed for giving her a hard time. "It was fun to watch you gawk." He motioned to the other man, whose eyes seemed to shine with amusement. "This is

26

Ian. He runs a psychology practice near ASU and moonlights here every week."

Kate sniggered at the introduction. *Great.* It would be her luck to run into a damn shrink.

Pink colored his face, and he scoffed. "Yes, let's announce to everyone that I'm a counselor. That'll make people want to stick around." Casting her a charming smile, he extended his arm in greeting. "So now you know who I am. What about you?"

"I'm Kate." She didn't trust herself to speak more than those two words.

Her voice was tinny, sounding more like a mouse than a confident woman. Suddenly warm, she fanned her shirt until remembering she wasn't wearing a bra. She flattened her palms against her thighs. Realizing she was staring again, she averted her gaze.

Needing to escape, she hopped to her feet then caught herself on the bar. If she didn't run away, she'd say something cringeworthy or embarrassing.

She didn't have Maddie's knack for flirting. Her sister was a social butterfly, willing and able to make friends with the entire world. All she had to do was flash her signature smile and flip her dark hair to have men lining up to buy her drinks.

Kate was too shy to flirt or approach the opposite sex. She'd only met Matt because her mother pressured her to go on a date with her best friend's son.

Thoughts of her ex soured Kate's mood, and she coughed to hide her scowl. "I think I'm gonna go. Nice to meet you, Ian."

She marched past them and stumbled. Carlos appeared by her side, positioning her against him as she slumped against his shoulder.

"Okay, let me call for a Lyft," he said, whipping his phone out of his pocket. "There's no way you're going home alone like this."

She shrugged, allowing him to navigate the crowd and steer her to the bar's exit. They'd barely made it through the door and passed a line of college kids waiting to get carded when a small group stopped them.

Someone pointed and jeered. "Nice wedding, Dr. Miller!"

Another kid whistled and yelled, "Nice panties! Wanna take them off next time? I won't say no to that ass!"

Oh lord. Not this. Couldn't she have a moment of peace?

"Keep moving and don't respond," Carlos whispered in her ear.

"You gonna post a sex video next? Lots of guys are into the whole teacher thing," another guy shouted.

His friends laughed, seeming to embolden him. He approached

her, leaning into her personal space and standing well above her. His light hair was shaved on the sides, and the top was styled with enough gel to remove an eye. A pair of sunglasses sat perched upon his head, despite the sun setting several hours ago.

His designer clothes and ripped skinny jeans screamed *Douchebag.* "I saw you in the news and heard you got fired. You can have sex with students now, right?"

She broke away and lunged at the bastard, but her friend was faster, and he restrained her, spinning her in the opposite direction. When she struggled, he urged her the other way.

"Jesus, Kate, let it go. They're recording everything with their phones."

She glared at him. "What happened to friends looking out for each other?"

He inhaled sharply. "If I attack him, I'll lose my job. Let it go. He's being a dick because he's with the boys. You're better than him."

Better would be men not treating women like they were objects. Wasn't the Me-Too Movement still supposed to be a thing?

Mr. Douchebag squealed behind her, and she whirled around. She gaped as Ian twisted the other man's arm behind his back, saying, "I'd apologize if I were you."

Sunglasses clattered to the pavement as he fought to break free.

"Okay, fine! I'm sorry!" he cried.

This kid didn't seem so tough anymore, especially as his friends roared with laughter and pointed their phones at him.

Ian released the guy and shoved him face-first into the sidewalk. He scrambled to his feet and swung before Kate could warn Ian. Not that it was necessary; he maneuvered away with a smirk.

A bouncer broke them apart, yanking the young man by his collar.

Like a petulant child, he screamed, "What the hell? He manhandles me and you're grabbing *me*?"

"He's a regular, and you're an asshole," the bouncer said in a bored voice, motioning for him to leave. "Why don't you run along home? I'm not letting you into a bar full of women who can do better than a boy trying to get into their pants."

Ian mock-saluted the bouncer before retrieving his guitar, greeting Kate and Carlos with a grin. Seeming oblivious to the indignant shouting behind him, he touched the small of Kate's back and guided her forward.

When had her life gone from blissfully boring to interesting? And since when did office boys become nighttime vigilantes? None of it felt real.

"Aren't you worried he'll press charges for assault?"

He shrugged. "Nope. The bouncers know me, and no one likes a pig. If he complained, the police would learn he sexually harassed you first, and he wouldn't have a leg to stand on."

"Thank you," she said, surprised by her unexpected knight in shining armor.

"It was nothing. Now, let's get out of here. Do you two need a ride home? I'm parked less than a block away."

His serene smile caught her off guard. The way a near-stranger was willing to offer her a ride was nice. She could use more people like that in her life.

"Um, sure," she stammered.

"No," Carlos clipped at the same time.

This is awkward.

He cleared his throat. "You don't need to go through the trouble, man."

"I don't mind," Ian insisted, lifting his eyebrows in a swift, challenging motion.

"That's not necessary. You live on the other side of Chandler, but thanks for the offer."

Kate snuck a glance between the men. Ian shrugged in a nonchalant manner while Carlos fumed. If his ears turned any pinker, he'd be spouting steam through them. It was almost like he was jealous.

To relieve the tension, she murmured, "Thanks for the rescue."

He ceased his staring contest with Carlos and offered her a genuine smile. "Of course. That kid had it coming. Are you all right?"

She coughed and dropped her gaze to the asphalt, unable to conceal the heat creeping into her cheeks. His self-assurance was attractive, and with the amount of alcohol she'd consumed, she worried she might say something stupid.

After a second, she said, "Yes, thank you. I don't have many people defending me at the moment."

"I'm glad I matter," Carlos grumbled after loudly clearing his throat.

A stab of guilt pierced her belly at the realization her words might have hurt him. "You do." She tightened her arm around his waist, grateful for his friendship. "I appreciate you bringing me here after my disaster at the altar."

"Altar?" Ian asked.

He looked between her and Carlos. He must have thought they were together.

Kate broke away from Carlos. Wobbling as she faced Ian, she said, "Don't ask. I'm sure you'll find it somewhere on YouTube, if it isn't already shared to your social media accounts."

"I know we just met, but you can talk to me," he answered without missing a beat. "I'm told I'm a good listener."

Yeah, because you're paid to do it.

She chose not to answer as a Lyft approached the curb where they were huddled, and Carlos waved at the driver. When his hand slipped around her, she resisted the urge to swat him away, angry with his attitude. Whatever happened to upset him, she couldn't help feeling like she was responsible for it.

When she reached the passenger-side door, she met Ian's gaze once more. "Thanks again."

His head bobbed once, his easy-going smile never wavering. "Anytime. Are you sure you're okay?"

Fumbling with the handle, she shrugged. "I'll live. I might need to sleep and hide from the world for a week after this, but I'll be okay."

"Running away from your problems isn't a solution," he said sagely. Taking his wallet from his pants, he produced a card. Then he whipped a pen from his front pocket and scribbled something onto it before giving it to her. "Here, feel free to call me if you ever want to talk. My personal number is on the back."

Heat seared her cheeks as she took it and stowed it away. Was he hitting on her? She hoped he wasn't insinuating she needed a shrink.

Carlos muttered something under his breath and unlatched Kate's door with a huff. "She doesn't need a visit with a psych. She needs her friends. I'll make sure she doesn't hide."

Ian's eyes widened, and he nodded curtly. "Right. I'll see you two later."

Was Carlos cock-blocking his friend? What was with his weird behavior? She wasn't his girlfriend.

Kate didn't want Ian to leave, yet she said nothing as he disappeared across the street. She slid into the vehicle and closed the door shut before Carlos could do it for her. He came around the car and took his seat beside her, silent and brooding.

Part of her wanted to snap at him for acting childish, but her head hurt, and she was in no condition to fight with her only ally. Besides, for all she knew, he and Ian could have an old feud, and he was merely being polite in introducing them.

Making assumptions wouldn't do her any good. Her week had been full of nothing but drama, and she was ready for peace and quiet.

Chapter Four

Kate spent most of the next morning heaving. She couldn't remember how much she had to drink, but it was enough to make her want to die.

She also couldn't recall Carlos saying much to her last night after dropping her off. The playful banter they'd shared earlier in the evening had disappeared. Also, when he walked her to her door, he stayed long enough for her to go inside, leaving without saying goodbye.

She staggered into the kitchen for coffee, toast, and aspirin. She wasn't sure how much of it she could stomach, but charred bread was better than nothing.

Placing a coffee pod in her Keurig, she hit start.

The coffee maker had been a gift from colleagues after she set the teacher's lounge on fire two years ago when someone asked her to make a pot. After that incident, Carlos bought her a fresh cup of Starbucks every morning on his way to work.

Before she could sit, let alone think, Dodger darted into the room and mewled, pawing at her leg. She grinned and followed him to his bowl, where he watched her with expectant eyes.

"Do you ever stop eating?" She searched her cabinets for his wet food before remembering she didn't have any.

She'd given her supply to the kennel and had forgotten to buy more. All she had was dry food.

She kneeled, scratching behind his ears. "Sorry, little guy. You ate the last can last night. Eat your regular food."

As if he could understand her, he hissed before stalking away.

Shaking her head, Kate sat on a barstool and looked around her apartment. Boxes sat stacked in the corner of the living room, ready to be relocated. The only remaining unpacked items were furniture she'd planned on donating when she returned from her honeymoon. Her family was supposed to move everything else while she was gone.

Her chest tightened as a scary realization hit her. The lease on her apartment would expire in two weeks. She'd given her notice a month ago, and someone else was scheduled to move in. She didn't have the funds to find a new place, especially on short notice. Or in the summer, when everything was expensive.

Her heart rate spiked at the thought of being homeless. Shoving her plate aside, she ran into her bedroom and picked up her phone. She needed to talk to someone, anyone, and discuss her options.

She cringed as notifications flooded her screen. There were thirty-seven missed calls since Saturday, twenty-nine of them from her mother. Kate needed to ring back her mom but had been ignoring her since their argument.

Why couldn't this woman give her a break? Kate knew the answer. Her mom hated not being the center of attention and loved to poke non-stop until acknowledged.

The others were from her sister, brother, Carlos, Matt, and Jordon. She hadn't expected that last one. She'd have to call him later.

As for Matt, she dialed her voicemail to hear what he had to say. "Hey, it's me. I know a phone call is a poor way to deliver an apology, but I want to tell you I'm sorry anyway. You're probably pissed about the honeymoon, but we couldn't get a refund, and I figured someone should go so the money didn't go to waste. I also wanted to give us some time apart so we can speak rationally when I get back. Please don't give up on us. I'll see you soon. I love you."

What a load of crap. He was using the refund as an excuse to party and flirt, otherwise, why would he add a hashtag to his photos announcing his single status?

She promptly deleted the message, choosing not to respond. He was on the cruise for another two days. She didn't want to think about him with all those women in bikinis and holding froofy drinks, let alone talk to him.

Right now, she needed to strengthen her resolve to face Mom. Asking for help wouldn't be easy, but it was better than the alternative.

She answered on the first ring. "I was wondering when you'd answer your phone."

Straight to the point. That was her, a shark out for first blood.

Pinching the bridge of her nose and slowly exhaling, Kate said, "Hello, Mom."

"What were you thinking? Your tantrum wasn't bad enough, so you stumbled around drunk on the street?"

Kate smacked her head against the counter and cursed. "How did it go viral already? That happened last night."

"It's easy, when tagged as the 'Social Media Bride,' and that video is still popular."

Was that what they were calling her? She had no desire to search for herself online. It was safe to say everyone judged her the moment the first debacle surfaced. Everywhere she went, people recognized her. It was like being a celebrity where her every move was filmed.

She rested her cheek against the counter, mumbling into the receiver. "This is crazy. I'm a Geology professor. I'm not important. I don't understand how my life is newsworthy."

"It doesn't matter who you are these days, entertainment is entertainment, and social media doesn't care who it ruins."

"I noticed that already. I don't need a reminder." Putting pride in her pocket, Kate forced herself to ask the question she'd been dreading. "I was supposed to move in with Matt, which didn't happen, and I can't stay here. The lease is going to expire soon, and I don't have a job or the funds to find a new place. I was wondering if I could stay with you and Dad until I find something again."

She wanted to kick herself for sounding so timid. Most adults moved back with their parents at some point. There was nothing shameful about needing help. Plus, she had no other options. It was her parents' house or the street.

She knew Dad wouldn't mind. It was Mom's reaction she was afraid of, considering their last conversation ended in an argument. Not to mention, this would be something else to hold against Kate.

Her mother didn't answer right away. Why couldn't the woman be normal and say 'okay' with no questions asked?

Finally, she said, "You know I won't say no, but I feel like you should at least try to hear Matt's side of the story. People make mistakes."

Kate shot straight in her chair and yelled, "Can you please stop justifying his behavior? Cheating is cheating. If he can't be faithful before saying 'I do,' what makes you think he'll be any better later? My only mistake was saying yes to him when he proposed."

"Don't use that tone with me, young lady. You and Matt both messed up, and you two need to fix this."

Oh, she had to be joking. "Excuse you? He whored himself around, and someone else posted a video, but I'm the one getting harassed. None of this is my fault."

"Maybe you shouldn't have shoved the pastor or hit Matt."

Inhale. Exhale. Inhale. Exhale again.

"Okay, that part was a mistake," she conceded.

"Come home. We can discuss Matt later. Everyone will forget

the video by next week. I can get your job back without much fuss, or you can take the next semester off while you get yourself sorted. We'll support you."

Kate held in a groan. Mom's idea of support was talking the subject to death and dissecting it until she could blame Kate for whatever went wrong. Then, she would give a lecture on the proper ways to conduct oneself. Living with her mother would be difficult, but it was better than being homeless.

"Okay. I'll come home." Rubbing her temples, she changed the subject. "There's something I need to know. The video was posted by a celebrity with more than a million followers. We didn't have any famous people at the wedding, so it doesn't make sense how they got a hold of it. Is that legal? Am I able to do something about it?"

"There's nothing to be done. It's not against the law to film people in a public setting," Mom said in a tired voice.

"What about Maddie? She's a model with loads of big contacts."

"Why do you always blame her when things go wrong?"

"Why aren't you answering my question?"

"Because I don't know," she shouted. Then releasing a sharp burst of air, she resumed her normal tone. "I can't keep track of Maddie's friends at the agency. She couldn't have posted it herself because she was with you, remember? A lot of people were present, many of us who have big clients. Anybody could have shared it with a friend, who shared it with someone else. In the end, it doesn't matter who uploaded it."

It mattered to Kate. Whoever had posted it had ruined her life overnight. Twenty years ago, this wouldn't have been newsworthy. It would have been gossip at family dinners or parties, but it wouldn't have been available to the entire world.

The worst part was that she knew she should never have lost her temper. She had a certain responsibility in accepting the consequences of her actions, but she was also human. No one was perfect, and she didn't deserve everything that followed.

She couldn't help wondering if her sister had played a role in what had gone wrong. Even though she had been the first person to dismiss Matt vocally, Kate had a horrible thought that Maddie might have slept with him.

What if her sister's attitude was a mask for feelings beneath the surface? Was it possible she had an intimate relationship with someone she disliked?

Kate was afraid to voice her concerns aloud, but she had to know if anyone else shared them. "Mom, is it possible Maddie was the one who slept with him?"

"Oh Kate, you don't honestly think she'd stoop that low, do you?"

"She could," Kate said in a tight voice. "Maddie said she hated him, but what if they were seeing each other on the side?"

"Why would she sleep with him, if she couldn't stand him? Listen," Mom commanded, "whatever you have going on with your sister, you need to fix it. You blame her for everything that goes wrong in your life. She can be spoiled, but I don't think she'd ever intentionally hurt anyone."

"Okay, but remember my college boyfriend?"

In Kate's third year at ASU, her sister had zeroed in on Chris. He'd been her first boyfriend, and it had taken months to build enough courage to ask him to have coffee with her. She'd been elated when he accepted, and their casual dates soon became a relationship.

They did everything together, from classes to outings with friends, and Kate decided to bring him home for Thanksgiving to meet her family. Everyone eagerly greeted him, and nobody more than Maddie.

Home for the holidays from Northern Arizona University, she immediately gravitated to him, plying him with questions and giggling when he joked. She told him stories of her childhood with Kate, giving him more attention than necessary or appropriate. The longer she chatted, the more Chris's attention shifted to her.

Halfway through dinner, Kate caught him with his hand halfway up her sister's thigh. When she confronted him, he told her Maddie was prettier, more charming, and appealing.

He hadn't left it there. To her humiliation, he went on to say he found her irritating and that he had accepted her first date on a dare from a friend.

Crushed, she'd shoved him out the door before retreating to her room in tears.

Maddie couldn't help who she was or that men naturally flocked to her. Kate should have given her the benefit of the doubt. Maddie hadn't hit on him, and Kate should have been less harsh on her sister, yet all she could see was Maddie's face as she flirted, seemingly oblivious to her effect on men in general and Chris in particular.

Their relationship became strained and awkward following Kate's breakup with Chris. It wasn't until her engagement with Matt that they'd tentatively begun speaking again, despite Maddie's insistence that he was no good.

It never once crossed Kate's mind that Maddie would sleep with Matt, but with the amount of drama her family indulged in, Kate couldn't help wondering. She'd heard co-workers trade stories and compare the horrible things their siblings or cousins had done. It wouldn't be farfetched to assume someone in her personal circle might pursue Matt.

"Sweetie," her mother said, cutting into Kate's dark musings. "Maddie would never do something like that. She adores you. Why can't you see it?"

Kate wished she had an answer. They'd been close before everything went to Hell in a handbasket. Maybe she was jealous of her sister's success, her ability to talk her way out of trouble, or the fact she could reel in a man without trying.

There was no point in dwelling on it. Kate was tired of brooding on her suspicions and everything that went wrong. All this conversation did was bring her down lower, and she wanted it to end.

Once the first hiccup bubbled inside her chest, she shuddered and whispered, "I need to go. I love you."

"I love you too. Try to stay strong."

Ending the call, Kate strode into the living room and sank onto the couch. Still holding her phone, she stared at it. How could such a small device be so destructive, and when did they start monopolizing everyone's lives? She scrolled through her apps until her photos appeared. She tapped the file, and dozens of images of herself and Matt beamed back at her.

She selected every picture until she reached the end and pressed the trash button. 'Delete image?' it asked. Her finger hovered above the words for a moment before clicking it.

The moment they disappeared, half the world's weight fell from her shoulders as the other half pressed against her, telling her what still needed to be done.

Bolstering her resolve, she closed the photo app and opened her contact list, going straight to Matt's name. Keeping his number was pointless since she had no intention of reconciling with him. *Delete.*

Now the heaviness had dissolved. She leaned into the couch and smiled. This was more therapeutic than getting drunk at a bar.

Next, she needed some answers, and she knew who to turn to, even if she had to beat it out of him. There was no hesitation as she dialed Jordon's number.

He answered on the third ring. "Hello?"

"Are you busy?"

"For you? Never. Are you okay? I saw the second video on Facebook."

Kate groaned and covered her face with a pillow. "Ugh, who hasn't seen it? I can't believe people think this is funny."

"Not that you read the comments, but in the first video there seems to be a huge debate on whether you should have been fired. Loads of people are rallying behind you. As for the newest one, that kid was a prick. He deserved what he got. Who was the other guy?"

"A friend of Carlos."

She hoped that kid learned his lesson, but he wasn't the one in the spotlight for poor decisions. Instead, people would enable his inappropriate behavior by blaming it on his age or because he was a man.

It was also another reminder of her unfair termination. It wasn't as if she'd been representing the university on her wedding day. And now she was being heckled. Didn't she have a right to be angry?

Yet, would the kid for last night be expelled? No. He was a man with a small penis complex and an ego. Meanwhile, the hard-working women of the world were shit on.

"Was this friend a date?" Jordon asked.

"Dude, he was some guy I met who did something nice. Just because he's a person of the opposite gender, doesn't mean I'm hot and wet for him. Besides, who he is doesn't matter. What does, is that people like this kid get to coast through life with no consequences while others are held to ridiculous standards. I can't leave my house without having to look over my shoulder for my next public mistake."

"I know you're not how the media depicts you. Plus, I should have chosen a better time to tell you about Matt."

"No, you did the right thing. It's better to have the truth before getting married than discovering it later and have to file for divorce. No matter how angry I was, I shouldn't have reacted the way I did, and that blame lies with me."

"Yeah, well, you shouldn't be the only person held accountable. I could have chosen a better time, and Matt could have avoided this by not having sex at the bachelor party."

"Would have, could have, should have," she mumbled. "None of it really matters, does it? I need to ask you something important."

A long pause ensued, and she waited for him to respond. He probably knew what she wanted to ask.

"Jordon?" she prompted.

"Okay. What is it?"

"Who was the woman? Was it a one-time thing or has he been seeing someone on the side?"

Another break followed. Finally, he said, "I have no idea. It's not like I stalk him or share his bed. You need to let it go."

This whole situation made her sick. "Why wasn't I good enough?"

"I'm not sure the truth would make it any better."

"Why are you afraid to tell me? Was it Maddie? Was it Mom?" she asked, grasping at straws. Oh God, she hoped not. She didn't believe either of them really did it, but she needed to ask anyway. "Please, I *need* to know."

"Ew, Matt can do better than your mom, no offense. Also, it wasn't your sister."

She laughed, relieved to cross her family off her list of suspects. "None taken. I'd castrate him on sight if he fiddled around with my family. If it wasn't them, then who?"

"You need to let it go. No matter what Matt says, your relationship is ruined. With you, there's no rebuilding bridges once they're burned."

Tucking her feet into the cushions, she wedged her phone between her cheek and shoulder. Her life was a mess, partially brought on by her actions. The rest had been influenced by circumstances out of her control.

Jordon was right. She was too unyielding when wronged. Matt could broadcast to the world he was sorry and that the woman he slept with was a nobody he'd met in the bar. He could proclaim his undying love for Kate, and it wouldn't matter. She'd never be able to trust him again, constantly wondering if he was imagining someone else or if she made him unhappy.

"Well, I guess there isn't much else to say," she whispered.

"Give it time. It hurts now, but I promise, it gets better."

"I want it to get better now."

"It's going to be fine. Call me if you ever need me, okay?"

They said their goodbyes and ended the call. She rolled to her back and rested her neck against the arm, staring at the ceiling. Sunlight filtered through the empty room, and dust motes floated like clouds on a lazy day. She started counting them, first to fifty, then to a hundred.

The entire time, unwanted thoughts and resentment plagued her. Matt, her family, her job—all of it taunted her, reminding her she'd screwed up.

As Jordon said, she needed to move on. Mom would tell her to see a therapist, but what good would that do? He or she would most likely tell her to exercise, meditate, or find a new hobby.

Without anything to anchor her, she was adrift. Everything she loved was taken from her, and her passion, Geology reminded her of her former job. The only familial fixture in her life was David and Carlos. Her brother had a family of his own, and she wasn't sure what was going on inside her friend's head after last night.

The apartment walls and her mind were closing in on her, so she sprang into motion. Her single-bedroom apartment with its patio no bigger than a shoebox didn't give her much room to prowl. However, she needed to move, to do something to release her negative energy.

Going through every cabinet, she finally found a small bucket of cleaning supplies beneath the bathroom sink. Retrieving her music, she inserted her earbuds and scrolled through her playlist until she found something upbeat.

With the volume loud enough to drown her thoughts, she set to work on scrubbing the bathroom. Soon, her skin was raw from the hot water in the bath, and her elbows were sore from the repetitive movement, but she pushed herself harder every time she brooded over the dismal state of her life.

When she finished with the bathroom, she moved on to the kitchen and then the living room. The morning gave way to the afternoon, and eventually, the sun began its descent, casting pink and purple hues across the sky outside her sliding door.

With the apartment gleaming, Kate threw her scrub brush into the bucket and stood. Her back popped, and her hips ached from bending over, but her emotional state had finally calmed enough for her to address a final, lingering question.

After a quick shower, she texted her sister. *'Did you have anything to do with my wedding video that a celebrity posted?'*

Given her prestige as a model and artist, Maddie knew a few famous people. Therefore, the link was possible.

Thirty seconds passed before she replied. *'I'm sorry I didn't tell you sooner. I had no idea my friend took the video from my phone until after she'd uploaded it to YouTube. I knew you'd be angry, and you already have enough going on in your life.'*

How was she supposed to respond to this? Why had her sister decided it was a good idea share to Kate's humiliation with other people?

She had dozens of questions but had a feeling none of the answers would make her feel better.

Yelling or hurling insults wouldn't accomplish anything. Several minutes passed without her answering until she eventually typed the only civil words that came to mind. *'We need to have a discussion.'*

With nothing left to say, she turned off her phone. Her energy was depleted, both mentally and physically. She didn't want to fight or dwell on what went wrong. Sooner or later, she'd have to confront Maddie, but not yet.

Maybe Jordon was right. Learning the truth wouldn't help. Finding out who was responsible for posting the video made her feel worse.

Would it be the same if she found out who Matt had slept with at his bachelor party?

Chapter Five

"I can't do it," Kate announced after arriving at Carlos's house. "If I move home again, I'll punch my sister for that video."

He handed her a glass of water and sat beside her in the small dining alcove. "Have you talked to Maddie yet?"

Kate bounced her knee until it shook the table and rattled her untouched cup. Nausea sank into the pit of her stomach as vessels throbbed behind her eyes.

She'd hardly slept or eaten since her conversations with Jordon and her family the day before. She was restless and exhausted, and no matter how hard she tried, she couldn't stop replaying everything that had led to the downward spiral her life had taken.

Rubbing her temples, she sighed. "Besides the text where she admitted her friend shared the video? No. What am I supposed to say? Loads of people filmed the wedding. I've seen it on Facebook, Instagram, and Twitter. At least twenty people I follow on social media have posted it to laugh at my expense, but *they* weren't celebrities. I might have been okay if it weren't for her."

"You need better friends," he said, wrinkling his nose.

"Tell me about it. I wish I understood what goes through people's minds. Maddie sort of makes sense because she's always shared everything with her friends. But what really irks me is that every time I see those snippets in the newsfeeds, no one mentions Matt. He cheated, confessed to it at the altar after he was forced to, but the articles trash me instead." Kate raked her fingers through her hair and expelled a loud breath, continuing, "And the best part is that Mom wants me to reconcile with him."

Carlos bared his teeth like a rabid dog and balled his fists until his knuckles turned white. "You're kidding."

"Nope."

"Ugh. I don't know how you tolerate your family. If someone

cheated on me or my sister, my folks would be hiding the body."

A smile tugged at the corners of her mouth. She'd never met his family, but based on the crazy stories he shared, his mother would do more than hide the body. She'd cut whoever was crazy enough to hurt her children. Then she'd probably get their relatives together to dispose of the corpse. She took Mama Bear to a whole new level.

"Is your family adopting?" Kate joked.

"I'll ask Mama if she's taking applications."

The banter lifted her spirits. It was like their awkward encounter at the bar never happened. She was relieved they didn't need to apologize for anything they'd said when drinking. The moment she'd texted to say she was on her way, he responded with a thumbs up and a 'See ya soon.'

They sat in companionable silence, not needing to fill the air with small talk. Kate's leg bounced again as she propped her chin on her hand, absently watching a butterfly through the sliding glass door that led to the backyard.

Its brown and orange wings fluttered as it landed on a potted plant in front of the door, flapping twice before settling in place. After a minute, it took flight and disappeared into the bright sky.

With the butterfly no longer available to distract her, she slumped into her chair. Carlos looked from his phone, and when their eyes clashed, he set it down.

"What are you thinking about?" he asked.

She sighed. "What am I supposed to do now?"

"What do you mean?" he asked, raising an eyebrow.

"I feel like I'm in a rut. I'm unemployed, and I have no choice but to move home with my parents. My family is *so* dysfunctional, and I can already see my mental health tanking within a week."

He caressed her arm, offering a cautious smile. "You could stay here."

She tilted her face and gnawed on her bottom lip, unsure how to respond. The offer was nice, but there were several reasons why it wasn't a good idea.

"That depends on a couple of different factors."

Trailing his fingers down to her hand, he traced small circles on her knuckles. "You're worried I'll hit on you."

He wasn't wrong, but he could show some tact. She worked her mouth, trying to find the right words. Unfortunately, nothing came to mind.

After a moment, she said, "Well, yeah. I mean, you were acting weird the other night."

He looked as if he'd slammed his thumb in a door and was trying to conceal how much it hurt. "You're a nice woman. Matt was stupid to cheat on you. I won't lie. I am attracted to you, but I respect that you recently came out of a serious relationship. If friendship is what you need, I'll give that to you."

"You say that now but what if you change your mind? Do you really want to risk our friendship over complicated emotions?"

Taking her other hand, he held them like he had in his office last week. The gesture was becoming more romantic than friendly, no matter what he said about giving her time to recover from her heartbreak.

She liked him well enough but couldn't picture them in a relationship. While she and Matt didn't have much in common, she and Carlos were too much alike with their hobbies and interests. She wanted a balance, someone she could occasionally argue with and wouldn't become boring after six months.

"I promise I won't complicate things," he pressed. "You need a place to stay, and I have an extra room. It'll get you away from your family, and you can get your life together without anyone knowing you're here."

She sat straight in her chair and fixed him with a frown. "There are two problems. One, I can't afford rent, especially if I need to place a deposit on a new apartment. Second, you got really weird when you introduced me to Ian. I don't want to feel like you're marking your territory every time I talk to a guy."

"I'm still a man, and you're a beautiful woman. It's a natural instinct for me to be protective of people I care for. I don't want to see you hurt."

Her eyebrows shot up. Ian was his friend, yet Carlos worried about *her* getting hurt? It sounded like he was jealous.

"More than I already am? I doubt that. Besides, what gave you the idea I'm the type of woman to engage in a fling or rebound relationship?"

He raised his arms as if in surrender, scooting away like she was a snake preparing to bite. "I wasn't implying anything. I'm worried you're emotionally vulnerable. If you wanted a fling or boyfriend, Ian wouldn't be the guy. He doesn't want either."

Ouch. Way to shut her down before she even considered it. She wasn't interested but found it curious that Carlos would warn her away from Ian. "Neither do I. He offered to talk if I needed a friend. That's not code for 'Ooh, let's bang!'"

Averting his gaze, he cleared his throat and said, "He was being nice. Talking is what he does."

"You acted like we were trying to get in each other's pants," she grumbled.

"You *were* ogling him."

"I was paying attention to the music," she lied.

There was no way he wanted to hear her admit she found Ian hot. Plus, she wasn't a woman who discussed men with her male friends.

"Right," Carlos muttered.

She shook her head and stood, meeting his gaze with a firm glare. "All I want is to rebuild my life. I came here for your advice, not for you to make implications about my love life. I need to pack and figure out how the hell to fix the mess I'm in. I'll see you later."

When she turned to leave, he stopped her and enveloped her into his arms. She froze, afraid he'd do something stupid, like kiss her in an act of desperation. His fingers fluttered along her arms. Eventually, his movements slowed until their hands linked and his breathing evened.

Swallowing, he said, "I'm sorry. I promise, I want what's best for you. Stay with me for as long as you need while searching for a new job. I won't charge you rent. Just buy your own food and keep your living space clean."

She had too many reservations. First and foremost, a man didn't suggest something like this without wanting more, no matter what he said.

Detaching herself, she met his gaze. "I'm sorry. I do appreciate the offer, but I feel like it would complicate our friendship."

The shutters closed behind his dark eyes, and his face became a mask. "Okay," he said in a defeated voice. "At least let me help you move?"

"Of course," she said around the lump in her throat.

His disappointment was a jab to the gut. No matter how much she didn't want to hurt him, she couldn't give him hope of anything happening between them.

Why did she have to ruin everything lately?

~ * ~

Two weeks later, she, along with her brother and Carlos, loaded a rental truck with her apartment contents. Like it or not, she'd be staying with her parents.

As tempting as it was to move in with Carlos, there was no way she could live with him. His attraction and her wanting to be friends made things complicated.

In another life or world, dating might have been an option. He was a good guy, but in this reality, they would never be more.

They hadn't talked since she'd rebuffed him, but true to his word, he'd come to help her move. Yet, when she greeted him, his response was curt.

He marched into her building and put himself to work, avoiding her. When he finished, he reached into his pocket for his keys, telling her he was leaving.

She'd brought Dodger's carrier last, and she set him down for a moment so she could draw Carlos into a hug. Releasing him, she rocked on her feet. "Thank you."

He shrugged, no longer her sympathetic and compassionate best friend. He may as well have been a stranger with the way he withdrew.

Her throat tightened, and she fought tears. It wasn't her fault she couldn't commit to living with him this soon after her break up. Any reasonable person could see it was a terrible idea.

"I feel like you're mad at me," she confessed.

He shook his head and exhaled. "Not mad. A little disappointed. There aren't many people you can trust at the moment, and I want to be here for you."

"You are in the way that matters. There's a lot that could go wrong if I moved in with you. Not to mention, if people found out, it'd look bad. They would call you my rebound or read between the lines of boss and subordinate. Neither of us need that kind of headache."

"You'd rather take your family's drama instead?"

Kate flinched. She hadn't confronted Maddie yet, but she couldn't put it off forever. "More like I've accepted the inevitable."

He shoved his hands into his pockets, seeming to absorb her words. After a period of silence, he said, "I have nothing but respect for you. You're beautiful and intelligent. You're the kind of woman a man would kill to be with because you're down to earth and real. What pisses me off is that guys like me don't have a chance when the Matts of the world snatch up the good women and then treat them like shit. I could be okay with us being friends if I knew you wouldn't let what he did keep you from dating again."

She was speechless. Here was the perfect man, standing in front of her, yet alarm bells kept ringing, telling her moving in or crossing the friend zone was a terrible idea.

She sincerely hoped he'd find someone worthy of his compassion. He deserved to be happy.

"I'm sure after some time, I'll be fine." She didn't know that was true, but she hugged him again, holding tight and trying to convey how much she appreciated him. "I'm sorry."

He detached himself and gripped her shoulders. "Stop. I told you, it's fine. You can't help how you feel. Just promise me you'll consider us if you decide to start dating again. Not every man is like

Matt."

Now it was her turn to be silent. There was nothing she could do or say without hurting Carlos more. It was bad enough to see him miserable, and upsetting him was like punching a kitten in the face.

Maybe with enough time, she could give him a shot. A month hadn't passed since the wedding. It was too soon to be pursuing anything. She needed to heal emotionally and didn't want the pressure of him waiting on her.

They parted without saying more than murmured goodbyes, and Kate sadly watched him drive off, hoping their friendship wasn't damaged.

A moment later, David approached with the keys to the moving truck. "You ready?"

"No. Mom and Dad's house is the last place I want to be."

"It's temporary. You'll find something before you know it."

"It's not just that," she said with a grimace. "Mom is difficult, but also, I haven't talked to Maddie."

He sighed. "What are you waiting for, Hell to freeze over? I'm not saying she's not culpable, but you need to stop blaming her for everything."

Her face tingled like she'd been slapped. It wasn't often that she found herself at odds with her brother. Their last serious argument had been when she was in college.

He'd eloped without telling anyone, and Kate was pissed he'd excluded her. She wanted to be there as his partner in crime, witnessing the happiest day of his life. Now, it was the other way around, where he cast her a reproachful glare, making her feel like she was five years old.

Unable to meet his gaze, she dipped her chin into her chest and hugged herself. "You're right. I've kind of been a bitch."

"I wouldn't go that far. You do need to stop putting this off though. At least try to get Maddie's side of the story. When I spoke to her, she was adamant she didn't give her friend permission to post the video. As for Mom, if she keeps bugging you, remind her your relationship isn't hers to fix."

"You make it sound so simple," she said in a shuddering voice.

He wrapped his arms around her, giving her back a firm pat. "Because it is. Mom bullies you because you let her. Once you stand your ground and ignore her crap, your life will be loads easier."

"Don't you remember what it's like to live with her?" she mumbled. "She'll pick at me until I explode, and then tell me why my behavior is unacceptable."

"That's when you disengage and leave the room. The same goes for Matt. With him, make sure you keep walking and stay away from him. I'll disown you if you get back together with him."

She laughed. "Don't worry. He's called a few times since he came home from the cruise, but I haven't answered or returned any of his voicemails."

"That's my girl." David let go of Kate. "Now let's go before I become a puddle of sweat. It's hot as hell."

"You should take a shower too," she teased. "Mom will flip if you walk into the house smelling like a locker room."

Sweat clung to both of them, soaking their clothes in the one hundred-and-eleven-degree heat. The only thing worse than an Arizona summer was moving during it. The evenings were cooler, though not by much. It would be close to triple digits by ten at night, and Kate wanted to be done long before then.

She waved as David drove past in the truck. Opening the passenger door, she allowed the shimmering heat to spill out before placing Dodger's carrier on the seat, firmly buckling the seatbelt around it. Then she slid inside and turned the ignition. Welcome cold air blew into her face, cooling her skin as she glanced at the building she'd called home.

Dodger howled beside her as if she stabbed him.

"Oh, my God, you silly animal. You'll be out of there soon enough. Hush."

He mewled even louder, headbutting the cage and hissing. Kate chuckled and turned her attention to the apartments again.

It would soon be nothing more than a residential structure that would house the next stranger. For her, it was a reminder of the time she wasted with Matt and shattered dreams.

Backing out of the carport, she bid the complex good riddance. As much as she didn't want to live with her parents again, she knew this was a step in the right direction. She was moving forward. The past and everything associated with it would fade into a distant memory.

Chapter Six

Kate parked in her parent's driveway and took a minute to stare at the ostentatious façade. Premium concrete in stamped circles meandered between the sprawling lawn of grass and rock, bordered by gray shale and artistically placed stones.

Considering her family lived in the desert, she found it funny to pay for special rocks when most of them could be found in an empty field. The wastefulness of planting grass was also ridiculous.

Two large shade trees covered the walkway. As kids, she and David used to climb them to see who could reach the top first. Being smaller, she always won, shimmying and bending through the limbs like a gymnast. Despite being the older brother, he wasn't as agile and tended to fall. Then, she'd scurry down to soothe his tears before sneaking into the freezer for a tub of ice cream.

Nostalgia expanded inside her chest, and she smiled. Her childhood had mostly been happy, filled with her and her siblings' laughter in every corner of the home. The basketball hoop stood near the garage, and toys for her nieces littered the side of the house. If she were to go to the backyard, she'd find the pool as well as the firepit and the curtained gazebo.

A loud honk interrupted Kate's musing. David climbed from the truck and motioned for her to exit the car. Getting out, heat whooshed against her face like an open oven door in a warm kitchen.

She fanned herself and whimpered. The truck wasn't big, and she was moving from a small apartment, but her limbs were wet noodles. When her brother slid the latch and pushed up the rear door, the boxes towered far above her, taunting her with the work she had yet to finish.

Reaching inside the cab of the truck, he produced two bottles of water and brought them over. After passing one to her, he unscrewed the cap on his. He chugged it before wiping his brow and following her gaze. "You have too much shit."

She laughed. "Me? You're one to talk. How many times have you snuck toys into the donation bin when your daughters weren't looking?"

He grinned. "Too many. You remember when Mom used to try that with us? Maddie would cry, and we'd go through the boxes to reclaim our treasures."

Neither of them could resist their baby sister's tears. When the princess demanded something, they delivered.

If she wanted a tea or makeup party, no force in Heaven or Hell would stop her from having it. When boys made her cry, David came home with a black eye, but he'd gotten his hits in too, bloodying the offender's nose.

Kate used to drag her sister outside in the rocks, where they pretended to go on expeditions for rare gems. It was fun until Maddie realized she preferred the real thing instead of an ugly rock.

Crossing her arms, Kate said, "I wish life was still that simple." Her idling car was parked next to the truck. She leaned against it, yelping when the metal burned her butt through her shorts.

"It can be, but you have to accept that shit happens. We might have grown up, but nothing has changed, not really. Instead of verbally attacking her, remind yourself that no one is perfect and try to listen before speaking."

"Yes, Master Zen," she teased, bowing like a student in a dojo.

He shoved her shoulder before bounding to the truck. She took off after him, spraying him with the meager contents of her flimsy water bottle. Once satisfied with her victory, she turned off her car and brought Dodger inside the house before unloading her boxes.

After bringing some to her room, she went downstairs to do it all over again.

A surge of water hit her in the chest, followed by David's boisterous laugh. He peeked around the column he was using as a shield, holding the garden hose, his finger hovering near the nozzle trigger.

"That's what you get for the water bottle!"

"You're dead!" she squealed, lunging for the hose.

He jumped away and ran, pausing long enough to squirt her with another burst before taking off again. It wasn't until he tripped on a rock that Kate reached him, and they fought for the hose.

Water splashed in every direction as her hand covered the nozzle, and they dissolved into giggles. David wrenched it from her grasp and raised it high above her, showering her in rainbow-colored droplets.

She danced away, shrieking as he pursued her. "What are you, twelve?"

"You're just mad because I outgrew the Halfling stage, unlike you."

"Are you calling me a Hobbit?"

Something shattered near the door, and she spun around to see David quickly turn the nozzle off. They stared at the remains of a tall clay planter. The hose had somehow tangled itself around the pot, sending it toppling to the ground when one of them tugged against the line. Soil littered the front doorstep with flowers ripped by the roots scattered on the concrete.

He dropped the hose and grimaced. "Oops."

The front door swung open, revealing Maddie in a pair of shorts and a pink tank top. Broken pottery shards crunched beneath her flip-flops, and she recoiled. "Oh, Mom isn't gonna like this."

Her gaze darted from the overturned plant to her siblings. When her gaze clashed with Kate's, Maddie chewed her bottom lip and retreated further into the house. Her feet shifted like she was preparing to run in another direction, yet she remained stuck in place, fidgeting with the hem of her shirt.

David lifted an eyebrow and cocked his head toward Maddie. "You can't put this off forever," he whispered. "Go talk to her."

Kate scratched her nose and looked away. Even though she told her sister they needed to talk, she'd delayed the conversation, not knowing what to say. It felt impossible to repair the burned bridge between them.

She squeezed the water from her hair and the front of her shirt on the porch, before stepping around the broken vase. Once inside, she kicked off her shoes and gripped her sister's arm.

After exhaling, she said, "I'm going to dry off so Mom doesn't have a stroke over me ruining the hardwood floors. Then we can talk."

"You're not going to yell at me?" Maddie asked in a small voice.

Kate clenched her teeth and puckered her lips. Two weeks ago, when she was angry, she might have. Today, she didn't have the energy to fight.

She shrugged. "No, but I do want answers. Let's get this done with. I need to help David and get the rest of my stuff moved in before the rental company charges me for an extra day."

Releasing her sister's arm, she trudged upstairs, ignoring her aching thighs and back from all the heavy lifting. Her old room was on the second floor, across from the bathroom, waiting to be lived in again.

On her way to retrieve a towel from the linen closet, she pushed on her bedroom door, glancing inside. The walls were sponge painted in shades of light and dark blue, reminding her of the ocean. The shag carpet had lines across it where someone had steamed cleaned it.

"Are you coming?" Maddie asked behind Kate, making her jump. She hadn't heard her sister approach. Holding out a towel and robe, she said, "You didn't return, and I'd rather have this discussion in my room without Mom. You know how involved she gets."

Kate took the items with a nod of thanks. If their mother came home in the middle of the conversation, she'd want to mediate. It was her way of gathering information under the guise of 'keeping facts straight.'

The entire family would be there because that was how they did things: together. Meanwhile, Dad would be downing several glasses of bourbon. Kate would pray for a swift death, Maddie would burst into tears, and David would seek the nearest exit.

Maddie was right. It was better to talk in private.

"Yeah, okay. I'll be there in a minute."

Giving her a wide berth, Maddie scurried to the next room without closing the door. Kate went into the bathroom and peeled off her clothes before hanging them on the shower rod to dry. Once she was reasonably dried off and dressed in the robe, she entered her sister's sanctuary.

Kate never understood why Maddie returned home after college. She had a stable career between modeling and painting, and she had a great propensity for saving money. Yet, despite her and Mom constantly butting heads, Maddie didn't show any desire of wanting to live somewhere else.

She sat on her bed, covered with a tropical comforter of orange and pink hibiscus flowers. Art supplies from paints to brushes covered an entire side of her room while makeup, jewelry, and clothes littered the rest of the room. Bottles of nail polish battled for space on her dresser beside bedazzled picture frames of friends. One was a blond man Kate had never seen, and in the middle, one of her and Maddie several years ago at a beach in San Diego.

The photo had been taken when Maddie had recently graduated high school. Kate surprised her with the trip. She'd wanted to create a final summer of happy memories together before her sister left for college.

They were both wearing sunglasses and wide-brimmed hats, hugging each other with huge smiles as they stood on the pier. The sunset covered the sky in deep hues of orange and pink, and the water glistened against the light. They'd spent the day combing the sand for seashells. It was the last time they'd spent together before drifting apart.

"That was always my favorite picture of you," Maddie murmured from her spot on the bed.

"Mine too," Kate admitted, tracing her fingers along the purple edges, smiling at the long-ago memory. "I wanted to make the trip special for you."

"You were with me. Of course it was special."

Turning away from the picture, Kate sank into a fluffy pink hang-around chair. It was hideous, like something My Little Pony regurgitated in the form of rainbows, glitter, and cotton candy. However, there was nowhere else to sit except the bed. Plus, the chair was soft, not to mention a safe distance away from her sister.

"Okay, we're here," Kate drawled, leaning forward and folding her hands in her lap.

Maddie picked at her fingernails, staring at them. Her dark hair tumbled past her shoulders, shielding her reddening face until only her nose was visible. When she spoke, her voice trembled. "I'm sorry. I never meant for my friend to share the video."

"Well, she did," Kate said in a clipped tone. "How did she even get a copy of it? Why would she share something like that?"

Maddie lifted her chin. Tears welled in her eyes, then trailed along her cheeks until they fell in fat drops onto her shirt. "Sharna and I had drinks together after you left the church, and I was showing her what happened. I swear, I was shaming Matt for cheating. I didn't know she was going to post it on her YouTube account or make fun of you."

Sharna, Maddie's dear friend, hadn't simply passed along something funny to her followers. The bitch had gone and inserted text, images, and sound effects throughout the reel. Everything was designed to defame Kate and Matt for the biggest wedding fail of the year. Then, she'd tagged Maddie in the comments, thanking her for the laugh and warning her to do better than her sister.

Kate's bottom lip quivered. The viewers were worse than Sharna, calling Kate a dumb bitch, cunt, and a full array of colorful insults. Several people wished she'd tripped and broken her neck, and nearly everyone else laughed at her stupidity.

A few called out Matt for being a sack of cheating shit, but most of the hateful criticism was directed at her. Reading the comments had hurt almost as much as the confession at the altar.

Maddie still hadn't answered her other question. It wasn't that Kate didn't believe her. What she wanted to know was how the video came to be in Sharna's possession. "Okay, what happened after you showed her the video? Did you send it to her?"

"No!" Maddie rubbed her nose and cleared her throat between

sniffles. "We were settling the tab when Sharna said she needed to borrow my phone to call her boyfriend. I didn't think about it because I forget to charge mine all the time. I didn't find out she'd sent the video to herself until the next day."

Squeaking sobs, muffled by her face buried in her knees, punctured the silence. Everything in her posture screamed she was sorry. Her long legs were drawn into her chest as she hunched, hugging herself.

It was hard not to be angry, but she looked so small and deserving of forgiveness wrapped in her little cocoon. Kate crossed the room and sat on the bed, joining her sister in her tears as they embraced.

Part of her wanted to berate Maddie for being foolish. To ask her how she could be so naïve. Kate couldn't fathom why she would associate herself with such horrible people.

However, she knew the answer. It lay in their past. Her sister craved social interaction, but Mom and Dad were never around to provide it. Kate and David did their best to fill in as playmates and companions, but they had lives too. When everyone brushed her off, Maddie had to entertain herself, leading to her surrounding herself with friends. Her peers were the first people she sought comfort and validation from instead of family.

When their parents lambasted her art career and refused to pay for the school, Maddie became a model and built a support group through her agency. When she felt like Kate or Mom attacked her, she ran to David. With their brother gone to raise his family, it made sense she'd run to someone else to vent.

Kate cleared her throat and sniffed. "Your friend sucks."

"I know," Maddie hiccupped. "When I called her, she told me to pull the stick from my ass. Everything she did was for her viewership and popularity at your expense. I feel so stupid."

"You didn't flash your panties to the crowd or beat Matt with the flowers," Kate joked.

"I already pose in my underwear for TV," Maddie scoffed. "I can't tell you how many times Mom has berated me for it. She called me a slut when I paid my college tuition with those commercials. Honestly, I don't see what the big deal is. It's my body, and I'm not ashamed of it."

"At least you're not filming porn," Kate teased.

"Dad would kill me."

"Before or after the heart attack?"

Maddie laughed. "Probably through the entire thing. Then Mom would cry to the entire world and tell them she raised me better than that."

Kate smiled. Most mothers would set the world on fire for their kids, but not theirs. She'd be carrying holy water and fire, standing at the front of the mob.

A soft knock brought their attention to the door where David waited. His shirt had partially dried, and his jeans had dark splotches of potting soil and water. "Hey, is it safe for me to come in yet?"

Maddie rubbed her face and croaked, "What, you weren't listening in the whole time?"

"Of course I was," he admitted with a remorseless shrug. "I just wanted to make sure no shots are going to be fired before I insert myself."

They made room for him, and he sat, bringing them into a damp hug between wet clothes and tears.

Whether things would be okay remained to be seen. Being perpetually angry wouldn't solve anything, and it was time for Kate to work on becoming a better person. Then, she would focus on picking up the pieces of her life.

With any luck, she might rebuild the frayed bond with her sister.

Chapter Seven

David helped Kate put her bedframe together before ditching her to unpack the boxes on her own. He wanted to be scarce before Mom discovered the broken planter.

Not that Kate blamed him. She'd have run too.

Freshly showered, she flopped belly-first onto her mattress. Dodger joined her and curled into a ball, purring when she stroked his fur. Boxes surrounded her, stacked on top of each other in every corner, but she couldn't bring herself to go through them.

If her body hurt this much today, she dreaded what she'd feel like in the morning. Unpacking would have to wait. She had all the time in the world.

Her phone sat nearby, plugged into the charger. Reaching for it, she scrolled through it for something to do.

A new text from Matt sat in her notifications. *'You can't ignore me forever. Please call me. I swear, I didn't mean to cheat. We can still salvage this.'*

She snorted. Not likely. Sooner or later, she'd have to respond, at least to return her ring, but that was something she could address later.

Once she blew through her lives on her mobile games, she viewed her social media for the first time in two weeks.

Dozens of messages from colleagues flooded her inbox, as well as a request and DM from Ian. Curious, she opened it, reading it.

'Hey, we met at the bar in Gilbert the other night. I wasn't sure if you wanted me to reach out, but I thought you could use a friend. My offer to talk is still on the table if you're interested.'

She didn't respond right away, wanting to know who he was first. The last thing she needed was to involve herself with someone clingy or creepy.

She wouldn't admit it, but Carlos's words nagged at her. She couldn't tell if he was jealous or warning her away from another potential heartbreak.

Ian's Facebook profile loaded:
Ian Anderson
Child Psychologist
Studied Psychology at Harvard University
Lives in Chandler, Arizona
Hometown: Boston, Massachusetts
Single

Everything else was kept private. Kate studied his picture, contemplating the information in his bio. Not many people were native to Arizona, and it wasn't uncommon to escape cold weather to live here. However, it didn't stop her from concocting a story for why he'd move across the country.

Maybe, he was a secret agent posing as a psychologist. She shook her head. That was cliché and overdone. She could do better. He could be a reformed hitman lying low after losing his inheritance.

Him, a hitman, counseling children? She laughed. Someone would have discovered his secret identity by now.

His picture was of him playing his guitar, with one leg crossed over his knee. She shamelessly stared at it since there wasn't anyone to judge her for it.

A five-o-clock shadow lined his jaw. Though he didn't face the camera, happiness radiated from his relaxed shoulders and how he held his instrument.

He appeared the same way at the bar, at ease without a care in the world. It was difficult to believe such a calm man would transform into a nighttime vigilante, ready and willing to defend her honor.

Whoever he was, he was worth getting to know. If his primary issue was an aversion to dating, that was fine by her. She wasn't interested in a boyfriend anyway.

Sucking in her breath, she sent a friend request before she could think better of it. Then returned to his message and typed a response.

'*Sorry for the late reply. I haven't been online. Still wanna talk?*'

His status changed to active, and dots danced below the text, followed by an incoming message. '*Hey! How are you? I guess everyone has asked you that by now.*'

If he only knew. Her phone pinged with a notification of him accepting her request. She continued typing. '*Yeah. Or they tell me how sorry they are for the videos. Not my finest moment.*'

'*I didn't want to mention it, but I'll be happy to listen. Would you rather talk in person? I'm free this weekend. We can go to a park where it's quiet.'*

Offering a public place to meet was brilliant. There was no pressure to be intimate, and people rarely paid attention to others at a park. She could be anonymous enough no one would recognize her, unlike at a bar. She could get away from her family and anyone else who wanted to offer an opinion. Also, if Ian turned out to be a creep, she could easily leave.

'I'd like that.'

'Great! Tempe Town Lake on Saturday at 7:00 PM?'

'Sure. See ya there.'

She sent him her number with a promise to add him to her contacts. His card was in her purse, forgotten between her hangover and the pressure of moving.

Curious, she dug it from her bag and traced her finger along the embossed print. The card was a brilliant shade of white with a picture of him in a suit on the front. Modern blue lines bordered the card with matching text.

Flipping it over, she studied his writing. His script was elegant in a calligraphic way, slanted and stylish. Beside his name and number was a smiley face, making her lips curve. It was such a little thing, but it was like he wanted her to be happy without telling her.

The remaining weight dissipated from her heart as she entered his number into her contacts. For the first time in weeks, anxiety didn't threaten to choke her. Tonight, she could conquer anything thrown her way.

~ * ~

Kate should have known parking would be terrible on a Saturday evening. Cars lined the street, regardless of strict traffic laws. Parking garages in Tempe were expensive, and it was impossible to find anything with a meter.

Cars tailed each other, music blared at unsafe decibels, and people jaywalked between the stop-and-go traffic. If she were smart, she'd have called for a Lyft.

By some miracle, a car backed out of a parking space right as Kate pulled into the tiny lot behind Tempe Beach Park. Being among one of the few free parking lots in the city, she sped into it as someone else slammed their breaks and honked their horn at her. She couldn't hear what they screamed through the window, but the middle finger said it all.

She didn't bother to return the gesture. Putting the car into park, she opened her phone to text Ian. *'I'm here.'*

'Where are you at? I'll come to you.'

'*I found a parking spot at the beach park. I'll meet you at the entrance beneath the sign.*'

'*You drove? Are you crazy?*'

What a thing to ask. With a snort, she typed another message before stowing the phone away. '*You tell me. You're the shrink. :p*'

Stepping into the dry heat, she expelled a breath and smiled, stretching as the late afternoon light kissed her skin. Tempe Town Lake sprawled ahead of her, glistening against the illumination of the artificial and natural light. The sun sat low in the sky, turning to a deep blue against the lake. Boats glided across over the rippling water as the orange sun rays danced across the horizon, creating an image of something she could find on a thousand-piece puzzle.

The gate loomed ahead, and butterflies flapped inside her stomach, asking her if this was a good idea. Since the night at the bar, she hadn't done much of anything. The closer she got to the entrance, the harder her heart drummed against her chest.

Inhaling slowly, she forced her feet to keep moving. Sweat formed along the ridges of her spine until they soaked her thin shirt.

When she saw Ian standing with his hands in his shorts' back pockets, her mouth went dry. As she looked at him, it seemed the already God-awful heat skyrocketed, sending perspiration to areas she didn't know could sweat.

He wasn't one of those clichéd men with muscles bulging from every inch of his body. Nevertheless, he was appealing in the way he confidently carried himself. He was self-assured and unshy, traits Kate lacked and wished she had.

Their eyes connected as she came closer, and he smiled, closing the distance between them. Carrying two bottles of water, he offered her one. "Hey."

The corner of her lips twitched. Like the night at the bar, his relaxed demeanor caught her off guard, sending heat creeping into her cheeks. She returned his smile and uttered a simple, "Hi."

"Wanna take a walk?" Ian indicated the winding dirt path around the lake.

She accepted the water bottle and swept her arm out in front of them in an after-you gesture. They fell in step beside each other, moving at a leisurely pace as people rode bikes or skated past.

Now that they were together, she felt shy and self-conscious. She remained silent, taking in the park's greenery against the Arizona desert landscape. Despite the sun disappearing behind the mountains, it was so hot the devil wouldn't visit.

Ian glanced at her. "What's on your mind?"

"I was thinking about how much I hate the heat."

He laughed. "You're in the wrong state."

She smiled and sipped her drink. Little beads of condensation formed rivulets, sliding down the length and dripping onto the ground. "What can I say? Arizona is my home. It doesn't mean I have to like the summer. What about you? I saw your profile on Facebook. What brought you here?"

Taking a deep drink from his bottle, he didn't answer. Kate wondered again what his story was, but without the hitman or secret agent part. She decided to prod a bit. The worst he could do was tell her to mind her business. "I don't mind talking, but you can't expect me to share my life story without doing the same."

He smirked. "Who's analyzing who now?"

"Did you see my Social Media Bride video?"

"I did."

She appreciated the lack of judgment in his tone. "Well, you already know my most embarrassing story, starting and ending with my life going to crap at the altar. All I'm asking for is a Cliffs Notes version of yours."

He led her toward the Neil G. Giuliano Park in front of the silver corporate buildings that overlooked the water. Painted metal picnic tables sat ahead of the sandy walkway before the lake. Behind the tables was a circular amphitheater with seating spaced out on the hill.

They found a shaded section outside of the common area and sat in the grass as they gazed across the man-made lake.

Watching the lights from the bridge bounce across the calm water made Kate recall the trip Matt took without her, and she sighed. "I was supposed to go on a cruise for my honeymoon."

"I'm sorry. If it helps to know, you could have made it through the vows and had a great trip, but many people don't make it past the honeymoon phase. Money, sex, and communication are big contributors to failed relationships, but approximately three quarters of couples divorce because they aren't prepared for married life. Statistically, most relationships dissolve within the first ten years, particularly between the fourth and eighth anniversary. Among that demographic, the rates are highest among partners in their early twenties. In fact, I'm part of that group. I was married for five years when my ex-wife left."

Kate couldn't decide if she should laugh or cry. He sounded like he was reciting a textbook, but his past made her wonder if her relationship with Matt was doomed from the start. She wanted to believe people could find their happily-ever-after, but Ian made it sound like the odds were slim.

"You make marriage sound like it's not worth it," she said thoughtfully.

She wondered how much time had passed for him. She could tell by the bitterness in his tone he hadn't moved on, no matter how much he hid it behind smiles and a pleasant demeanor. When he mentioned his ex-wife, he looked like he wanted to punch something.

Perhaps that was why Carlos told her to avoid pursuing anything with Ian. Depending on how close they were, he might have been aware of his friend's past.

He shrugged, watching the lake ahead. "I'm sure it is, but I wasn't lucky enough to hold on to my wife. I know your breakup was bad, but at least it happened before you got hitched. I was in grad school when I got married, and it was with the understanding we'd start a family once I finished." He paused, and a cloud darkened his features as his shoulders slumped, and he draped his arms around his knees. "During my last year, Sonya, my wife, wanted to expand our family since she'd already finished school and we were mostly stable. That was when we found out I couldn't have kids. Long story short: she left and found someone else who could."

Wow. What kind of person left their partner because of something they couldn't control? "Ian—"

He signaled her to stop. "Don't. It was several years ago. I told you this because I understand what you're going through. Not from a psychologist's point of view, but as a human being who's been dealt a crappy hand. The only advice I can give you to make it easier is to give it time and try not to isolate yourself."

"That's easier said than done. There's no one I can trust at the moment, and I'm constantly between angry, sad, and embarrassed. I'm mad because Matt, my ex, didn't end things with me, even though he was unhappy. I'm upset because I'm alone again. I'm humiliated because my sister went and shared a mortifying moment of my life with her friend, who in turn made me a joke. I'm exhausted from every other emotion running rampant in my head."

As she rambled, she studied Ian's face. There was no judgment in his eyes, and he was listening as if he cared.

He took in her words and stroked his stubble, downing the rest of his water before speaking again. "Your emotions are normal. It's going to take some time, but once you accept what's happened, you'll begin to move on."

She raised an eyebrow. "You've never had your fifteen minutes of mortifying fame. That's difficult to move past."

"You're right, I haven't, but that doesn't mean it's the end of the world. It's more like a giant speed bump in the road. You get jolted around a bit, swear, and then get back on track."

"'Back on track' would be finding a job and not having a constant reminder of my failures. I've started putting in applications, but no one has called or emailed yet."

"You need to let it go. Everyone will eventually forget about it. Besides, choices have a way of catching up with us. You might believe people perceive you as crazy, but I guarantee there are others who aren't impressed with your ex cheating on you, especially the night before your wedding. Last I checked, adultery is still frowned upon. You can think of people's judgment against him as your silver lining."

"What's your silver lining?" she asked curiously.

"My work is fulfilling."

She wrinkled her nose. "That's not moving on. That's like, I don't know, admitting defeat. Moving on would be to consider the potential to love again."

Bitterness flashed through his eyes as he scoffed. "No, thank you. I've always wanted children. I could never be with someone who doesn't want kids. Yet, if I was to find a woman willing to try adoption or fertility, I still couldn't guarantee either option. If it failed, she'd be trapped and disappointed. I couldn't put anyone through that, and I've accepted being alone and shifted my focus to helping others. When I'm not playing music or working, I volunteer at a children's home. It's enough for me."

Wow, and here she thought she had problems forging ahead after being hurt. Two weeks ago, his eyes had been the window to a tortured soul as he'd played his music. She saw it again now, during his confession.

She had an overwhelming desire to nurture him. She carefully pondered her next words. It was a touchy subject for most people, and he was almost a stranger. The last thing she wanted to do was alienate him.

"You need to take care of yourself. You shouldn't push everyone away just because the wrong woman hurt you. Life happens, it is unpredictable, but a loving couple would lean on each other for support, not leave when things get hard."

"That's a nice fantasy, but reality is harsh."

Sheesh, he was stubborn. What did he tell kids when parents got divorced: never get married? Did he say Santa Claus wasn't real? "Does this mean you're celibate too?"

He snorted, and the humor returned to his features. "That's a very personal question."

"I was teasing." She blushed furiously and mentally kicked herself for making such a flippant comment. She changed the subject before her face became redder than a lobster. "Back to what you were saying though, I get that a lot of marriages are unsuccessful. God knows Matt would have been a disappointment, but I'd like to find someone to fall in love with again someday."

Ian shifted in the grass and smiled. "I understand. I've been on the occasional date from time to time, but it gives me anxiety because I'd worry about the strings that come with it. I could tell her I don't want anything serious and find one of us developing feelings anyway."

Poor guy. That didn't seem like a fun way to live, always shutting himself out when someone came along. The perfect woman could fall into his life, and he'd never realize it.

No wonder Carlos warned her away. He'd acted jealous, but after listening to Ian, Carlos's actions made more sense.

"How well do you know Carlos?"

She didn't realize she'd asked until Ian regarded at her with a bemused expression. "We play basketball at the gym sometimes. We don't have Tuesday night poker or anything, but I'd say he's all right. Why do you ask?"

She lowered her eyes, unsure if she should voice her concerns or betray her friend's confidence. What if he didn't want their conversation to be shared? Would he be mad if he knew she'd said something? Most importantly, would Ian be offended by what Carlos had insinuated?

"Uh, after the night at the bar, he told me you weren't the type of guy to have a fling with. Not that I want one," she added quickly.

Geez, why did she have to put her foot in her mouth? Now Ian was going to get the wrong idea and think she was looking for a rebound.

Understanding appeared in his eyes, and he chuckled. "Oh. I'm not sure if I should tell you this, but he, uh—"

"Likes me more than a friend?" she finished.

He grimaced. "Yeah. It was pretty obvious. At first, I thought you two were a thing until you mentioned the wedding. Did he tell you how he feels?"

"Yeah."

She didn't tell him about Carlos's awkward invitation to stay with him, but her stomach dropped as if she was having the conversation anyway. She had her suspicions the night they went drinking, but hoped she'd been wrong. Now, with everything laid bare, only time would tell if their friendship lasted after this or if he'd walk away.

"Do you reciprocate his sentiments?" Ian asked.

"He's my friend," she said honestly. "I admire him, but I don't share his feelings."

"Have you told him this?"

She nodded. "We haven't talked since he helped me move. I swear I wasn't mean to him, but he dropped this on me right after my engagement ended."

"I see. At least you told him the truth. He'll respect you more for your honesty."

His validation was a relief, yet she couldn't shake the anxiety that she'd destroyed one of her closest friendships. It wasn't her fault; she knew this, so why did she feel guilty anyway?

She turned her attention to the lake, letting her mind drift. A small sailboat sliced through the water, carrying two men in life jackets. She couldn't see their faces, but based on their gestures, bobbing heads, and the drinks in their hands, they seemed happy. All around her, the park teemed with activity. Joggers kept an even pace on the trails, a young woman walked her dog, and a family with young children rode bicycles.

While they talked, the sun took the final hues of orange and pink to give way to the dark sky against the city lights. Tempe Town Lake didn't compare to the major cities of the world, but the way everything reflected off the water was no less beautiful than if she'd been on the California or Washington coasts.

When her legs itched from sitting in the dry grass for too long, she pushed herself up and brushed her shorts. Ian stood too and stretched, reaching high over his head and revealing toned abs. Kate pretended not to notice and hid her disappointment when his shirt lowered with his arms.

There was no denying he was a good-looking man, though it'd be prudent not to pursue anything with him. However, that didn't mean they couldn't get to know each other, and she wasn't ready for the evening to end.

"What do you think of walking down Mill Avenue?" she asked.

"Sure," he said, offering his elbow to her. "I'd like to learn more about you."

They walked at a comfortable pace, and soon, Kate's legs ached from hiking through the park's path. It would have been easier to drive, but they'd spend more time finding a parking spot.

When they arrived at the main street, back-to-back cars crawled through traffic, next to a sizeable crowd of pedestrians. Teenagers, ranging from high-schoolers to college-aged, filled the sidewalks. There were also couples holding hands beneath the bright streetlights. Neon signs flashed overhead, and a blend of food from the different establishments filled the air.

In the dense throng, Kate took Ian's hand, lest she found herself lost. The contact sent a jolt of giddy excitement into her chest, making her a bit dizzy.

His hands were warm and his fingertips calloused, most likely from playing the guitar. For a moment, she visualized where else he could place them before dismissing the thought.

Don't go there, girl. It's too soon and not at all appropriate.

An ice-cream parlor sat on the block's corner, and Kate led him inside. A bell pinged overhead as they entered the busy shop. The low conversations of patrons in the line were nothing compared to the loud nightlife outside, and she relaxed as they stepped in line.

Ian nudged her. "You okay?" he whispered.

"Yeah. I get a bit nervous in crowds. Too much mental stimulation with the lights, people, and noise."

A grin crept onto his lips. "And yet you're here in the busiest part of Tempe. Very brave."

"I can't always keep myself locked away in my parents' house. Plus, I like to keep busy."

"That's fair. So, tell me, what do you do for a living?"

Oof. She hadn't expected the question, and her good mood fizzled. "I taught Geology at ASU before the video. After it went viral, they fired me."

He dipped his head. "Ah, crap, I'm sorry. I didn't mean to—"

She waved him off. "It's not your fault. I'm sure I'll find something once my wedding disaster fades into the background." Needing to change the subject, she said, "I saw on Facebook that you moved here from Boston. Were you a psychologist there too?"

He rubbed the back of his neck as if he was now the one uncomfortable. As they sidled through the line, she noticed his feet shift from side to side and his other fist curl at his side.

Finally, he said, "No. George, my adoptive father, endorsed me to study at Harvard. He's an alumnus and continues his practice off campus. He initially wanted to bring me into his practice, but when I expressed a desire to leave Massachusetts and start with a clean slate, he encouraged me to start my own."

She puckered her lips. If they kept touching on uncomfortable topics, they were headed into a downward spiral. "We might be safer asking what we wanted to be when we grew up."

"Indeed."

Thankfully, he didn't seem ready to flee. In fact, a gleam appeared in his gray eyes, and his mouth curved into a wide grin.

"What are you thinking about?" she asked.

"Instead of playing Twenty Questions, we should try a different game. I'm going to guess and order your favorite ice cream flavor. You do the same for me."

It was silly but interesting and cute. She loved it. "What if I get something you hate?"

"I could order something just as bad for you. I guess we'll have to see who survives."

"Any food allergies I should know about?" She didn't want their evening spent in an ER.

"Nope."

She directed her attention to the rainbow of colors in front of her. Small calligraphy place cards identified the different flavors. The assortment was huge, stretching from one end of the bar to the other, curving until it met the wall near the door. Sprinkles, nuts, and sauces were near the register.

She peeked at Ian, trying to figure out what kind of dessert he liked. Should she play it safe or be adventurous? As she glanced through her peripheral, she saw him rubbing his stubbled jaw and leaning close to the divider. He did that for several flavors, especially the more interesting ones like jalapeño or honey avocado.

If he was going to be adventurous…

A girl with braces and a white apron tied around her waist greeted them. "Hi there! What can I get for you two?"

Kate cleared her throat and decided to go for it. She chose the first weird flavor she could find, a green vanilla with marshmallow and caramel. "Okay, I want the booger flavor."

Ian choked, and Kate bit back a giggle. She had a feeling she was going to pay for her choice in a minute.

The girl's lips twitched, and her eyes widened as she looked between them. She spun around, keeping her back to them for several seconds before facing Ian with a watery gaze. Her voice trembled with mirth when she asked, "What will you have, sir?"

An evil grin filled his lips as he pointed to the flavors. "Can I get a scoop of beer and also of bacon? Is there any way you can blend it into a smoothie by chance?"

When the girl rushed away in a fit of muffled laughs, Kate folded her arms over her chest. "Beer and bacon?"

He shrugged, and his lips trembled as if he was trying to repress a laugh. "You're the one who ordered booger flavored ice cream. I don't wanna hear it."

"I feel like we've dived into the world of Harry Potter. Who comes up with these crazy flavors?" she teased.

"That's a good question. I've seen flavors for everything, and I don't recommend trying it fried at state fairs. It's gross."

"Worse than boogers?"

He laughed and moved around her, closer to the register. When the girl brought their ice cream to the counter, he swiped his credit card before Kate could offer to pay.

"I could have gotten that," she said as they took a seat at one of the corner tables.

He dipped a spoon into his cup and took a bite before answering. He made an appreciative sound and smacked his lips. "Hm, not bad. Anyway, you could have paid, but this was my idea, and you got the weirder flavor. Consider it my treat."

She eyed the shake as if it was something stuck to the toilet. She wasn't against beer or bacon by themselves, but as an ice cream flavor? At least this place didn't sell desserts with crickets. That's where she would have drawn the line.

Flipping the lid off the top, she jabbed her spoon into the cup, not bothering to unwrap her straw. If it tasted as bad as it smelled, she wouldn't get past the first bite.

The beer was pungent. Not in a horrible way, but it had a yeasty smell to it without the rich qualities found in darker ales. The bacon aroma was worse. It was something people put on cheeseburgers or added to a side of sausage and eggs. The combination of the two smelled like something from a fast-food grease trap.

Bile rose when the flavor touched her tongue, and she stabbed the spoon in her ice cream, reaching for a napkin to cover her mouth. Dropping the cup onto the table, she waved her hands. "Oh my god, I can't. I'm sorry."

"I'm sure it's not that bad," he said, reaching for the oversized container and taking a sip. He twisted toward the window and gagged.

"Okay, maybe it is," he wheezed. "This is disgusting."

He pushed the smoothie away and offered her his. "Wanna share this one?"

Plucking her spoon from her cup, she wiped it off on a napkin before skimming a bite from his. Vanilla and caramel assaulted her tastebuds, chasing away the gross concoction mocking them at the edge of the table.

"Well how about that? Snot isn't so bad after all," she said.

Ian laughed. "I think next time, I'll take you out for seafood."

She paused, holding her spoon in the air. "Is there going to be a next time?"

He straightened in his chair, resting his forearms against the edge of the table. He scraped his bottom lip through his teeth, watching her as if he wanted her for dessert. "I'd like there to be a next time if you're interested."

She was, even though she'd recently exited a serious relationship, and Ian came with an entire suitcase of commitment issues.

They shared a connection, a spark that promised more, and Kate wanted to follow it. Something passed between them during their talk at the park, an understanding of each other's pain. *And* they possessed a similar sense of humor.

In a short time, she wanted to know more than the basics, like his favorite color or which music he kept on his playlists. She wanted to learn about the things that made him tick.

He was comfortable to be around, allowing her to be herself without hiding behind a mask.

Grinning, she closed her mouth around her spoon, sucking on it in satisfaction as his eyes dilated and his breath hitched. She swallowed and said, "I'd like that."

It was the easiest decision she'd ever made.

Chapter Eight

After her time spent with Ian, Kate went to bed with happy thoughts and not a worry. When she woke up to check her email, her mood soured.

She clicked on a new message, and another form rejection greeted her with the standard, "We thank you for your interest in a career with us. However, we have chosen to go in another direction at this time."

This was one of many nonsense replies that filled her inbox. Others suggested she was overqualified or unsuitable. The rest ghosted her.

No matter who she contacted, the unspoken response was, "We saw you online, and there is no way in *Hell* we would hire you." She couldn't decide if she'd feel better with the truth or the lie.

Closing the email, she scanned job sites for new postings. When the search yielded nothing useful or relevant, she shut the laptop and slumped in her office chair.

This is hopeless.

The frenzy surrounding her wedding disaster had mostly dissipated when the next big scandal swept through the media. As everyone said, the ordeal lost its excitement, taking the attention away from her. The problem was the damage had been done. With over a million views, her status on the internet as the #socialmediabride was cemented, making job hunting impossible.

Her phone pinged with an incoming message. Thinking it might be Ian, her heart jumped. It was Matt. '*We need to talk.*'

After the last several ignored messages, why couldn't he take a hint and piss off? She considered blocking him or changing her number, but she wanted to return his ring.

Yet, she wasn't comfortable with responding. It was too soon, and the pain was too fresh. She was afraid of exploding and giving him more ammunition against her.

However, if she didn't acknowledge him, he'd keep poking.

'Now you want to talk? You went on our honeymoon and took pictures with women on each arm. In case you forgot, you also captioned yourself as living the #singlelife in your photos, dumbass. I have nothing left to say to you.'

'Can we be adults about this?'"

She ground her teeth, holding her phone in a death grip. She wanted to say a multitude of things, to use every profanity she knew, but that would play into his hands.

Every time she typed a response, she deleted it before pressing send. Her words were too angry or antagonistic.

Finally, she replied with the most civil thing she could come up with, one that didn't color her vision red.

'What is there to say? You cheated, and I don't want to talk or take you back. If it's all right with you, I'd like to send David to return your ring.'

'That's just like you. The moment you get uncomfortable, you run. You don't try to see another point of view or hear what other people have to say. You demand everything be your way, and you blame the world for your problems.'

His words stung as if he'd slapped her. She wasn't like that, was she?

Yet, she'd been swift to condemn her sister for things that weren't her fault. Then she'd harshly judged the college student at the bar when he harassed her. Now she was refusing to listen, convinced there was nothing Matt could say to justify his actions. If she walked away without talking to him first, she'd prove him right.

'I don't want to argue. You cheated, and I have no plans to reconcile. I feel it's best if we go our separate ways with no further contact other than to return each other's things.'

The phone chirped with another message. *'I poured two years into our relationship. I gave you my time when I could have gone out with friends or stayed late at work to earn more money. I never complained when you needed to grade papers or stay late to tutor students. When you begged me for that cat, I gave in even though I didn't have time to take care of him. The least you can do is give me five minutes of your time.'*

She set her phone face-down on her desk and stood, pacing. A migraine throbbed at the base of her neck, spreading into her shoulders as nausea churned her stomach. She took shallow breaths, sinking to her knees when dizziness overcame her.

Matt's accusations weren't fair. She'd put as much effort into their relationship as he had, canceling class trips and research opportunities to spend time with him. When he brushed her off to pursue work, she said nothing. When she was too tired for sex, he coerced her until she said yes. He had no right to imply she'd been a poor girlfriend.

Seeing him was a terrible idea. He'd find a way to make her listen and forgive him. Matt would work his charm, first through begging and then gifts if the former didn't work. Or he would make her question herself until Kate was certain she was wrong. In the past, she'd apologized for things that weren't her fault. At the time, she thought she'd done something wrong that she'd missed. Now, she wasn't sure.

The chorus to *Just What I Needed* blared from her phone, playing cheerful lyrics as if it would make her feel better.

"Feck, does he ever give it a rest?"

Silencing it before his persistence ruined one of her favorite songs, she jabbed the screen harder than necessary. "What!"

"Well, that's hardly polite," he said, calm as ever. "Your temper is going to land you in trouble. If it hasn't already."

She squeezed her eyes shut and counted backward from ten. That was a low blow. He had to know she'd lost her job because of that damned wedding video.

When confident she wouldn't snarl into the receiver, she said, "Your behavior is inappropriate and bordering on harassment. I will send David with a police officer if I need to. We are through."

"You wanna talk about crimes?" Matt asked. "How about domestic violence? Are you aware that it's a Class One Misdemeanor in the state of Arizona, punishable by up to six months in jail, substantial fines and fees, community service, and counseling?"

Where was he going with this? She wasn't abusive. She'd never touched…oh, shit. Her heart leaped into her throat, and she clutched her chest. He wouldn't.

"That was in the heat of the moment on a very emotional day for me," she said, her voice trembling.

"Assault is assault. We can argue semantics all day, but you are as guilty as I am. The only difference is that I am choosing to forgive you. Can you do the same for me?"

Frack. She was so screwed.

~ * ~

His threat had worked, and against her better judgment, Kate agreed to meet with Matt the next day. She couldn't go to jail. The stress alone would kill her if an inmate didn't get to her first. She'd never work again if convicted.

The odds of winning a domestic violence case based on a crime of passion wasn't unheard of, but she'd be spending a fortune on legal counsel with the *hope* the judge would dismiss it. Also, Arizona wasn't a forgiving state when it came to abuse.

Checking her appearance in the bathroom mirror, she fluffed her curled hair. Matt wasn't worth the effort, but she didn't want him to think she'd let herself go.

She wore an off-the-shoulder white and black pinstripe shirt and tight denim capris, paired with black sandals in a low heel. She'd borrowed Maddie's nail polish and had done her best with the bright red while wondering if she'd gone a tad overboard. Frills were not Kate's thing, and she considered changing into a pair of shorts and a tank top.

Anxiety thrummed through her. She needed to speak to someone about meeting with her ex but hadn't wanted to hear Maddie tell her, "I told you so." Mom was out of the question too. She wanted them to reconcile.

She texted Carlos to tell him what was happening, but that was another disappointment. He didn't respond, and the rejection stung.

She hated feeling guilty over not reciprocating his feelings and wanted her friend back. However, it seemed he was done with her. He'd updated his Facebook with a trip to the Grand Canyon. Every summer, they went with a group to collect samples and categorize them. This time he'd gone without even inviting her. Seeing those pictures was another painful reminder of the friendship she'd lost.

At least, she had her brother. Yesterday, when she called David, he promised to come with her as moral support and step in if needed. The fact that he was sacrificing his time, going with her instead of taking his girls to the park meant everything to her. When the world abandoned her, he was the person she trusted most to remain by her side.

When she walked into their parent's living room, David's eyes narrowed as his gaze landed on her. "You don't like makeup, and Maddie has to force you to wear a dress. I hope this doesn't mean you're getting back with Matt. You're better than that."

Kate laughed. "Please, I have more dignity than to beg for a man who cheated on me. I want him to see what he's missing."

"Okay, if you aren't trying to reconcile, then why are you agreeing to meet with him? You told me before that you wanted me to go there alone."

Groaning, she reached into her purse for her phone. Opening yesterday's conversation with Matt, she handed her cell to David. "He called me right after insinuating he'd press assault charges if I don't go."

Red splotches darkened her brother's cheeks, and his nostrils flared. "Douchebag! He doesn't get to whine like a little bitch when *he* cheated!"

"Yeah, well, the sooner I deliver the ring, the sooner I can be done with him. He won't give up, and I'm hoping talking today will give us closure."

"This is your life, not his. He shouldn't be manipulating you into something that makes you uncomfortable."

She wiped her palms against her pants and shook her head. "What can I say? He has me trapped."

"Can I castrate him?"

Kate giggled. She'd give her entire savings for Matt to lose his manhood. "As tempting as that is, you'd lose your medical license and go to prison. I'm pretty sure Tracy and the girls wouldn't appreciate that. Besides, orange isn't your color."

David gave the phone back and sniffed. "I don't like this. You should bail."

"I can't, so let's get this over with, okay?"

He withdrew his keys from his pocket, scowling as if they were offensive. "Fine. Do you have anything there worth bringing back?"

"Just some clothes. I left everything else at my apartment. You and Dad were supposed to clear everything out while I was gone."

"Good thing we didn't. It's awkward enough going to return the ring. Imagine having to spend the entire day moving your stuff."

Kate would rather not think about it. Matt had tainted everything she associated with their relationship, including the home they were meant to share. She'd be happy once this was behind her.

She followed David to his truck. Once inside, she buckled her seatbelt and kept quiet. She wasn't in the mood to continue their conversation. They didn't speak until they got on the road.

"I want to remind you to be strong in there, no matter what he says," her brother said. "Nothing is worth staying in a toxic relationship. Do you understand?"

She watched the mile markers pass by while cars zipped through traffic, all in a rush to go nowhere. Meanwhile, she dreaded the confrontation to come. As much as she wanted to be done with this, she equally wished they could put it off.

Leaning against the window, she kept her gaze outside, resisting the urge to tell David to shut it. She could sense a lecture coming on, and she didn't have the energy to listen to it.

"I mean it. If you go back to Matt, you will enable him to keep taking control. He wants you to feel guilty while he minimizes his actions. He is deflecting everything he did on to you so he doesn't have to shoulder the blame. When you go in there, hold him accountable."

His words made sense but didn't ease the knots in Kate's stomach. Logically, she knew he was right. Matt wanted control. He had no intention of claiming responsibility for his part in their failed relationship. But if she held her ground, she risked going to jail.

When she didn't respond, her brother squeezed her shoulder. He said nothing, and they spent the rest of the ride in silence.

The trip was too short, and soon, Matt's house loomed ahead. On either side of his driveway, bicycles, skateboards, and scooters littered the lawns and sidewalk. Kids kicked a soccer ball in a yard, cheering when they got past their friends. Kate envied them for not having a care in the world.

The last time she'd been here, she'd made a list of plans: It was an older house in suburban Chandler, rooted in a middle-class neighborhood.

She'd wanted to paint the interior while Matt set up the backyard similar to her parent's house. They'd have a barbeque pit, a small garden, and maybe a shaded area to sit with friends. Nothing fancy, but something that made it feel like their home, a place where they built memories, cuddling at night and having meals together.

They'd also planned to have kids. She'd always wanted them, little people to shower love upon and give them a happy family. In her daydreams, Matt would play sports with them while Kate shared her passion for science and crafts.

Everything she hoped for was gone, shattered the moment Matt cheated and lied. The house had become a painful reminder of everything she could have had and lost.

She exited the truck and stared at the cracked cement beneath her feet. David's legs entered her line of sight. She lifted her gaze and followed his sour expression to the lawn in front of them.

"Does this dude ever do yardwork?" he asked.

Dandelions sprouted between the rocks, and ugly brown weeds covered the landscape. The yard looked like nature was reclaiming it. If the neighborhood had a homeowners' association, Matt would be fined out the wazoo.

They approached the front door where Kate adjusted her purse strap around her shoulder, pressing the bag to her chest like a shield. Her finger hovered over the doorbell, and she flexed it.

"You can do this," David murmured. "I'll be right here with you."

I can do this. Matt can't do anything with someone else here. Return the ring and leave. That was simple enough, right?

Bracing herself, she pressed the small button.

"Be right there," Matt shouted.

Kate's stomach flipped and somersaulted, threatening to project her breakfast onto the porch.

Matt opened the door and stood inside the threshold, raking his gaze over her body appreciatively. With nothing separating them, she had no choice but to focus on him. When their eyes met, he grinned and threaded a lock of her hair through his fingers. "I like your hair. Is that a new shirt?"

She didn't respond as she stepped out of reach, forcing him to let go. Then she took him in, and though she hated to admit it, he looked good too. Jeans hugged his hips, and his casual gray shirt clung to his chest. He wasn't buff or overly muscled, but he exercised twice a week, keeping in good shape. His skin glowed with a deep Caribbean tan, and his crew cut had filled in around the sides. The expensive cologne she'd gifted him for his birthday lingered between them.

When his eyes drifted to her brother, his lips tightened before lifting into a polite smile. "Hey, man. I wasn't expecting you."

"Try not to look so thrilled," David said in a dry voice. "I'll cut through the crap and save us time. I'm here for Kate, so don't pretend to be my friend or talk like we're asshole buddies, all right?" Without waiting for a response, he pushed past Matt, shoulder-checking him on the way inside.

Matt's nostrils flared as a glower replaced his fake smile. "Feel free to come in, jackass." Clearing his throat, he readjusted his features and motioned for Kate to follow. "It's hot outside. Make yourself at home."

Kate tentatively crossed the threshold, relaxing in the cold air. She hadn't been in the heat for five minutes when the sun threatened to melt her into a puddle of sweat.

A glance told her Matt hadn't bothered to clean. Not that he'd ever kept his living space tidy. It was the same as always. Mail was scattered across the coffee table, clothes draped on the couch's armrest, and baskets of unfolded laundry sat on the floor. On the bright side, at least the house didn't smell.

Clearing a space off the couch, she took a seat, tossing his laundry to the other end and setting her purse beside her. Matt dropped into the recliner facing the long end of the coffee table.

The toilet flushed from the bathroom hallway, and David appeared soon after, eyeing the clutter with his lip curled in disgust. "Dude, you're a slob. Do you ever pick up after yourself, or did you plan on my sister acting like your little woman from the Stone Age? Do you want her to cook too?"

Her brother was too decent to say it, but Matt would be safer eating from the garbage than to sit through her culinary efforts.

Matt's cheeks and ears flushed a deep red as his eyebrows furrowed like two caterpillars mating. He shifted in his chair to glare at David. "I don't recall inviting you into my house. Either grab yourself a beer and be quiet or go wait outside in your truck. I don't need your commentary."

David wiggled his fingers like he was back in high school. "Ooh! What are you gonna do? Threaten to press charges against me too? What kind of asshole move is that anyway? I thought you were trying to win my sister back, you little cunt-waffle, not push her away."

He didn't seem to notice the steam practically spewing from Matt's ears as he beamed at Kate. "Where's your stuff? I'd like to get the hell out of this dump."

If looks could kill, David would be six feet under. He seemed unfazed as the blood drained from Kate's face.

She pointed to the hallway. "Uh, My clothes in the bedroom closet. Would you mind getting them?"

He could do that, while she gave back the ring to Matt. Working as a team, they could be out the door and on the road in ten minutes or less.

"Great! I'll leave you to it." Swaggering into the kitchen, David opened the refrigerator and grabbed a beer, popping the tab with a loud 'psh.' Slurping loudly, he saluted with the middle finger behind Matt's back and said, "Thanks for the free beer!"

Kate covered her mouth, frozen in place long after her brother disappeared down the hallway. If her ex didn't murder David for his antics, she might. Her face burned with mortification at the way he was behaving. She wished the messy room would swallow her.

A pregnant pause engulfed them. Kate kept her eyes trained on the floor, waiting to see if Matt would speak.

When it became clear he wouldn't talk, Kate brought her purse into her lap. She fumbled around inside, forcing it wide open. Of course, it would be at the bottom, behind the keys, wallet, and receipts. When she found the box, she withdrew it and presented it to Matt.

When he stared at her with down-turned lips, she set it on the coffee table and shrank into the couch cushions. "I think it's best if we don't postpone the inevitab—"

"I want to go to couple's counseling." He sprang to his feet and crossed the room to her, expertly navigating around the heap of junk in front of the couch.

He was so far into her personal space she had to set her purse on the floor and scoot backward until her butt rested at the edge of the cushion.

Ignoring her non-verbal cues, he enclosed her hands into his and murmured, "I'm sorry for what I did. I hurt and embarrassed you in front of our friends and family, and it was wrong of me to cheat."

Despite the confession, she couldn't bring herself to believe him. His eyes flicked toward her, wider than a puppy's, pleading with her to forgive him.

She carefully detached herself from him and pressed her thighs together, rubbing her legs. "I appreciate you apologizing, but my answer is no. When Jordon said you cheated, it was like being kicked in the chest. I never imagined you'd betray my trust like that, especially right before our wedding. Did you even consider my feelings before you did it?" Her voice rose an octave with each word, coming out in tiny squeaks as her throat squeezed shut and tears blurred her vision.

She thought she'd finished crying over the wedding, but talking to him was like she was back at the altar, hearing the confession for the first time. He pricked at her heart, piercing through it with hundreds of pins.

He lowered his eyes and bit his bottom lip. Snatching an accent pillow from the mound of laundry, he fidgeted with one of the embroidered edges. It was as if he was a completely different person, switching his charm on when it suited him. He did and said the right things, but he had no qualms manipulating her.

Yesterday's phone call was fresh in her mind. He'd tried to deflect everything onto her as if she'd been in the wrong. It reminded her of times when they argued over innocuous things, and he'd twist things around. Such as when he'd lie about skipping the gym to eat at his favorite café. Then snap at her when she asked about the powdered sugar on the corner of his lip. He'd demand to know why she had to call him out and make him feel guilty when all she'd wanted to know was why he needed to hide it.

Or, even more troubling, when he'd come home late, and Kate was already in bed, he'd coerce her into sex. When she said no, he'd accuse her of not caring while he peppered her neck with kisses. She'd hated it, smacked him away a few times, but ultimately gave in just so she could get some sleep.

In hindsight, Kate realized she should have broken up with him sooner. She loathed herself for enabling him to objectify her or make her feel like a terrible girlfriend.

"What else do you want me to say? I've apologized, and I can't take it back. I woke up confused with a killer migraine. When I realized where I was and what I'd done, I knew you would have hung me by my toenails if I told you. That's why I didn't say anything at the wedding. I wanted to get through our vows so we could talk in private. I'm sorry, okay?"

More like he wanted to trap her in marriage. It would have been easier for him to manipulate her into staying.

She sniffed, brushing the tips of her thumbs beneath her eyes. "Why didn't your conscience kick in before your little brain took control? Was this fling worth destroying our future together? This isn't like you blew money in Vegas or called me fat. I'm afraid of you doing it again. How many times is too many before I'm supposed to walk away? You didn't make it to our vows, and you refuse to tell me everything."

He said nothing, and she hung her head. "Who did you sleep with?"

Drawing several shallow breaths, he clawed at his chest beneath the collar of his shirt. Then he fanned himself and shifted in his seat. "I—" He shook his head. "I can't, all right?"

Why was he holding back? It didn't make sense.

He went from scratching his chest to his arms, something he always did when he was nervous or anxious, leaving trails of red marks on his skin. As he sat there in visible discomfort, she felt a moment of pity for him. Matt wanted to sweep his issues under the rug if it meant preserving his image. He wasn't strong enough to be honest, no matter how much it destroyed his relationships.

If he lied to her now, she wouldn't be able to trust him later. She didn't want to question everything, from whether he was fudging something as small as not doing his chores or if he was with another woman. The doubt would always be in her mind, gnawing at her.

She pinned him with a pointed glare. "Unless you can tell me who you were with, I can't believe anything you say. You've already hidden too much from me. For the sake of us, for our relationship, you need to come clean."

"Yeah right," he scoffed, dropping the pillow. He threaded his fingers through his hair and tugged on the ends. "I know you. Once you make up your mind about something, that's it. No matter what I say, you'll judge me."

Kate watched him, mouth hanging agape. "That's it? You made all these demands for me to come see you, pleaded with me to go to therapy, but you can't say who you slept with?"

"I can't!" he shouted, startling her.

David came into the room, interrupting whatever Matt was going to say. He wore a latex glove, pinching a small, clear bag between his fingers. Rage etched every line of his face, from his hardened eyes to his deep scowl and creased forehead as he glared at Matt.

"Do you want to explain why there's a bag of cocaine in your room?"

Oh shit. As far as she knew, Matt didn't do drugs of any kind. She had never seen them in the house before today. She turned to him, praying there was a reasonable explanation for this. Yet when he met her questioning eyes, he deflated, slouching and wetting his lips as the color left his face.

Her heart raced in shock as the pieces clicked into place—Jordon's discomfort at the wedding, his evasive answers on the phone, and Matt adamantly resisting telling her what happened the night of the bachelor party. She struggled to catch her breath, finding it hard to believe he would get entangled in drugs.

The room spun for a moment when she looked at the white powder clinging to the bag in David's hand, and she dropped to one knee.

"Please tell me those drugs aren't yours," she wheezed, clutching the coffee table for support.

"Give me one good reason why I shouldn't call the cops," David demanded, shaking the bag until the powder threatened to fly out.

Kate hoped he sealed it before confronting them. She frantically motioned for him to stop, cringing at the repercussions if she didn't de-escalate the situation.

David rolled his eyes and slammed the bag onto the counter behind him. Then he strode to the front door and leaned against it, folding his arms over his chest as if he was a bodyguard. "Don't hold your breath for the truth. He's already lied about his affair, and I doubt he had any plans to tell you about the coke. You have no reason to trust a word he says."

Anger churned her insides, fueling an intense desire to smack him. She needed to put space between them before she lost control. She shoved old mail to the back of the coffee table to make room for her to perch on the edge.

Her mouth was drier than sandpaper, and her tongue seemed to stick to her mouth as she tried to keep her voice even. "Well? Were you going to tell me that you had drugs in the house?"

Matt kept his gaze fixed on his lap, where he clenched and unclenched his fists. His jaw twitched, and he worked his mouth for a minute before muttering, "No."

The admission hit her like a sucker punch to the gut.

The lump in her throat grew, making it difficult to swallow. "How long has this been going on?"

He lifted his shoulder in a half-assed shrug. "Once or twice."

Kate's head snapped as if a marionette string pulled her spine until it was straighter than a rod. Gaping, she blinked several times, trying to make her voice work. "Wait, what? Once or was it twice? It can't be both."

"Fine, I did it every time I saw Dean."

There wasn't a word to define the abhorrence that surged through Kate when she heard that man's name. Of all of Matt's friends, she disliked Dean the most. Alarm bells had gone off the moment they met, and her skin crawled at the way he'd leered and made sexual innuendos.

When Matt suggested him as a groomsman, an explosive argument erupted, but Kate relented when he'd dug in his heels. Dean wasn't Matt's best friend, but he was his oldest, dating back to elementary school.

Kate should have fought harder to keep Dean away. It wasn't fair to ask Matt to stop seeing him, but the man was poison. She wished it didn't take drugs and a wild party to prove her point.

She took several calming breaths, counting backward in her head, but nothing worked. Red colored her vision, and adrenaline surged through her body.

Breathe. In. Out. Don't hit him. Better yet, don't murder him.

She needed air. Launching to her feet, she ran to the sliding glass door and stumbled outside, gasping until she was hyperventilating. Her knees buckled, and she sat on the concrete patio, violently trembling. The blood rushing through her ears was deafening.

Someone touched her shoulder, and she swung.

"Woah, calm down! It's just me!"

Her brain couldn't connect a voice to anyone. All she saw were images of Matt, snorting and entwining himself with a faceless woman. The apparitions mocked her, laughing every time their gazes clashed.

"Kate, look at me," the voice commanded.

It didn't belong to Matt, and the image shattered, breaking her trance. David kneeled in front of her, gripping her shoulders as he shook her.

When her focus returned and locked onto his hazel eyes, he asked, "Can you get up?"

She took his elbow and hugged her arms. "I-I want to go. I don't c-care what he did. I n-need to go home."

"Okay," he whispered, drawing her into his arms. His heartbeat marched steadily against her ear, soothing her rage.

She sobbed into his chest, bunching his shirt into her fists. They stood together until the wails became sniffles, and her breathing steadied.

When she finished, she wiped her eyes. "I'm sorry, I—"

"Don't apologize," he said, keeping an arm around her shoulder. "We can leave whenever you're ready."

"What about Matt?"

"We've come to an understanding," he said, leading her toward the house. "While you two were fighting over the coke, I started filming the argument from my phone. When he tried to follow you outside, I punched him. Then I threatened to share the video if he bothered you again."

"What if he presses charges on either of us for assault?"

"He won't, not if he doesn't want his job to know what he's been doing. Employers don't tend to turn a blind eye to drug use."

Kate didn't know if she should laugh or cry. She'd already done the latter, and a maniacal giggle ripped from her throat. She'd come to Matt's house, intending to return his ring and grab some of her clothes, not involve herself in a domestic dispute. This was a scene straight out of a soap opera.

After the stitch in her ribs abated, apprehension weighed on her chest. Walking through the house meant seeing Matt one more time, and she didn't trust herself to look at him without hitting him too. How could he be such an idiot?

Stepping inside again, Kate's gaze immediately landed on her ex-fiancé in the kitchen, who was holding a bag of ice to his cheek. When they made eye contact, he brought the ice down and scowled, revealing a large, fresh bruise.

He opened his mouth to say something, and David stepped between them. "Remember what I said," he warned, lifting a finger. "If you press charges against Kate, that video will go online for the entire world to see. If you go near her, if you harass her, or if you even think about speaking to her, you'll wake up with a special surgery you didn't ask for. You got it?"

Matt deflated faster than a balloon punctured by the sharp tip of a needle. Relief flooded Kate's veins, and she wanted to hug her brother. Him towering over her cowering ex and protecting her was sublime.

Casting a final glance at Matt, she sighed. Anger and indignation burned in his features, but he kept to himself. Without saying goodbye or bothering to pack her clothes, she collected her purse and left, closing the door behind her and followed her brother to the truck.

She might not ever learn who Matt slept with, but he was no

longer her concern. His affair, the lies, all of it was his problem. She was better off without him.

Chapter Nine

The moment Kate got home, she went to her room and dialed Jordon's number. He answered on the third ring.

She spoke before he could say hello, saying, "David found drugs in Matt's house."

He uttered a curse and sighed. "I don't know what to say."

Kate imagined this must be awkward and uncomfortable for him. He hadn't been the one to cheat on her, and as Matt's best friend, he was obligated to protect him. "It's okay," she assured him. "Let me explain."

She told him everything that happened, and he listened without interrupting. When she finished, he said, "I'm sorry I didn't tell you the truth sooner. When we woke up the next day, the place was trashed, and I panicked. I was going to tell you before the wedding, but Matt convinced me it was a bad idea. He mentioned the police, and I got scared, but when I saw you, I couldn't keep quiet."

"I don't blame you. I would have been afraid too." With the truth revealed, she wondered if he would answer her questions. "I need to ask you something."

"You want to know who Matt slept with."

"I need closure."

The line went silent for a moment. Then he sighed. "I understand. I wish I could tell you it was the stripper or an ex-girlfriend he invited to the party, but I've never seen her before. There were loads of people there, and everyone was blitzed. Whoever she was, Matt threw her and her clothes on the porch the next morning. When I asked, he said he'd never met her."

"And you believed him?"

"He's my best friend. Well, he *was*," he corrected. "I've known Matt since college. You aren't roommates with someone that long without learning a few things. We think she crashed the party. It wasn't like we were screening the guests."

Yikes.

The reveal was anticlimactic. Kate wasn't sure what she expected, but given everything else that had happened, she almost expected something big, like Matt snorting coke off the stripper's stomach and making a sex tape. However, she'd received her answer, and that was what mattered.

"Thank you for telling me. This couldn't have been easy for you to admit."

"I am sorry," he said again. "You deserve better."

She thanked him again and ended the call, immediately texting Carlos with the news. She didn't feel comfortable calling him yet. Every attempt she'd made to communicate was met with silence.

This time was no different, and she pocketed her phone. If he wanted to speak to her, it was on him.

However, talking to Jordon wasn't enough. She wanted to process the day's events, dissect it with someone uninvolved. She approached Maddie's room and knocked on the door, expecting her sister to greet her with a cheerful smile and begin chattering away. When she didn't answer, Kate peeked inside. The lights were off, and the bed was its usual mess, littered with clothes and a cosmetic bag.

Treading back to her bedroom, she laid across her bed and turned on the TV. Dodger leaped onto the mattress and curled beside her, purring as she stroked his fur. Flipping through the channels, she looked for something to curb her boredom, but everything was the same. Angsty teenagers, crime dramas that got the legal details wrong, or shows that took bizarre turns halfway through the series.

Soon, her eyes grew heavy, and her surroundings faded. It wasn't until her phone pinged that she jerked awake with a snort. A text lit the screen, and her heart dipped and rose when the message wasn't from Carlos but Ian.

'Wanna hang out tonight?'

Did she want to see him? Yes. No. On the one hand, she could use some time away from all the crazy in her life. On the other, being with Matt left her drained. Why did everything have to happen on the same day?

Half asleep, she typed a response. *'I'm not sure you'd want to, I'm probably bad company.'*

'Why?'

"I learned my ex is a junkie, and my attempt to return his ring ended with my brother punching him.'

Her phone chirped again.

'Sounds like you had an exciting day. Why don't you come over?

I promise I'm not trying to get in your pants or whatever else you're assuming. I'm always happy to listen if you need someone to talk to.'

She laughed. *'lol what am I assuming, o' wise one?'*

'Okay, I probably shouldn't have said that. I won't twist your arm, but my offer for you to come by is on the table. I'll order food. :)'

Food was nice. She looked at Dodger, who meowed.

When she scratched his neck for two seconds and returned to her phone, he slithered between her arms and head-butted the phone, making her bungle the text. *'Sounds like a plumber.'*

'lol plumber?'

'Plan,' she replied, glaring at the evil purring creature in her lap. *'My cat is being a butthead.'*

'Cats think they rule the world. Anyway, I promise to give you my undivided attention and not say anything weird. If you don't want to talk about the ex bf stuff, we can watch a movie and chill.'

'You had me at food. I'll be there soon. Thank you.'

He gave her his address, and she ended the text with a bunch of smiling emojis. When she shoved Dodger away, he swiped at her arm before bounding to her window, tangling himself in the blinds as he perched on the small platform.

She went to the bathroom to recheck her appearance. Her hair needed a good comb, and her pimples seemed to glow like a homing beacon. With a sigh, she worked on covering the blemishes and eye baggies before untangling her uncooperative hair. When finished, she searched her dresser for something that wasn't boy shorts or muddy jeans.

Appearance shouldn't matter. If Ian were interested, he'd like her for who she was, but she wanted to feel desirable. She was tired of everyone treating her like a Plain Jane, commenting on the state of her clothes or lack of makeup. Even Matt had taken jabs at it sometimes, asking if she planned to change.

She settled on a pair of jean shorts that showed the curves of her butt and an off-the-shoulder top she "borrowed" from her sister's closet. Satisfied, she twirled in front of Maddie's full-length mirror. Kate's curly hair bounced, and for the first time in a long while, she felt glamorous.

Excitement bubbled in her stomach at how Ian might perceive her, and a blush warmed her cheeks. She reminded herself this wasn't a date, not really, but she hoped he appreciated her effort. It would be nice not to hear a jab at how she could do better. Tonight, she would have fun.

Slipping into her flip-flops and securing her purse, she smiled and skipped outside.

Ian greeted her with parted lips that slowly curved as his eyes dilated.

"Hi. You look good." His words were breathless as he swayed in her direction before motioning for her to come inside the house.

She tried not to appear too thrilled, but it was impossible not to bite her bottom lip or blush at the way his gaze settled onto her.

Sneaking a peek as she crossed the threshold, she took in the contours of his body beneath his fitted shirt. She wouldn't compare him to a weightlifter, but he had a decent physique. Also, he was masculine and naturally attractive. Between his height, dark hair, and a well-timed smolder, he could easily model for the biggest names in the fashion industry.

She hugged herself and took in the room around her, unsure what to do. From where she stood in the foyer, the walls were sponge painted in shades of gold, and a clawed sofa sat against the far wall. Two sitting chairs were angled to face the couch, leaving the rest of the room spacious and open. Light streamed inside from two windows, showing floating specs in the afternoon sun.

She didn't think this was where he entertained people. Yet, she could imagine herself sitting comfortably with a cup of tea or having a casual conversation with him.

Her stomach rumbled like a starving jungle creature. She smoothed the fabric of her shirt and hoped he didn't hear.

Ian chuckled. "Good thing I promised food. Do you like Thai?"

"Better than boogers and bacon mixed with beer."

"I don't feel that adventurous today," he said with a laugh. "Are you okay with spicy food?"

It was like he'd descended from her mother ship, knowing exactly what she wanted. "The spicier the better."

She followed him further into the house, where a large kitchen adjoined the second living room. Mahogany bookshelves lined one wall, and a large sectional couch separated the living room from the kitchen. A large television was mounted to the last wall, where a turntable sat on the entertainment unit below.

She couldn't help herself, beaming as she touched it like a kid at a tourist attraction. Crates of records, old and new alike, arranged by genre in alphabetical order, greeted her. There was a lot, and by the weight and perfect condition of them, she could tell he was an aficionado.

"You like vinyls?"

He joined her and opened the turntable casing. "I love them. My mom and I collected them for years when I was younger. Do you have a favorite band?"

Kate beamed. Records were nostalgic, and she was briefly transported to the past, where she'd spent hours with her own system. She had loads of preferences, nothing that could be confined to one artist or label. "I like all the old stuff. The Cars, Elton John, Metallica, Coldplay, The Beatles, Queen, Pink Floyd, and anything that isn't Country. I'm not a fan of songs about breakups and crying. Dying cats sound happier than those singers."

He snorted. "Those poor musicians."

When he laughed, she wanted to absorb his joy. His laid-back nature made it easy to forget how much her life sucked. "Those poor singers? My poor ears."

Casting her a grin, he thumbed through his assortment, occasionally stopping on a title before returning it to continue his search. Finally, he picked up a Led Zeppelin album.

Where had this man been her entire life? Records were making a comeback among the younger crowd, but it was rare to see a collection this large in someone's living room. He had too many to count, sitting where Blu-rays or an Xbox would typically be in a house. His love for music was apparent, and her heart melted that he shared her passion for old relics.

The old record crackled for a moment before the music played, and Kate relished the sound only an analog device could make. It transcended her to childhood, one filled with cassette tapes and her blue Crosley. She spent hours listening to them while she did her homework in her room.

"You look happy," he said.

"It reminds me of my childhood, back when things were simple."

"Everything seems easier in childhood. The world is a bigger place during that stage, and kids see things in broader terms."

That was true. Kate's worries didn't consist of money or boyfriends back then. Her focus had been whether she would get through class without being picked on or if she would make good grades.

"Ready to eat?" Ian asked.

"Definitely."

They entered the kitchen, where several containers of rice and food sat. Strong spice permeated the air, and the rising steam had her salivating.

"Help yourself," he said, handing her a container of yellow curry.

She plopped onto the stool beside him and poured it on top of her rice. The chicken mixed with mustard seed and coconut milk was heaven in her mouth. If food orgasms were possible, she'd be having one now.

She refrained from shoveling the food into her mouth, lest she behave like a street urchin with no table manners. "Oh my god, this is amazing."

"Do you have any other favorite foods?" he asked.

"I don't care what it is as long as it has cheese in it. I could live in my own cheese block and be happy for the rest of my life."

"That's quite the obsession," he said with a chuckle. "I'll have to remember that."

"It's my happy food. Well, sad food too. I guess it's my comfort meal. It's uncomplicated and versatile. What's your favorite?"

Ian put down his fork and wiped his mouth before resting his chin on his knuckles. A far-away look settled onto his features, one of nostalgia and sadness. A moment later, his lips quirked up, and he murmured, "Arroz con pollo. My mom used to make it at least once a week. We didn't have a lot of money, but it was easy to prepare, and no one made it better than Mama."

Kate could have sworn she detected a hint of a South American accent. The way he pronounced the dish and referred to his mother made her curious about his heritage. Part of her wanted to ask if he was bilingual. She wanted to discover more about him, but the last time she prodded into his past, he changed the subject.

"It sounds good," she said awkwardly, returning to her food.

They finished their meal to the classic rock, neither of them engaging in small talk. Ian bobbed his head and tapped his foot in rhythm against the stool, humming lyrics to old songs between bites. Soon, his shoulders joined the dance, and Kate's lips quirked upward into a grin. The way he absorbed himself with music was endearing.

She took a moment to consider him. If she had to describe him at a glance, she'd say he was a people pleaser. He was easy to get along with and had a way of making other people smile. He shared bits and pieces of himself, but his core was inaccessible. The moment certain aspects of his past were questioned, he steered the subject back into safer territory.

The music stopped, and he turned to her with a quizzical expression. "Why are you staring at me like a science experiment?"

She averted her gaze with a cough. She hadn't meant to be so brazen. "Sorry, I was spacing out."

A smirk tugged at his full lips, making her blush. "Oh, really? Nice to know I can't hold your attention."

Oh, geez, that came out wrong. "What? No," she said, wildly waving her hands. "Trust me, you don't have that problem."

His mouth widened in a huge grin. "I'm teasing. Relax."

Easy for him to say. He wasn't the one digging himself out of holes he'd created. She wondered if he fretted over his words, always replaying them in his head and worrying if he'd said the wrong thing.

He shifted, angling his body to face hers. When their knees brushed together, she moved her leg a fraction of an inch, needing the space. The spark between them was present again, tempting Kate to seek more contact with him.

It was hard to resist the impulse to graze his arm or touch his knee when he directed his full attention to her, watching her with deep irises of gray steel. It made her want to drown in their depths and spill her deepest secrets.

"You said you're a scientist, right?" he asked, switching gears.

Finally, an easy question. She could discuss this topic all day long. "Geologist. My primary field was structural geology. It's the study of how mountains are formed and the folding of rocks."

"Did you always want to study science?"

"Yes. My family thought I was weird as a kid because I brought rocks home every time we traveled. I like the different textures and how no stone is the same. They can be big or small or smooth or rough. Kind of like people. They're all different, but they're still rocks."

He opened his mouth and closed it, tilting his head to the side. "That's an interesting analogy."

With no music to fill the pauses, Kate nodded to the turntable. "May I flip the record?"

"Of course. Or is there something else you'd like to hear?"

"Do you have The Cars?"

"Are they your comfort band?"

"One of them."

"The Cars it is." He crossed the room and knelt, leaning forward to scan his collection. Kate ogled way more than she should, especially when his shirt revealed black underwear over the edge of his waistband. The color made his skin pop, accentuating his butt. She briefly wondered if he had the full package before reeling her mind in, telling herself to stop being a perv.

With the record in hand, he replaced the Led Zeppelin album and started the music. After returning the vinyl to its sleeve, he returned to the kitchen and began packing away the food.

As he cleaned, he glanced at her and then at her half-touched bowl. "Are you okay?"

"Yeah. It's been one of those days."

That was an understatement. The scene at Matt's house was dramatic, a scene straight from reality TV.

She didn't want to complain, despite Ian's offer earlier to use him as a sounding board. The afternoon had been fun, and she didn't want to ruin it by rehashing her drama.

"You can talk to me," he prompted. And damn it if he wasn't melting her inside with those eyes.

He should come with a sign: *'Lady killer that will turn you to goo with one look.'*

She puffed her cheeks, expelling a long sigh. "I don't know where to start."

"I'm told the beginning is a good place."

"Smartass."

"Better than a dumbass."

She stuck out her tongue. "That's so cliché. But since you asked, I'll tell you. You've seen the videos, right?"

"Yeah."

Kate launched into her horrible morning with Matt. Then she told Ian about her conversation with Jordon and how he'd been manipulated. When she finished, Ian whistled.

"Wow. I'm sorry you went through that. How do you feel about what happened?"

"Honestly? I'm waiting for the dominos to stop falling."

"I understand. It's hard to keep up with the momentum. Until you get through it, you need to find a way to cope with what is happening."

It wasn't as if she didn't try. She wanted to see that light at the end of the tunnel, but that was far in the future. "I'm open to suggestions."

"Are you working right now?"

"Nope. Still putting in applications after getting fired the day after my wedding."

Ian's eyebrows rose to his hairline. "Geez, you *can't* catch a break, can you?"

"I loved my job. My favorite part was when my students grasped a concept after they'd been struggling to understand it. There's a moment of satisfaction I share with them because their hard work paid off."

"Have you applied for other teaching positions?"

"Yes. Dozens of them, but no one will hire me."

"I'm sorry," he said, taking her hands into his. The zing returned, racing the Indie 500 through her veins. The happy dance he ignited in her heart was almost enough to chase away the stress.

"It's not your fault I'm a mess," she said.

His thumb caressing her knuckles sent butterflies into her stomach as he said, "You're not a mess. You're in a rough spot, but you will get through it. It's just going to take time."

She said nothing, watching his finger trace patterns over her skin. Every spot he touched tingled with electricity until every fiber in her body hummed with excitement. It was difficult not to close her eyes and grin like a fool as she envisioned what it would be like if he did more.

She wondered what his lips tasted like, what he'd feel like melded against her. She wanted to discover if he had a spot on his neck that would make him shudder. Hell, she wanted to discover all the things that turned him on.

The room was too warm, and her body sensitive from her indecent thoughts. Her neck pulsed as she tried to steady her breathing. If he elicited these sensations from a simple touch, he'd be a volcano in bed.

Was it too soon to move on? Her mother would think so, as would everyone else. Any logical person would tell her this was a rebound, not meant to last.

She had loved Matt, but had she been with him for the right reasons? What if her feelings weren't as strong as she'd thought? Shouldn't she still be wallowing in self-pity? No, she decided. She refused to be broken by this. He wasn't right for her, and moping didn't do anything but breed negativity.

She subtly severed their connection and rubbed her arms. If she didn't stop fantasizing, she worried she would launch herself at him.

The moment gone, she tried to come up with something to say, but her mind drew a blank.

He spared her from an uncomfortable pause. Cocking his head to the side, he asked, "Have you considered publicly sharing your story?"

"What do you mean?

"I mean, is there a way for you to stream yourself online?"

He had to be joking. "Being online is what ruined me."

"It could also help you. People have only seen the wedding. They don't know who you are. This could be an opportunity to show the internet that you were unfairly judged for your actions."

"And how would I make my video go viral? You need subscribers and popularity. Mine would be buried beneath millions of other posts."

"How did it happen with your first one?"

"My sister's *friend* posted it," she spat, still salty over Sharna's disregard for everyone she deemed beneath her. "She has a large following, and her friends shared it, and so on and so forth."

"Okay, but let's say you recorded a small clip of yourself. Do you know anyone who could get it seen? Does your sister?"

Oh, Maddie had tons of friends. That wasn't an issue. The question was if Kate should put herself on the internet again after what happened the first time. Would anyone care at this point? Would it be enough to repair the damage done to her reputation?

She rubbed her face. "She definitely has the contacts, but this doesn't seem like a good idea."

"What do you have left to lose?"

She looked at him through her fingers and groaned. "My self-respect? I don't need another fifteen minutes of fame where people tear me apart."

He gently tugged at her wrists and brought them down until their faces were inches apart. Her eyes widened, and for a moment, she thought he might kiss her. The air halted in her lungs, and she swallowed.

"I'm asking you to consider it, okay? Maybe nothing will come of it, and that's fine too. You might find it cathartic to express what you're feeling."

It was an excellent point, sort of like writing in a journal. She could try it, and as he said, it could give her a chance to present her side of the story. Unlike the first time, she would be in control of what was shared.

She'd discuss it later with Maddie and David. Kate didn't know if she could go through with it on her own, but if they stood by her side, it wouldn't be as daunting. For now, she didn't want to dwell on her problems. She wanted to enjoy the rest of the evening without a dark cloud looming above her head.

"All right, I'll think about it," she promised. "I'd like to finish listening to the record and then perhaps we can watch a movie or something."

Releasing her, he stood and motioned for her to follow him into the living room. They walked together, and she sank into the corner of the sofa, kicking off her flip-flops. He slid onto the cushion beside her but not close enough to touch.

She was tempted to tuck her feet beneath her, but that might be too comfortable since she was visiting for the first time. Instead, she stretched her legs and relaxed, following his cues as they bobbed to the music.

Whatever happened would happen. She refused to worry any longer over the future when she could enjoy herself in the present.

Chapter Ten

Kate woke with a start, her heart pounding at the unfamiliar surroundings. Her neck ached from sleeping at an awkward angle, and she shifted, trying to find a better position.

Something pinned her down, and she froze, realizing there was a hand on her breast. She rubbed the sleep from her eyes, blinking to make sure she wasn't having a vivid dream. Her "pillow" was Ian's lap, and his hand was definitely on her boob.

Her pulse raced. She was half-asleep and fully clothed, yet the contact was erotic. It was also inappropriate, especially when Ian squeezed, making her nipples tingle and heat pour between her thighs.

Don't go there. He's asleep, you dummy.

She carefully removed his arm as if he was a ticking bomb. He didn't budge, and Kate slipped free, sliding to the corner of the sectional couch. Sitting, she popped the kinks out of her joints and glanced at Ian.

His neck rested on the backrest of the couch while his legs disappeared beneath the coffee table. He couldn't be comfortable. Kate assumed he'd fallen asleep watching the telenovela he put on earlier in the evening.

Not wanting to wake him, she rose with the grace of a mouse and reached for her purse near the table, digging for her phone to check the time. The numbers stared back at her, taunting her with Mom's inevitable lecture at being gone the entire night. It didn't matter that Kate was a grown woman. She was living at Mom's house and therefore had to follow her rules.

Scooping up her flip flops, she tried to step over Ian's ridiculously long legs. He chose that moment to stir in his sleep, and Kate tripped. Her bag and shoes went flying as she landed on the floor with a loud curse.

Ian jerked awake with a snort, swiveling his head from side to side. "Kate?"

She twisted around onto her backside and propped herself up on her elbows. "Sorry, I didn't mean to wake you."

The TV flickered in sleep mode, and Kate squinted in the dim light as he stretched his arms high and yawned. He inhaled deeply and dropped his hands into his lap, his lips curving into a lazy grin.

"It's okay. There are worse ways to wake up." He helped her to her feet. "Are you okay?"

Her face was so hot, she was surprised it hadn't burst into flames. She coughed and took his hand. "Yeah. I'm fine."

Sore knee and stung pride aside, she was A-Okay. Not aroused at all from his hand on her breast earlier. *Liar.*

"Are you hungry? I can make breakfast before you go."

Hungry for him, oh yes.

Frack, what was wrong with her? She needed to go home and take a cold shower.

Desperate to get herself under control, she uttered the first excuse she could think of. "It's four in the morning."

He shrugged. "So? I'm hungry, and I'm gonna make something. You should eat too. You'll feel lousy later if you don't."

Kate was ravenous but needed to get home before her parents noticed she hadn't come home last night. If they saw her coming in at this hour, the inquisition would be awful. "I don't know. My mom—"

"Isn't you. You're an adult, capable of making decisions for yourself."

She dipped her head and sighed. "Yeah, I guess you're right. Her opinion matters to me, and I try to keep the peace."

"Is it tense there?"

She shrugged. "I've been avoiding her since I moved back, which isn't hard because she's always at work. When she comes home, she brings her job with her and locks herself in her room. When Dad leaves work and walks through the door, they start arguing, and I don't stick around to have a conversation."

He wrinkled his nose. "That does sound stressful."

"You have no idea."

He paused, opening his mouth as if to say something. Then he closed it and walked into the kitchen. Kate was tempted to ask what was on his mind but decided against it.

Whistling an unfamiliar tune, he turned on the light, then set everything he'd need for breakfast on the counter: eggs, bread, sausage, and condiments.

Hugging herself, Kate watched him, wondering what was going through his mind when she spoke of her parents. "Ian?"

"Hm?" His back was to her as he reached into the refrigerator, and he turned to face her.

Just ask, you big coward.

"Um, I hope this isn't too forward, but why did you give that funny look when I said you have no idea?"

He adjusted his shirt and pressed his lips together before closing the refrigerator and leaning against it. Folding his arms over his chest, he stared at the ground. "I guess you could say I know what it's like to dread parents arguing because mine fought a lot when I was younger. Dad used to hit me and my mom, and it wasn't until he put her in the hospital that she took me and left.

Shit. Kate felt like such an asshole for venting about her mom. She wouldn't be surprised if he thought of her as a whiny brat. Sure, her mother was overbearing, but her issues were trivial compared to him. She never had any reason to fear her parents. She might as well be a thirty-year-old princess in her parents' mansion.

Hearing him describe the abuse he suffered was like listening to another language. It was almost an abstract concept, something she'd read about but hadn't experienced.

How many times had Ian's dad hurt them? Was it possible he started out a decent guy, then something triggered him? Or was there always a monster lurking beneath the surface? The reality was too abhorrent to ask about, and she dropped her head.

"I'm sorry. That's awful. I shouldn't have—"

"It's okay," he said with a reassuring smile, crossing the room and touching her shoulder. "It was a long time ago."

"But didn't you say she died when you were fifteen? How did you end up getting adopted, instead of living with your biological father?"

She internally groaned. She might as well add insensitivity to her list of negative qualities.

"It's complicated, but the important thing is I was placed with George almost a year after Mama passed."

He'd dodged the question about his birth father. It was clear he didn't want to talk about him, and it wasn't her place to press for details. Some things were better left unsaid.

The longer they stood there in silence, the more awkward it became for her. If Ian was offended, he didn't acknowledge it. He resumed his task again, leaving Kate with anxiety and a dozen questions. Had she gone too far with her inquiry? Did he believe she was a spoiled princess with first-world problems? What if he didn't want to see her again?

She was tempted to snatch her purse and take off, but that would be rude. Plus, it was possible he wasn't judging her, and she was having a panic attack for nothing.

Thankfully, he saved her from having to devise an excuse to flee. When he faced her again, holding an egg in his hand, he asked, "What do you want in your omelet?"

She sighed in relief that he wasn't sending her on her way. Her stomach growled before she could reply, making them both laugh. The tension melted away, and she patted her flat tummy. "I'm fine with whatever you make."

Ian's eyes glittered as he tossed an egg in the air and caught it behind his back. Then he cracked it over a bowl, using one hand while reaching for a whisker. "One omelet, a la Ian, coming up. Make yourself at home and have a seat."

~ * ~

The sun was barely making its ascent when Kate parked in her driveway at a quarter after five. The sky was dark in one direction, coalescing with different colors of nature's palette as it brightened in the east. Birds chirped to announce the start of a new day.

Resting her head on the steering wheel, she closed her exhausted eyes while cursing the birds for their cheerful tune. She was too tired for their happy songs this early in the day. If not for the temperature reaching triple digits before eight o'clock, she'd be tempted to lay the seat back and fall asleep where she sat.

A car door closed, and Kate looked for the source of the sound.

Mom was leaning through the window of a silver Cadillac, kissing someone who *wasn't* Dad. Her highlighted hair was mussed, and her clothes were rumpled. Her body hid the man's face as she reached inside, standing on her toes as if she was a giddy high school girl instead of a woman in her late fifties. When she backed away with a wave and an air kiss, her *friend* exited the driveway, leaving her with a besotted smile.

Not once did she check to see if anyone was watching. She withdrew a set of keys from her purse, not bothering to pay attention to anything but the front door, approaching it with a bounce in her step.

Kate's heart thundered with indignation as her world crumbled at her feet. The flimsy glamor shrouding her parents' marriage was stripped away. She knew they were on rocky terms, but she didn't want to believe Mom would have the audacity to flaunt her affair in broad daylight.

She needed to say something before Mom walked inside and pretended like she wasn't just with another man. Kate stumbled out of her car and tried to speak, but the words got stuck in her throat.

Determined to get her mother's attention, she slammed the door shut and coughed.

Mom whirled around, dropping her keys on the porch as her eyes widened. "What are you doing here? I thought you were inside."

That was it? She wasn't going to acknowledge what she just did?

Trembling, Kate dug her fingernails into her palms. "Who the hell was that?"

Mom's cheeks flushed, and she retreated, bumping into the door as she stooped to retrieve her keys. "I-he—"

"Does Dad know?

Gripping her keys, Mom's knuckles whitened as her mouth formed into a thin line. "I don't need to explain myself to you. What I do with my life is my business."

Mom spun on her heel and unlocked the door, marching inside the house. Kate stomped across the driveway, chasing after her. When she crossed the threshold, she threw her purse down. Loose change spilled from it, spinning across the hardwood floor.

Kate's emotions burst with the force of a pyroclastic blast. "You are such a hypocrite!"

Mom halted mid-step and turned, glaring with unadulterated fury. "How dare you use that tone with me."

"How dare *I*? You hounded me to speak to Matt and listen to the garbage he had to say. You defended him instead of supporting *me*. Now I see why."

"When it comes to Matt, did you ever stop to think that you're the problem?" her mom shot back. "He wouldn't have needed to seek the company of another woman if you'd met his needs."

Kate stumbled, catching the wall for support. "That's not fair," she breathed, swallowing past the lump in her throat at the hateful comment.

"Is it fair to be ignored?" Mom pressed. "Relationships are a two-way street. Matt used to tell me how lonely he felt all those times you blew him off for work. You should have paid more attention to him. The same goes for your father and me. I'm tired of coming home to him drowning in a bottle of bourbon." If those words weren't bad enough, she drove the knife in further. "You're as emotionally clueless as Jeremiah. It's your fault Matt strayed, not his."

Kate's chest constricted. It wasn't her fault. She'd tried to be attentive to Matt's needs. Sinking to a nearby chair, she wheezed, "Matt is a pig, and you're as bad as he is. Nothing excuses cheating."

"If you think I'm such a terrible person, you can leave. I don't have to listen to this."

"I have nowhere to go."

"That's not my problem," Mom said coldly. "I don't need your judgmental attitude. You've been nothing but a disappointment, and I wish I'd never had you."

Heavy tears splashed onto Kate's chest, and she sniffled as she tried to contain her emotions. She wanted to scream, to convince herself Mom was only saying these things because she was angry. Yet, her mother never said what she didn't mean.

Footfalls thumped down the stairs. Dad and Maddie appeared at the bottom, rubbing sleep from their eyes. Maddie rushed to Kate, wrapping her into a crushing hug.

Dad glowered their mom with the most hateful look Kate had ever seen. "What the hell is wrong with you?"

"Stay out of it!" Mom snapped, directing her fury at him.

"Not this time," he snarled. "Only a fucked-up person would say that to their child. If anyone made a mistake, it was me. I should have divorced you a long time ago. Seeing you with your boyfriends is one thing, but I won't stand here and watch you reduce our children to nothing."

Maddie closed her hand around Kate's wrist and hauled her to her feet, stopping to grab the discarded purse. "Come on. Let's go upstairs."

Kate blindly followed her sister, half-climbing, half-running. When she reached the top, she gasped for air. She drew her legs into her chest, convulsing with sobs. Maddie's arms encircled her once again, and they sat there as their parents' shouts carried upstairs.

"...completely uncalled for," her father yelled, his previous words cut off from the sound of blood rushing through Kate's ears.

"She came at me, not the other way around. This is my house, and it's my right to tell her to go."

"No, it's *our* home. I make decisions here too. You don't get to expel her just because you didn't show more discretion. Who were you with this time?"

Hold the phone, Dad knew? Kate lifted her head to see if this was news to Maddie, but she shrugged and murmured, "I'll explain later."

"Does it matter?" Mom continued. "We agreed to keep our affairs private. Kate has no right to preach to me. I'm not the one all over the internet making a public fool of myself."

Maddie blew a raspberry and mumbled, "No, we get to listen to her air her dirty laundry behind closed doors." Then, turning to Kate, she whispered, "I would have slapped Matt too. And those videos were not your fault."

Kate huddled tighter into her sister's chest. "You're too good to me."

A piece of furniture smashed downstairs, followed by more yelling. "Real mature, Nancy, let's throw things when you can't have your way. I've tolerated a lot from you, hoping you'd find yourself or whatever bullshit you contrive to make yourself feel better, but this is exhausting. I supported you when you finished your law degree and embraced your career. I worked insane hours to keep the finances afloat, paying on the house, your loans, and your comfort. You don't thank me for anything, and you bring nothing but stress and misery to everyone around you."

"Don't you start," she shouted. "I've endured your crap for years. I'm the one who had to hide your liquor bottles from the kids, so they didn't ask questions. Then there was your god-awful mother constantly driving a wedge between us. If she wasn't nagging me to be a better wife and wait on you hand and foot, she was complaining about the house or my parenting skills. She didn't like the way I dressed; nothing was good enough. Did you ever defend me? I asked you for years to step in, and you told me to ignore her."

"Jesus, let it go already. It's not like you see her anymore. You whine about how she treats you, and yet you're the one criticizing Kate for everything. Matt was a piece of shit, and I'm proud of her for walking away and doing what I couldn't."

"What's holding you back? It's pretty clear we're never going to be happy together."

"You're right," Dad said in a cracked voice. "Maybe we should go our separate ways."

Kate couldn't listen anymore. She didn't want to be the reason her parents decided to end their marriage. Not that their problems were her fault. They'd been fighting for longer than she could remember, yet she hoped someday they'd find a way to reconcile their differences.

She abandoned her seat at the top of the stairs and trudged into her room. Maddie trailed behind, and once they were inside, Kate locked the door. She changed into comfortable clothes before dropping onto the bed, wrapping herself into her sheet like a burrito.

Her sister joined her and rested on her elbow, using her arm as a kickstand to prop up her face. With her free hand, she smoothed Kate's hair behind her ear. "I'm sorry you had to hear that. Mom sees a different guy every weekend. I probably should have warned you."

"You're not the one who needs to apologize."

Kate curled into the fetal position and tucked her blanket tighter beneath her. Another migraine pulsed at her temples, throbbing until her stomach lurched with the urge to vomit. She squeezed her eyes shut, forcing her breakfast not to make an appearance.

Everything had been going so well with Ian. Unlike when she was home, being with him didn't cause stress or anxiety. He didn't belittle her or act like she was weird. Kate had laughed more in a single night than she had all month.

As if Maddie were reading her mind, she asked, "Where were you last night?"

"I stayed with a friend." The memory of Ian's hand on her breast suddenly surfaced, and Kate tried not to giggle.

She couldn't control the heat on her cheeks, and it seemed her sister noticed. Her mouth lifted into a conspiratorial grin as she waggled her eyebrows. "A friend or a boyfriend?"

"A friend," Kate reiterated, fighting the smile creeping onto her face. "We had dinner, listened to music, and watched a telenovela."

Maddie snorted. "Did you understand any of it? I remember in high school, you couldn't string more than two words of Spanish together unless it was to say, '*no comprende*.'"

To this day, that held true. Kate was hopeless at learning languages. It was the only class she ever got a grade lower than a B. She would have failed if the teacher hadn't taken pity on her and given her a C. "There were subtitles."

"No dessert?" Innuendo laced Maddie's tone, and her eyes gleamed with mischief.

Kate opened her blanket to toss a pillow at her. "Shush."

Her sister caught it and playfully smacked her with it before settling onto her side. "Sounds like you enjoyed yourself."

"I did," Kate said after a yawn.

Her heart had returned to a normal rate, and exhaustion tugged at her. Snuggling deeper into the mattress, she changed the subject. "Why do you still live here?"

Maddie flopped onto her back with a sigh and interlaced her fingers on top of her stomach. "I work too much with modeling and painting to get a place of my own. It didn't seem practical to waste my money on an apartment I never stay in."

"But doesn't Mom get to you?"

"Oh God yes. She's constantly telling me how worthless my art is. If it wasn't for my agent talking me down every time I have a panic attack before showings, I'd be a mess. I've sold my paintings for thousands of dollars, gotten into elite venues in LA, yet I still don't feel good enough at what I do, and it's probably thanks to Mom."

Maddie was born with a crayon and paintbrush in each hand. Ever since she was old enough to move around, she scribbled on anything she could find: paper, walls, furniture, and her face. She spent hours at her sketchbook, drafting and erasing the masterpiece she visualized until it was perfect. She'd gone from butterflies and stick figures to nature, stills, and three-dimensional paintings. Art was her calling, a passion she nurtured and refined. Mom was a bitch for making her feel inferior.

"Your work is amazing. Don't ever let anyone tell you otherwise."

"It's hard not to when the one person you want to believe in you is always tearing you down."

"Trust me, I get it, but you *are* awesome."

A tear slipped down Maddie's cheek, and she turned, biting her quivering bottom lip. "Do you mean it?"

Kate threw off her blanket and hugged her. "Yes. You've been supportive, and I was awful to you. I'm sorry."

It was a start in repairing the broken bridge between them, but her apology felt inadequate after years of resentment. She needed to make amends with Maddie and prove how much she valued her. "We should find a small apartment together. Mom is too toxic and being here is unhealthy. What do you say?"

Maddie bolted upright, bumping her head against Kate's mouth. "Oof! Sorry."

"It's okay," she said, rubbing her lip where her sister smacked her.

"I'm surprised you want to be around me after everything that's happened between us," Maddie confessed. She looped her arms under her knees and hunched forward. Apprehension lined her face as she grimaced. "Also, as much as I want to, I can't."

Kate pushed herself up and arranged her features into a neutral expression. Her stomach knotted like she'd been punched, but it would be wrong to make her sister feel guilty for not wanting to live together. "Oh. It's not a big deal. It was a dumb idea."

"No, it's not what you think," Maddie said, waving her hands wildly. "I would *love* to live with you, but I've been saving my money to move to England."

Europe? "What's over there?"

Maddie looked away, cracking her knuckles and twisting her fingers around each other. "Um, well nothing really. I wanted to expand my art, that's all."

Kate's eyebrows shot into her hairline. Something wasn't right.

It wasn't like her sister to keep enormous ideas to herself. When she planned, she went big and shouted her thoughts to the entire world. "Is there a boyfriend I don't know about?"

She rapidly shook her head before clearing her throat. "No. Nothing like that. I went to Somerset after my last year in college, and I've always wanted to go back. Now that I'm making a name for myself, I can, but I want to be financially stable first. That's the real reason I haven't left yet. It's also why I can't go in on a place with you."

"Are you sure? You can be honest if you're upset with me. I understand I haven't been nice to you."

Maddie stuck out her tongue, then kissed Kate on the forehead. "Yes, you silly goose. We buried the hatchet weeks ago. If you find a place, I promise to help. I'll set aside some money for a deposit so you can get a better place, okay?"

"All right." Whatever her sister was hiding, she wasn't going to come clean. Maddie would tell her when she was ready.

Pulling her sheet over herself, Kate lay down with a loud yawn. "Sorry, I'm falling asleep. Can you lock my door when you go?"

"Sure. I'll let Dad know not to bother you until you're ready to talk about what happened."

Best. Sister. Ever. Kate didn't have to ask or tell her what she needed. When she woke up, she was going to think of something special to do for her. "Yes, please. And Maddie?"

"Hm?"

"I love you."

"I love you too, sis."

Chapter Eleven

'I know you're not talking to me, but I need you to call me. It's important.'

Kate stared at the words she'd sent to Carlos shortly after waking up. She'd spent ten minutes drafting the message, typing some form of the same sentence at least four times before she settled on this version, and it still felt weird.

Maybe she was being unreasonable, but she needed her friend to let go of his wounded pride and call her.

He hadn't responded, but what did she expect? He'd been avoiding her since she rejected his offer to move in with him. Now she was ready to reconsider, but they were estranged. Irony was a bitch.

She set her phone aside and stared at her laptop in dismay. She'd lost count of the job applications she put in, and she hadn't received one bite. During a low moment, she put in an application for Hooters, and even they ghosted her.

One video. That was all it took to derail her life. She closed the job listings tab and went to YouTube, despite her better judgment. Searching for 'The Social Media Bride,' she clicked on the first post in the results and wished she hadn't.

Though the momentum slowed since it hit a million views, new people commented on it every day. On the bright side, some viewers were finally demanding justice and asking why no one gave Matt a hard time, but most of the focus remained on Kate and her epic fail.

She exited the screen and propped her elbows on the desk, staring ahead and letting her mind wander. She didn't have a job, yet she couldn't stay with her mom. She didn't have a boyfriend or any close friends. David didn't have room for her in his house, and Maddie couldn't move out. Kate couldn't ask Ian because that would be awkward. That left Carlos, her only friend who wasn't speaking to her.

Frack.

She sighed, returning to her career, the root of her problems. No one would hire her.

Yet, what if she *could* turn her reputation around? Would telling her story help? Also, she needed to consider the time frame and visibility.

Currently, the hashtag was trending but no longer in a viral status. Also, if she streamed herself online, she needed people to see the video, or the effort would be meaningless.

However, if she gained traction, she might save her image and be taken seriously again. She could make them understand that she was as human and susceptible to mistakes as anyone else.

She drummed her fingertips on the desk. She didn't want to go through a news outlet. Most people watched clips on YouTube or Twitter, preferring something short and catchy. She also remembered the movie *Mr. Deeds*, where the media roasted Adam Sandler's character, twisting everything he did for a better story.

On the bright side, if they do twist my words and edit footage, at least they won't get another video of me screaming and running around in my red underwear.

She needed another opinion.

Turning off her laptop, she went to her sister's room. Pop music blared through the walls. There might as well have been a sign that read, "DO NOT DISTURB!"

Given the decibel level and the happy vibes, Maddie had to be painting.

Kate banged on the door and waited a minute before trying again, pounding hard enough to rattle the frame. When Maddie didn't answer, she slipped inside and grinned.

Her sister was on the far end of her room with her curtains drawn, shaking her ass to the music. Kate crossed the distance between them and waited for Maddie to lift the brush from the canvas before interrupting her.

When Kate tapped her shoulder, Maddie jumped and whirled, splattering them in light pink paint. Depositing the palette on her workstation, she turned off her music. "Shit, I'm sorry!"

Kate wiped her palms on her shirt as she laughed. "No worries. I wasn't attached to this shirt. You have paint on your cheek by the way."

She didn't mention the several colors dotted across her sister's overall dress. Damn, she even had it in her hair.

Maddie wiped her face, smearing the paint everywhere. Then she studied her hand and shrugged. "What do you need?"

Kate picked at her chipped fingernails, bitten down after weeks of stress. She'd been considering a lot of ideas lately, a vlog being one of them. "I wanted your opinion on something."

"Oh?" Maddie's smirk was both playful and irritating, especially when she put a hand to her ear and leaned forward. "Can you say that again? I didn't hear you the first time."

"You're a brat," Kate muttered.

Maddie wrinkled her nose. The smudge was still there, giving her the appearance of a pocket pet. The only thing missing was a set of whiskers.

"What's going on?" she asked, taking a seat on a covered chair. Sheets were over most of the nearby furniture. They were dotted with splotches of paint in a rainbow of colors, probably from hours of dancing to music.

After climbing onto the bed, Kate hugged her knees. "Well, you remember how the video destroyed my career, right?"

Guilt flashed through Maddie's eyes, and Kate waved her hands. "Stop, I didn't say it to make you feel bad. A friend of mine suggested that I should record my side of the story and stream it. What do you think?"

Maddie's shoulders perked up, and she cocked her head to the side. "What would you say?"

Kate hadn't thought that far ahead yet. When Ian suggested it, it was an abstract idea. "Beats me, but something that would make me seem more sympathetic."

Her sister tapped her chin. Gaze shifting far away, she sat in a trance-like state for a minute before expelling a breath and redirecting her attention to Kate. "Okay, I have an idea. Everyone has a personal brand, something unique to them that makes them noticeable. There are gamers, makeup influencers, foodies, etcetera. For this to be successful, you'd need *a lot* of viewers."

"I have no online presence."

"All you need is the right contact, someone who could interview you and stream it on one of their social media accounts."

"Could I use you? You have a big following online, right?"

Maddie shook her head. "I do, but that doesn't mean I'm the right person. My accounts are either about art or modeling. I can share the link and get viewers, but you need someone bigger and whose fan base is closer related to your story." She leaned back, interlacing her fingers over her head. With her tongue between her lips, she bounced her legs. "Give me a second." After a moment, she produced her phone, swiping the screen.

"What are you doing?" Kate asked.

"I'm trying to find someone who can help. I don't know anyone personally, but that doesn't mean one of my friends doesn't."

There had to be at least one person in Maddie's rolodex with enough followers to put Kate on the map. A fluffy purple pillow laid across the bed, and she grabbed it, holding it to her chest as Maddie continued to peruse her phone. When Kate's foot went numb under her knee, she readjusted her legs, wondering what was taking so long. Six degrees of separation was a real thing, but Maddie couldn't possibly be acquainted with that many people.

After what felt like a wait in line at a theme park, Maddie pressed a button on her phone, holding it to her ear. Kate listened to one side of a conversation.

"Hey Marla. I'm good! I have a question. You remember my sister Kate, right? Yeah, that's her. Uh-huh. Okay, well you wouldn't happen to have any vloggers in your contacts, would you? I need to get in touch with someone with a big following who'd be able to stream an interview or small segment with her."

Kate bit the inside of her cheek as her sister slumped forward. She couldn't hear the other person, but between Maddie's furrowed brow and annoyed tone, Kate was nervous.

"First, this wouldn't be an issue if Sharna hadn't been a bitch and used my phone to upload the video. I know she's not your client, but she still goes through the agency." She paused, narrowing her eyes. "Okay, I didn't want to go there, but remember that venue you lost for me in LA because you slept with the owner's dad? Great! I can't wait."

She ended the call and tossed the phone onto the bed with a smirk. "She's gonna call around."

Kate sat stunned for a moment, at a loss for words. If she ever said something like that at the university, she'd have been escorted away by security. When she got her voice to work, she asked, "Isn't she your agent?

Maddie nodded.

"Aren't you worried she'll drop you as a client?"

"Nope. She owes me after losing that venue, and she knows it. Besides, if this brings in good publicity for one of her existing clients, she'll be happy."

"Do you think this is a good idea though? What if they twist everything I say?"

"Have a little faith. All it takes is the right person to get you on YouTube. And I'm going to screen whoever Marla finds before you get on camera. It'll be okay."

Fair enough. If Maddie insisted it would be okay, Kate would have to take her word. Dropping the pillow, she stood and examined the half-finished painting next to her sister.

She couldn't discern much besides brush strokes and outlines of blobs. They didn't look like anything in particular, even when she tilted her head from side to side the way she would for one of those lenticular photos that changed depending on the angle.

When she couldn't determine what it was, she asked, "What's this supposed to be?"

Maddie blocked Kate's view, blushing furiously. She didn't like showing her art to anyone until she unveiled her work. "You'll see it when it's done. I'm supposed to be working on a special theme for my next show, but I'm procrastinating and doing something else." She waved her hands toward the door. "Now shoo. This is my sacred space. I'll tell you when Marla calls me back."

"Rude."

"I love you and you know it, but I'm kicking you out. Go call your friend who isn't your boyfriend," she said, shoving Kate into the hallway.

"He's not—"

The door slammed behind her before she could finish saying Ian wasn't her boyfriend. She spun around and stared at the barrier between her and her sister's room with a gaping mouth, curious as ever to learn why a bunch of abstract lines were so classified.

Shaking her head, she plodded downstairs to make a sandwich. She was adding avocado mayo to her bread when her mother's meek voice spoke behind her, raising the hackles on Kate's neck.

"Hi, sweetie."

Kate's shoulders tightened as she stared straight ahead. Setting her knife on her plate, she turned in a slow circle until she faced her mother.

She was dressed in a cream pantsuit, and her makeup and hair were flawless. She was nothing like the carefree, rumpled woman from the other morning. There also was no sign of rage or shock. Today, she was calm and collected, an emotionless mask.

A dozen hurtful things came to mind, all of them beginning and ending with how she could be such a hateful person. Or why'd she become a mother if everyone around her was always such a disappointment.

Kate's jaw hurt from clenching her teeth and holding back an angry response. She couldn't face her mom right now, maybe never. The morning was too fresh, just like everything else that happened lately.

When she didn't respond, Mom came closer, forcing Kate to step backward. Stopping, her mother said, "I want to talk."

That's it?

Kate bit back an angry retort. Mom didn't get to act like nothing happened. It wasn't right.

Plus, her mother wouldn't listen to anything Kate said. Mom would deflect and make everything about herself, avoiding the blame without accepting responsibility for her actions.

Inhale. Exhale. Four beats in. Hold. Eight counts out.

Kate busied herself with cleaning the counter and putting the leftover food into the refrigerator. She kept her back to Mom the entire time, unable to make eye contact. "There isn't anything for us to say. You made your feelings clear the other morning."

"I didn't mean any of that," she murmured.

"I wish that was true."

Clamping her mouth shut, Kate took her plate and spun around. When she tried to make a hasty exit, Mom touched her arm.

"Kate, please. We should sit down."

"I don't want to," she said, trying her best not to cry again. Her patience hung by a thread, threatening to snap if she didn't get away.

Mom sighed. "I cancelled my appointments this afternoon so we could talk. You can give me five minutes."

Seeing no way around this, Kate trudged to the table and sat, picking at the lettuce poking from her sandwich. Her appetite was gone, replaced by a stomachache.

"I owe you an apology," Mom said, sitting across from her.

A diamond bracelet slid down her wrist, clinking on the wooden table. Kate studied it for a moment to distract herself. Her mother liked material possessions, wasting ridiculous amounts of money on unnecessary things. If she didn't buy them herself, she charmed Dad or other people until they showered her with presents. Was this a gift from her new beau?

Kate shoved her plate away. The correct response would be to say she forgave her. Instead, she said, "Yes, you do."

"You're not a disappointment."

Yeah, right. "Okay."

"Come on, what do you want from me? I'm trying to apologize."

That was just like her. Mom would sweep the issues under the rug with a simple "I'm sorry," and think that made everything better.

"It doesn't take back what you did or make me feel better. And, while I already suspected you were cheating on Dad, when I confronted you, you screamed at me like it was my fault."

"Who I see is none of your business," Mom said in a cold tone.

Pushing the topic wouldn't achieve anything except to incite another round of insults. Switching gears, Kate steered the subject to something more personal. "Fine, but when Matt cheated, you told me to resolve our differences anyway, knowing how much I value honesty and trust. You don't care about me or how I feel."

"That's not true."

Mom would never understand how her words and actions affected those around her. Nothing made her happy, and no matter how hard Kate tried, she remained a disappointment in her mother's eyes.

"I can't do this with you," she said, standing and knocking her chair backward. "If I stay in here, I'm going to say something that will upset both of us."

Halfway into the living room, her mom called, "Please don't walk away from me."

Kate kept going. The angel on her shoulder told her to stop and listen, but the devil said, "Hell no!"

Every time she stayed, she got hurt. Matt, Carlos, Mom—they'd all wounded her in one way or another, and she was falling apart.

Increasing her pace, Kate ran. In her haste, she stumbled over a stair, slamming her shin into the wood. Scrambling to her feet, she hobbled until she was safely inside her room.

One deep breath followed another as she leaned against the door, willing her racing heart to steady itself. Dodger slithered between her legs and meowed, and she sat on the floor beside him. He jumped into her lap and purred while she cuddled him and scratched behind his ears. It was as if he knew what she needed to calm her down, and after a minute, her nerves settled.

"Are you hungry?" she whispered.

He headbutted her hand and mewled, taking a few steps toward where she kept his food, looking back as if to make sure she was following.

Climbing to her feet, she retrieved a can of food and opened it, setting it on the floor where he greedily gobbled it up. She ran her fingers through his fur until her phone buzzed from her desk.

Dodger ignored her when she left him to cross the room. She stared at the innocuous device, debating whether she should check it. Mom wasn't beneath texting to have the final word, but it might be Carlos, finally returning her message. Good or bad, she needed to see what he had to say.

Closing her eyes, she counted to five. She wouldn't indulge any more time in her anxiety. Then she could bolster her resolve.

One. What if it's Mom?

Two. I can't handle any more bad news right now.

Three. What if it's Carlos? Is he still upset with me?

Four. Frack, I'm gonna be sick. Is this what a heart attack feels like?

Five. Time to put on your big girl panties.

Holding her breath, she reached for the phone and unlocked the screen. Sure enough, there was an incoming notification from Carlos. With shaking fingers, she scanned the contents. When she finished, her heart plummeted into her stomach as she fell into her chair.

'I'm sorry I haven't been in touch. I know how much honesty means to you, so I'm going to just say it. I love you. I've felt this way since our first Christmas party. I've tried to accept the fact you don't reciprocate my feelings. Before you blame yourself and feel guilty, I want you to remember it's not your fault. You can't help how you feel just like I can't carve my heart out and lock it away somewhere. You're amazing and everything I've ever wanted in a woman. You're fierce, intelligent, and a little badass when you forget to be self-conscious. Your loved ones mean the world to you, and you're loyal. I want you to be happy, even if it's not with me, but I can't be friends with you. I think it's best for us to end our friendship. I'm really sorry.'

The phone tumbled from her hand, clattering against the floor somewhere beneath the desk. Kate's world slowed to a stop until all she could see in her mind was the last part of his text. She remained rooted to the spot, trying to process what she'd read. She valued friendship almost more than romantic relationships, both of which were few and far between for her, and each person lost left a painful void that was impossible to fill. With everything that had happened in a short amount of time, Carlos's decision to cut ties hurt almost as much as Matt cheating.

It wasn't until her gaze flickered to a quartz stone on her desk that she unfroze. She took it, clenching her hand around it. They'd found it together on a summer trip. She hurled it as hard as she could, watching it shatter. If this was how he wanted to end years of friendship, fine. She could learn to live without him too.

Chapter Twelve

Tuesday

    Maddie: '*Guess what? We booked Ava Montenegro for your vlog interview! I'm squealing in excitement! She's HUGE! Happy dance! EEEEEEEEE!*'

    Mom: '*Sweetie, I'd like to finish our conversation. I don't regret having you. I know how hard you work in your career, and it was wrong to take my insecurities out on you. I shouldn't have pushed you to speak to Matt. I'm so sorry.*'

    Maddie: '*Did you get my text?*'

    David: '*Maddie called and said you aren't answering your messages. She also told me what happened with you and Mom on Sunday. Are you all right?*'

    Maddie: '*Is everything okay?*'

Thursday

    Maddie: '**It's been two days and your door is locked. Answer your phone!**'

    Ian: '*Hey! I haven't heard from you in a few days. I hope everything is going well for you. Are you doing anything on the 4th? I'd like to see you again. :)*'

Group Text, Maddie/David:

    Maddie: '*Okay, you need to leave your room. David is having a game night tonight at his place, and I'll pick the damn lock on your door if I need to. Bring your guy friend if you want, but you're spending time with us.*'

    David: '*I wasn't going to be THAT dramatic, but Maddie is right. You've been through a lot, and it's not healthy to shut yourself away. We love you. Also, who is this friend of yours? I want to meet him. :)*'

'P.S. When Maddie picks the lock, I'm dragging you to the truck. :p'

Lying on her side, Kate frowned at the latest text. She wanted to be left alone, not forced to socialize. Every message went unanswered while she indulged in her black hole of negative emotions. Her heart skipped at Ian's text and performed a tiny hop when Maddie told her about Ava Montenegro's interview, but Kate didn't have the energy to respond to anyone.

However, Maddie *would* pick the lock on the door. If that didn't work, she'd drop-kick it until the hinges came off.

As if on cue, someone pounded on the door with the force of a battering ram. Dodger tried to jump from his perch on the windowsill but got himself caught in the blinds. Before Kate could untangle his leg, the slats snapped, and the rod fell to the floor with a crash. Yowling, he darted beneath the bed.

Maddie shouted from the other side of the door and banged again. "Let me in! I'm gonna keep knocking until you answer me!"

"Jesus, give me a minute!" Kate stomped across the room and flung open her door. "I appreciate you checking in on me, but I'm not in the mood."

"Too bad," Maddie said, elbowing her way inside and whirling around to give her the stink-eye. Her gaze traveled the full length of Kate's body, and she scowled. "You look like shit."

"You barged in here to tell me that?"

Maddie scowled. "No, I'm here because you won't answer your damn phone. Seriously, what is going on? You were fine the other day when we talked about the vlog, and then you freaking ghosted me. Ava is big! You should be happy dancing, but instead you're hiding."

Kate shrugged and dropped onto her unmade bed. "I'm not hiding, I'm simply not in the mood to be around anyone."

"It's the same thing."

Falling onto her back, Kate spread her arms and stared at the ceiling. Maybe she was hiding. If she kept to herself, no one needed to see how much she was hurting inside. They didn't need to hear her whine or cry for the umpteenth time.

The effort to keep her expression neutral was like climbing Mount Everest. If she blinked, tears would fall, and if she breathed, her breath hitched. She needed to be alone.

Maddie didn't seem to notice. Sinking onto the bed, she settled beside her until their shoulders touched. "What happened?"

Her tenacious spirit was touching. Annoying as it was, Kate was happy *someone* cared enough to ask. "You remember my friend Carlos from the Geology department?"

"Really hot guy who looks like he got lost in the Geek Squad department at Best Buy?"

A shallow smile formed on Kate's lips. That was one way to phrase it. She told Maddie the whole Carlos drama.

"Ugh, I'm sorry. I will never understand men. And they say women are complicated."

"I keep feeling like I'm responsible for hurting him. It's not true, but there's that voice in the back of my head, telling me I should have let him down differently or something. And then there was all that stuff with Mom and Matt. I'm tired. I keep waiting for the universe to drop the other shoe on me."

"Aw, don't think like that. Sometimes life sucks, but you have to stay positive, or you'll drive yourself crazy."

"How do you stay so cheerful?"

"Bright side," Maddie trilled in a sing-song voice before turning serious. "I went through a period of depression right after college. It got to the point where I had to see a therapist. Rather than focusing on everything wrong, my doctor had me concentrate on my art as well as exercise, meditation, and the whole shebang."

"I had no idea."

"I didn't tell anyone. We have enough issues in our family without me crying about my problems."

Kate sighed, squeezing Maddie's hand. "You shouldn't have to repress it."

"You know what Mom is like. It's her I don't want to deal with."

"Is it possible she has a disorder?" Kate asked, releasing Maddie and rolling to her side.

"Oh, she definitely does. I love her, but she's a narcissist. She'd take credit for the sun shining if she could, but when things go wrong, *nothing* is her fault. When I broke down after college, Mom told me the depression was all in my head. Though, Dad was there for me. I asked him once why he won't divorce her. He told me he's with her because he doesn't want the family to fall apart."

Kate couldn't stay in an unhappy union. On the one hand, marriage vows were a big deal, not to be thrown away on a whim. However, if things were toxic with no hope of reconciliation, staying would harm her emotional well-being.

Sitting up, she crossed her legs and faced her sister. "She does bring stress everywhere she goes, and she's made me feel like crap long enough. It wouldn't hurt to consider therapy."

Maddie beamed and sprang off the bed, bringing Kate with her. "Great! But first, you should take a shower. You stink."

She didn't need to raise her arm to do the sniff check. Maybe this was a sign of spiraling into depression. Before, she couldn't go a day without showering or cleaning her room.

Lately, she neglected everything, telling herself she'd do it later. Her clothes spilled onto the floor, shards of broken gemstones littered the corner of her room where she'd swept it into a pile but didn't dispose of, and empty soda bottles filled her trash bin. The broken blinds added to the mess, summarizing the state of her crumbling life.

Sliding off the bed, she trudged to her dresser and grabbed her last clean pair of undergarments. Then she turned to address her sister. "Maddie?"

"Hm?"

"Why are you so good to me? I'm horrible to you. I shut you down out of jealousy, and then I made you feel bad about the video even though it wasn't your fault. I don't deserve you."

"You do," Maddie insisted. "It would be different if you didn't feel any remorse. Plus, with the wedding clip, I get it; you were going through a lot, and the fallout was huge. I'd probably want to fling blame around too."

"If you say so." Guilt was a tricky thing. Some people went through life without regrets, while others, like her, were eaten alive by it.

After gathering her clothes, she left the room to shower. She stopped in front of the mirror and stared at her reflection. Her hair hung in greasy tangles, stress acne dotted her face, and dark circles settled beneath her eyes.

Maddie was right. Kate looked like shit.

She stepped into the shower and turned on the faucet, reveling in the hot spray. Long after she washed away the grime, she remained there, clearing her mind of everything dragging her down.

When finished, she went back to her room with a spring in her step, towel drying her hair. Maddie was still there, sweeping the debris into a dustpan.

"Oh, you didn't have to do that," Kate said, overcome with guilt again.

"It was nothing. I started your laundry too."

That didn't ease Kate's conscience, but she was secretly glad she didn't have to deal with the mess later.

She hung her towel on a hook behind the door and scanned her room for anything else that needed tidying. She didn't want Maddie doing all the work.

Stripping the bed, Kate said, "You texted earlier to say you wanted to do game night at David's house. Is that still happening?"

"Yeah, we were talking about Cards Against Humanity or Phase Ten."

"Do you think Cards Against Humanity is appropriate around the girls?"

"They'll be in bed by then," Maddie said dismissively. "I promise not to corrupt their innocent minds."

It would be a miracle if the girls made it to adulthood without assimilating their father's potty mouth. David did his best not to swear around them, but his filter disappeared when he was angry or excited.

When he was in those moods, he was the type of man mothers would run away from, ushering their children to safety while covering their ears. Not that he'd ever unraveled in public, but Kate could picture the scene.

"Don't bring out Risk," she cautioned. "He gets mad every time we team up against him."

Maddie giggled. "Good thing I hate that game, but it's fun to push his buttons. Do you remember the Monopoly incident?"

"I try not to," Kate replied, horrified on her brother's behalf. "That poor table. Does Tracy let him play Candyland with the girls?"

"Yeah, with supervision."

And they wanted to do game night? That was like throwing a match into a canister of fuel. Maybe we are better off watching a movie where pinching and eye-poking wouldn't commence.

Kate laughed nervously. "Okay. I'll go, but only if David behaves."

"No promises," Maddie said with a grin. "Oh, and I'll message Ava and tell her we'll chat on Monday, okay? She already sent a list of questions for you to rehearse for the vlog."

Oh right. The last shred of Kate's reputation hung on this. "No pressure."

"One thing at a time," Maddie said, tying off the end of her trash bag. "You'll be on your road to success before you know it."

Placing her hands on her hips, Kate eyed the messy room around her, mentally comparing it to the state of her life. Both required cleanup, but with enough work, they'd transform into something she could be happy with. "I hope so."

~ * ~

The next day, they sat cross-legged on Maddie's bed, rehearsing the questions Ava sent to them.

Kate was cranky, and the list's material wasn't helping her mood. "This is stupid," she grumbled.

"No, it's not," Maddie grumbled.

"Yeah, it is. It's one of those questions people ask in job interviews, designed to learn more about you. Ava isn't hiring me."

"No, but the world judged you, and you need everyone on your side. These will help."

She rotated her shoulders and neck, shaking her hands to loosen her body. "Okay, read it again."

Maddie flicked her wrist, straightening the paper with a snap. Then she cleared her throat and repeated the question again in a bubbly voice. "Tell me about yourself."

Who am I? "Uh—"

"Stop! No filler words."

Kate groaned. "People say um and uh all the time!"

"Not in an interview. You can pause but don't stammer, or people will think you aren't confident."

"I'm not."

Scowling, Maddie clenched her fists and crumpled the paper. Then, she closed her eyes and took a deep breath. When she looked at Kate again, she splayed her fingers over her knees. "The first rule of any audition is to treat the room like you own it. No matter how nervous you are, you have to exude control. Nothing else matters."

"Fake it 'til you make it, got it." Kate scratched her neck and sighed. Everything was riding on her success. "Okay, let's try again."

Maddie's finger flew to the corner of her lip. "Confidence is key. And a smile. Always wear your happy face and don't let the wolves smell your fear."

Speaking of rabid animals, Mom knocked once before opening the door. "May I come in?" she asked, stopping at the threshold. Swallowing, she glanced back and forth between them. "I'm sorry to barge in, but we need to talk."

Maddie's smile disappeared as she dipped her head. Her silence stretched between them like an ocean, threatening to swallow them into a whirlpool of familial dysfunction.

Mom smoothed her manicured nails along her shale-colored blazer. Then she swept a lock of highlighted hair behind her ear. Her face was an emotionless mask, giving nothing away as she watched them with an expectant gaze.

Kate worked her mouth, trying and failing to speak. After a moment, she stared at her fingernails, waiting for someone else to open the conversation.

With a noise of disgust, Maddie slammed the paper onto the bed with a loud thwack. Uncrossing her legs, she scooted toward the edge. "Should I give you two some space?"

Kate's head snapped up. Maddie wouldn't leave them alone together, would she?

Mom spared her the anxiety, waving for her to stop. "No. I need to speak to both of you. It's time we cleared the air."

There was no avoiding the inevitable. Kate slipped off the bed to take the rainbow chair before her sister could claim it.

Rolling her eyes, Maddie positioned herself at the headboard while Mom daintily sat on the edge of the bed, folding her hands in her lap.

"Have you come to hurl more insults at us?" Maddie sneered. "Everyone knows apologies are beneath you."

Ouch.

However, it was true. Mom never begged forgiveness for anything before saying those awful things last week. Still, Kate didn't have the gall to confront her about it. She figured it never did any good to poke angry bears.

"You are being childish, Madeline. I am trying to fix things so it won't be awkward between us."

"That's enough," Kate chided, meeting Maddie and Mom's disdainful glares. Pursing her lips, she directed her gaze at her mother. "I don't mean any disrespect, but I agree with Maddie. You act like nothing is your fault, and the moment someone condemns you for your behavior, you get pissy. We went from me catching you with another man to you screaming that you wished you never had me. And when Dad came in to stop it, you whaled on him and brought him and Maddie into it. Your words were completely uncalled for."

Kate's entire body trembled. Her heart raced, threatening to leap from her throat, and her head swam. There was no way she could get through this conversation if her body swooned after firing the first shot.

To her surprise, instead of yelling or deflecting blame, her mom said, "I know. I was shocked when you saw me, and what I did was unforgivable. Your father and I should have told you about our arrangement sooner. I married Jeremiah at a time when this state was very family-oriented, and expectations were different. Women didn't have the same opportunities that we have now, and I initially struggled to find work. I stayed home with you three, and our fighting started because I had a law degree I wasn't using."

She dropped her gaze to her hands, and Kate's flew toward Maddie. She appeared as shocked as Kate. Mom had never been this candid. According to her, there was no room to examine feelings. It made people weak. Crying was never an option. They were expected to be strong and weather the storm, often at the cost of their emotional well-being. Her admission shined a new light on her, one where she was a victim of societal oppression.

After a few moments of dead silence, their mom continued, "Once you were old enough to watch your sister, I went back anyway. By then it wasn't as difficult for me to find work. I was good at my job, and I loved it. I was quickly promoted, proving I didn't need a penis to do work that was barred from us a century ago. I became the voice to women who struggled to overcome stigma in the workplace."

"Was Dad mad you were working?" Kate asked.

"Yes. Jeremiah is a very conservative man. He never considered what I wanted and insisted his money was enough to support the family. I could have remained home as his trophy wife, playing the part of the loving mother in the perfect family, preparing hot meals every night, keeping the home tidy. But that wasn't me. I tried it."

Maddie brushed her hair aside and leaned forward. Her features softened until she was no longer glaring, but her expression remained guarded. "Why didn't you leave then?"

Kate was curious too. Dad's supposed transgression seemed to be rooted in masculine ignorance. His and Mom's ideas were different. She should have tried to compromise, or she should have left if she was unhappy.

"We'd been married for almost twelve years by the time I went to work," Mom said, tucking her knee beneath her. "I didn't see much point in leaving. Not only is divorce expensive, but we'd invested so much into this home and personal lives. We'd be on our own again, and that's more terrifying than staying with someone you no longer love. Jeremiah and I have learned to pursue our hobbies as long as they don't affect anyone else."

Maddie scowled, clenching her fists in her lap. "Your attitude affects everyone and not in a good way."

Mom said nothing. Either she was too proud to admit the truth, or she didn't believe she was wrong.

"You didn't come here to apologize, did you?" Kate said quietly. "You want us to forgive your outburst and bury it, like we always do, but nothing is accomplished by doing this. You are the problem, but you can't see that. You know something is wrong, and you put on a front for the world to see while treating the rest of us like shit."

Maddie's eyes glistened, and her mouth trembled. In a thick voice, she said, "I think it's obvious we aren't going to see eye to eye.

You should go." She jerked away when Mom reached for her.

"You're overreacting," she said. "I came here to have a discussion, not argue."

"Get out." Maddie's voice was firm. "You bring nothing but stress everywhere you go. You crossed a line the other morning, and I am done making excuses for you."

Kate propelled herself from the chair and joined them on the bed. When Mom opened her mouth, Kate cut her off. "Don't. Maddie is right. I understand how frustrating it is to work as a woman in a man's world. I've been there. I'm glad you told us how you felt trapped with Dad, and it explains a lot about how you act, but it doesn't excuse your behavior or your resentment towards us. I'm tired of you making me feel like less of a person."

Mom slapped her thighs and stood up. "If this is how you choose to see things, who am I to argue with you? I'm not going to listen to you try to make me feel guilty after I have sacrificed everything to make you three happy."

"There you go again, playing the victim," Maddie scoffed. "What did you sacrifice? I'm the one who paid my way through school, not you. I lived through you calling me a slut and saying I'd never amount to anything. If I owe anyone gratitude, it's Kate and David for being by my side."

"If you're so independent, you can find your own place," she snapped. "This is still my house, no matter what Jeremiah says. As I told Kate on Sunday, I don't need your attitude."

"Great, you can tell Dad how you chased us away," Maddie shouted. "I'm sure he'll be thrilled to be living alone with the shrew he married."

"Okay, that's enough," Kate cried, crawling on her knees until she was between them, extending her arms to each woman. "Maddie, calm down. Mom, please leave. You've both made your points."

Mom spun on her heel and exited, leaving the door ajar. Her shoes clacked down the tile hallway, echoing long after Maddie closed the door.

The paper with the printed questions lay on the comforter, crumpled from the abuse. Taking it between her fingers, Kate smoothed it until the words were legible again. The text stared back at her, beckoning her to take the interview seriously and rise from the ashes of her digital demise.

Then, a thought struck her. This video would be more than telling the world why she deserved a second chance.

She could make excuses all day like her mother. She couldn't please everyone, but it was her chance to stop focusing on what she couldn't do and seize control of her life. By giving a candid interview, she'd be accepting responsibility and telling her side of the story.

With determination in her eyes, she patted Maddie on the back. "Forget about Mom. You're a strong, amazing queen."

"You're right," she huffed, flopping onto her stomach with an oomph, toying with a heart charm on her bracelet.

Kate placed the paper aside and dug between the fluffy pillows for her phone.

"What are you doing?" Maddie asked, lifting her head and dropping the bauble with a plink.

"*I* am responding to my secret friend," Kate said with a sly grin, opening her messages from Ian and typing a short response. '*4th of July sounds great!*'

Her phone pinged before she could set it down again. '*Awesome! I'll see you then. Wear jeans and tennis shoes.*'

'*Where are we going?*'

'*It's a surprise. Until then, don't forget to smile. :)*'

And she did. Not only because her heart buzzed with warm fuzzies every time they talked, but because she finally felt like she was going with the tide instead of against it. The negative cloud over her head shifted, making way for a sunny forecast in her future.

Chapter Thirteen

"Please tell me you are not wearing that," Maddie demanded, plucking Kate's blouse from her grasp. "You hate flowers."

"I don't *hate* them," Kate lied, trying and failing to retrieve her shirt from behind her sister's back. "Flowers appeal to my youth."

"If you're a granny! You're burning this after the interview." Maddie flounced into the closet, calling over her shoulder as she disappeared among the clothes. "Sis, I love you, but you can't wear any of these." Hangers zinged along the rack, and fabric rustled.

Kate followed after her sister. "What's wrong with my wardrobe? I wore these all the time when I taught at ASU."

Maddie poked her head out and arched an eyebrow. "You need chic and fashionable, not something you found in an excavation."

"I dig up rocks, not people," she said flatly. "And even if I was an archaeologist, most fabric would have deteriorated long before we discovered the remains. Meaning, I'd be appearing naked. Which wouldn't do me any favors."

"That depends on who's watching," Maddie said with a coy smile. "I bet your *friend* you've been texting wouldn't mind."

"We've only hung out twice," Kate mumbled, blushing furiously. "We're friends. Nothing more."

"Then why do you have a goofy grin on your face every time I mention him? You're doing it now."

She touched her scorching face and cleared her throat. "It's not like that. Ian and I have seen each other twice, and we haven't even kissed."

"Oh, his name is Ian!"

Damn it. She walked straight into that. "Maddie," she warned.

"Oh, please. You're totally into him. Why can't you admit it?"

"Because I'm not his type?" The truth was that Kate was afraid to get her hopes up. Living in denial made her feelings seem less real.

"If you aren't his type, why'd you stay at his place last Saturday?"

Kate crossed her arms and pinched her lips. She was tempted to send her sister away, but she couldn't because she needed moral support. "I fell asleep watching TV. I told you that on Sunday, remember?"

"I do, but I also think you're fooling yourself," Maddie said with a knowing look. "It's okay if you like him. He probably feels the same way. Have you thought about asking him on a date?"

Kate had ogled him once or twice when he wasn't paying attention but hadn't considered asking him out. He'd made it clear dating wasn't for him. "Nope. Ian isn't a car on the market. Can we discuss something else?"

"You can admire the car even if you don't buy it." Maddie grinned as she pretended to hold a steering wheel, circling as if making a sharp turn. Then, she lowered her voice and spoke as if delivering commentary. "First stop, the sexy love interest's house. Second stop, dinner and a show, preferably with his shirt off. Third stop, they're in the hallway, ripping off clothes. The final stop, his bed. Can I get some sirens for all the flames?" She finished by fanning herself before dissolving into giggles.

"Why do I tell you anything?" Kate shoved past her sister to search for clothes.

Her temperature rose, and it had nothing to do with Ian and everything to do with her growing mortification.

"Because I'm awesome, and you'd be lost without me," Maddie said, popping Kate's bra strap. "The moment you finish this interview, I want details. I know you're dying to tell me."

"You're just nosy. I'm content to keep my plans to myself."

"You made plans?"

"No." Another lie. Her sister was so infuriating. With Maddie's eyes boring holes into her back, Kate huffed, "Fine, I'm seeing him on the fourth. Although, he hasn't told me what we're doing. It's a surprise."

"Hello? Fourth of July? Fireworks? He's planning on a surprise that ends with a bang, if you know what I mean."

Her face and neck burning, Kate yanked an outfit from a hanger and held it up. "What about this?" she asked, quickly changing the subject.

Maddie wrinkled her nose at the pink shirt with spaghetti straps, a strawberry print, and pink lace. "Strawberry Shortcake called and wants her clothes back."

That was being kind. It looked like a cake vomited antacid medicine onto it. Kate's lips twitched, and laughter bubbled in her throat.

"Okay, it's hideous. Let's burn it."

"Agreed. I need to take you shopping before your big date."

Were they back on this subject again? "Nope. Ian said to dress casual and wear tennis shoes."

"And he won't tell you where you're going?"

"Nope."

Kate had tried a variety of methods to coax it from him, but he kept the secret locked tighter than a vault. Casual with sneakers could refer to many things, from minigolf to hiding a body in the desert. If he brought a shovel with him, she was hightailing it to the nearest police station.

Maddie discarded another shirt with a humph. "I'm drawing a blank. No swimsuit?"

"He didn't say, and before you ask, I'm not going skinny dipping with a stranger."

"Don't knock it 'til you've tried it," she said with a scoff.

"Have you?"

Now it was Maddie's turn to blush and avert her gaze. "Erm, once, when I went to Europe after college."

That was news. "Who was he?"

"No one." She cleared her throat and kept her back to Kate.

"Oh, he sounds like someone," she prodded, lightly touching her sister's arm.

Maddie dipped her head. "It was a casual fling." Her voice was sharp, cutting off any further questions.

Kate let it drop. It wasn't her place to pry if her sister didn't want to discuss it.

She redirected her attention to the clothes on the hanger, spotting a blue maxi dress shoved between her other summer outfits. When worn, it flared at the waist, and embroidered lace decorated the shoulderless sleeves. Not only was it perfect for the Arizona heat, but it was also casual and feminine.

Taking it off the hanger, she spun around to reveal it to her sister. "How do you like this?"

Maddie pinched the fabric and held it up, smiling as she inspected it. "I like it. Blue is totally your color."

"All right," Kate said with a grin, folding the dress over her arm. "Let's restore my reputation."

~ * ~

Kate sat at her desk, waiting for Ava to come online. Maddie sat nearby, invisible to the camera, ready to help.

The light was configured so it wouldn't make Kate difficult to see when the call started. She and Maddie spent the weekend cleaning her room and rearranging things so the walls weren't bare or dirty laundry didn't spill from the basket.

Dodger was permitted inside as a cameo from him would be welcomed. Maddie reasoned that people loved animals. Pets were relatable, and it would show Kate's loving nature.

Her sister also had the crazy notion of painting the room in shades of teal and purple, placing abstract paintings from her personal collection on the wall. The overall effect was beautiful, even if it was overdone. Plus, Kate did feel less depressed now that her space was no longer bland.

Waiting, she tapped her foot, trying not to think of all the different ways this could go wrong. She spent the weekend running through the questions, rehearsing until she could respond without hesitating or using filler words.

The computer chimed with an incoming call, and she answered it. A heart-faced woman with voluminous chocolate curls, sparkling brown eyes, and a wide smile appeared on the screen.

Thin bangles jangled against each other as she waved enthusiastically. "Hi!"

Kate lifted her arm with half the vigor. "Uh, hi."

Maddie hissed, gesticulating until Kate looked in her direction. A scowl crossed her face as she mouthed the word "no."

She was about to ask what no referred to when her sister crossed her arms in an X and pointed to the computer. Kate returned her attention to the screen and cleared her throat. "Hi, sorry. I'm nervous."

"I totally understand," Ava said, emphasizing her words. "I saw your videos when they went viral and watched them again when Marla called me. I would have died if that had been my wedding."

Anxiety washed over her, making her sway in her seat. She gripped the edge of the chair and inhaled through her nose. "Yeah, not my finest moment. If I could go back in time—"

"Ah-ah-ah!" Ava wagged her finger. "Save this for the interview. I want to go over a couple of things before we start."

"O-okay," she stammered.

"Did your sister explain my vlog to you?"

"Yes. You're a social media influencer."

Kate was overwhelmed by being in this rising star's presence. Ava had more than seven million Instagram followers. Her page was filled with makeup, clothes, and pictures of her travels. However, her YouTube videos were the bread and butter of her brand, and she had almost a million followers. She'd started at a young age, covering social issues ranging from injustice to minorities in America to women in the workplace.

"That's one way to put it," Ava said with a chuckle. "I started my foray online when I was fourteen, where I streamed myself at an immigration rally. My abuela was deported when I was in middle school, and it shaped me into who I am today. I couldn't sit at home doing nothing, knowing that so many people are being dragged from their homes just because they have brown skin. Then there were those kids were put in cages with inhumane living conditions while those in power did nothing. It was traumatizing to grow up, wondering who else I was going to lose, and I marched with everyone else to protest the government's cruelty."

"Shit, I'm so sorry," Kate said, horrified by the memories of the news articles. It was one thing to read about it and another to speak to someone who'd been affected by it.

Ava took a breath and composed herself, offering a ghost of a smile. "I wish I could say it's okay, but it's not. So many families are still in the system and not yet reunited. Children are separated from their parents, and some may never see them again. The system is wrong, and it's why I worked hard to keep my grades up in high school. I studied U.S. history and government policies, going further with my content, covering discrimination and its impact on us as a country."

"How old are you?" Kate blurted.

Ava didn't appear to be more than eighteen years old, yet she had the insight and maturity of someone twice her age. "I'm nineteen. I'm studying Sociology at the University of West Florida."

Holy moly, she was young for someone so accomplished. "Wow."

Ava waved her off. "I get that a lot, but marginalized women is a cause very dear to my heart. When I was approached for this interview, I couldn't believe it. We're supposed to be progressive, and your video is proof that women are still being held to unfair double standards. Anyway, I'm getting ahead of myself. When I start recording, we're going to introduce ourselves and go over the questions I prepared. Once the interview is done, I'm going to post this to YouTube and my vlog."

"That's it?" This was too easy. There had to be a catch.

"Yep. I recommend posting the video on your social media and sharing it with your friends. The more people who see it, the better." She took a sip of water before setting it down and fluffing her hair. "Okay, I'm ready when you are."

Kate would never be ready. She took a deep breath and exhaled slowly. Then, she drew another before cracking her knuckles and saying,

"Okay, let's do this."

A red dot flashed, indicating the camera was on, and Ava introduced herself. "Hi everyone! I'm Ava Montenegro, and I have something special for you all today. A few weeks ago, a video of a woman at her wedding went viral after the best man dropped a bombshell, revealing that the groom had cheated. What should have been the most magical day of her life became a nightmare, made worse after she was roasted by the public and lost her job. While the internet laughed, she lost everything after being humiliated at the altar. I'm here today with Kate Miller, former Geology professor at Arizona State University. She is going to give you her side of the story."

Ava was a natural, working the camera and speaking as if she was born in the public eye. She never stuttered or lost her excitement, keeping her focus straight ahead on the "audience." When she signaled for Kate, she gave the screen an expectant gaze, as if they were sitting next to each other.

"Why don't you tell us about yourself."

No matter how much she rehearsed this question, Kate wasn't good at public speaking. Forcing a smile, she straightened her spine and began. "Hi. I'm Kate Miller. Most of you know me as the Social Media Bride."

She chuckled nervously as Ava joined her. "You're more than that. Who are you when you're not teaching?"

Focus on the question. Be confident. Own the room. "Well, I'm pretty normal. I was born here in the valley, I graduated with honors at ASU, I like to travel, and spend time with those close to me." As if anticipating her words, Dodger jumped onto the desk, pressing his nose to the screen. Kate laughed and shoved him away. "My cat wants to be acknowledged."

"Aw, he's adorable! What's his name?"

Holding him to her chest, she scratched his ear. He squirmed for a moment before curling into a ball and purring. "This is Dodger. I got him from a shelter last year. They had trouble placing him with a family because he was scared and antisocial. I took him anyway. He spent the entire first day hiding in the closet and refused to let anyone touch him, but he's since adjusted and allows me to hold him, especially when I give him a can of his favorite food."

Ava jutted her lip into a pout. "That's so sweet! I think it's great when people give animals a loving home, and it's clear how much he likes you."

Kate wouldn't go that far. If she had to describe Dodger's feelings, she'd say he tolerated her. He settled onto her lap if he wanted attention, food, or to claw her arm. The rest of the time, he sat perched on her windowsill unless he wanted to drop a dead lizard on her bed. Not that the public wanted to hear that. "Yeah, he's great."

When she didn't offer more, Ava moved on, not allowing the pause to sit too long. "Let's talk about why we're here. During your wedding, the best man dropped a massive bombshell on you and the guests. What was going through your mind when he revealed your fiancé had cheated on you?"

Kate froze, squeezing her cat until he wriggled out of her grasp and hissed. Going through this question with Maddie was one thing, but airing it for others made her anxious. She shifted in her seat and averted her gaze, locking eyes with her sister.

Maddie scooted forward and took Kate's hand. "It's okay," she whispered.

She blinked away the tears burning behind her eyes and faced the laptop. "I was blindsided with the news. When you get married, you want everything to be perfect. I don't think anyone expects to receive that kind of news at the altar. There was a moment I thought it was a horrible joke."

"And when you realized it wasn't?"

"I felt like I couldn't breathe. I remember looking at Matt and telling myself, 'This can't be true,' but his eyes gave it away. It was like meeting a different version of him instead of the man I fell in love with."

"How long were you two together?"

"Two years. Our moms are best friends, and that's how we met. He was charming, he treated me well, and I never once saw him check out other women. There weren't any signs that indicated he would do something like this to me."

Ava brushed a strand of hair behind her ear and tilted her head. "Is there a chance this was an isolated incident?"

Kate recalled Matt when David had confronted him with the coke. He'd appeared small and pathetic as he pleaded for her to understand and forgive him. And she might have if he hadn't tried to manipulate her first by threatening to call the police and claim domestic abuse.

"I do believe he hadn't planned on cheating. It was a result of too much partying." she confessed, forcing the past away. "Matt probably isn't a serial cheater, but everything he did afterwards made me confident I'd made the right decision to leave him. His first reaction was to lie to me. He went on our honeymoon without me. When I offered to return the ring through my brother, he manipulated me into seeing him. All he's done is deflect the blame and hide things from me. If he'd been honest from the beginning, with enough time and space, I might have been able to forgive him."

"Wow," Ava said.

Her smile had faded, and her eyes widened with each new piece of information. "That's awful. I mean, obviously you're not the first person to be cheated on, but he should have had the decency to call or say something after the viral video and fallout. Did he ever ask how you were feeling?"

Kate shook her head. "No. Every time he called or texted, it was to beg me to take him back. He never checked to see how I was doing or offered support. I would have gone through this alone if it hadn't been for my brother and sister."

"Jeez. And you said he blackmailed you?"

Kate scratched her nose, so she didn't snarl at the screen. "First, he sent me a text, listing the reasons he was a good boyfriend, while also insinuating I was a terrible girlfriend. Then he threatened to press charges for domestic violence if I wouldn't meet with him. In the end, I went to his house to return the ring and permanently end things."

"I would have done the same," Ava admitted. "Going through that must have been demanding on your mental well-being. I'd be a mess at the wedding, forget about everything else you weathered after. This leads me to my next question, which concerns your job. Earlier, I introduced you as a former professor at ASU. Why did they let you go?"

She'd considered the possible reasons a dozen times. Employers stalked a person's social media before and after hiring, even though personal lives should remain separate. Then there was the issue of the university president, who had never liked her. The video had been the perfect excuse to let her go.

She sighed. "The day after the wedding, I received a call from my boss, asking me to come to work. That's when he told me the university was dismissing me due to my temper. The logic was that if I acted that way at my wedding, I had the potential to do the same to the students."

"Do you feel betrayed by the termination?"

"Yes. I was a great teacher, and my reviews were excellent every year. My student's engagement scores were high even though I was tough on them. Many of the Geology majors found good careers, and I feel like I prepared them. It's heartbreaking to know I have so much to offer these kids, but can't because I was let go."

"Why not? You may not be at ASU anymore, but that doesn't mean it's the end of your career. There are other colleges who need passionate teachers."

Kate dropped her hands in her lap and stared at her feet. "Ever since my termination, I haven't been able to find work. Social media was the death of everything for me. I'm barely online, and I got caught in the crossfire anyway, just because someone thought my meltdown would be good for her followers. I'm here today to tell you and your followers I made a mistake, but that one video doesn't define me."

"That's important to remember," Ava agreed. "Even though the internet has been commonplace since the nineties, we're discovering its dangers daily. We live in a time where almost everything we do is online, and new rules are formed every day. We have to learn how to navigate them as we fall under the microscope. We might mean or say one thing, but the world will see something different as they dissect our actions."

She paused as if waiting to see if Kate had anything to add. Taking the silence as her cue, Ava spoke again. "Okay, y'all, that's it for today. I hope this was as insightful for you as it was for me. I'd like to thank Kate for her time and remind everyone to think before you post. If you liked this video, don't forget to subscribe to my channel. My name is Ava Montenegro, and I'll see you soon."

The red light turned off, and Ava smiled into the camera. "Thank you for doing this interview. I'm going to upload this tonight and send you a link. Don't forget to pass this along to your friends and post to your profiles."

"It's me who should be thanking you," Kate said with a laugh. "I couldn't have shared my side if you hadn't agreed to this."

"It was my pleasure. I know how judgmental people on the internet can be, and I was happy to hear your side of the wedding. I hope you find success in your job search. You seem like a nice person. Honestly, seeing you stay strong like this is inspiring to me."

That was the kindest thing anyone could have said to her. This teenage influencer proved that there were good people in the world. "I appreciate that. The same goes for you, and I can see you going far in life."

Ava inclined her head. "I hope so. Most of all, I wish you the best. Promise to stay in touch?"

Suffice it to say, they both had separate lives outside of this meeting. Ava would end the call and do her thing. She didn't have to remember Kate. Yet, she was extending the branch of friendship. Her generosity touched Kate's heart, filling it to bursting with gratitude. Though miles and an age gap separated them, Kate knew she'd keep in contact with her new friend.

"You bet," she replied.

Chapter Fourteen

"Where are we going?" Kate asked, standing in Ian's foyer on the Fourth.

He waggled an index finger and shook his head. "It's a surprise."

She wasn't sure if she liked those anymore. "Come on, can't you give me a hint?"

"Nope."

Jutting her lip into a pout, she tried to appeal to his sympathy with her best puppy-dog eyes. "Please?"

They went outside, and after locking the door, he grabbed a large backpack from the porch. Then, he walked toward his truck, and Kate followed him.

Turning and digging into his pocket, he produced a hair tie and handed it to her. "You'll need this."

She took it and slipped it around her wrist like it was a bracelet. "Okay. I didn't expect that for an answer." She stood on her toes, trying to catch a glimpse of anything that might hint at his plans. "Are we burying a body in the desert? Where's the shovel?"

"No bodies today," he said with a laugh, heading back toward the house and hefting a cooler that sat beside the front door. Once it was secure in the bed of the truck, he wiped his brow. "How do you feel about a small adventure? One that preferably doesn't involve violence."

"Depends. Are we exploring?"

"In a sense."

Curiosity burned in her chest at the secret, and Kate bounced on her heels. "Okay, are we going far, like to Sedona or Flagstaff?"

Tilting his head to one side, he stroked his chin. "No, we'll definitely be home long before the fireworks start. The view will be spectacular."

That could apply to any number of places. Arizona was filled with scenic deserts and mountains. "All right, I'm game. Let's go."

They moved to the front of his F-150, where Kate struggled to climb inside. "You couldn't drive something smaller? I feel like I'm inside a carnival funhouse."

Ian gave her a boost into the cab, chuckling. "Guess you should sprout up a few more inches to meet the height requirements."

She twisted around and blew a raspberry. Her sister and brother inherited the tall genes, whereas she was got stuck with her mom's short stature. There were twelve-year-olds taller than her. "Hardy-har-har. Better a hobbit than to bump my head into things."

He shrugged. "Tall people problems."

"Careful who you tease. Some might take offense."

"Do you?"

"Nah. My mother has said much worse to me."

The words tumbled out of her mouth before she could stop herself. Today was supposed to be fun, and she wouldn't dwell on her depressing home life.

She cleared her throat. "Sorry."

Ian cast her a brief side glance. "Why are you apologizing?"

"Because it's nothing. I didn't mean to mention my mom." She looked out the passenger window.

"It doesn't sound like nothing."

"No, really, I shouldn't have said anything."

Family drama wasn't something brought into a conversation this early into a relationship. The things her mother said weren't even six-month material. The dysfunction in her parents' dynamic was on such an epic level they could have their own reality show.

Breaking the silence, Ian said, "I understand not wanting to talk about it, but you should probably speak to someone. It's not good to hold everything inside. Trust me, I know."

Oh, right. His dad. "I'm s—"

"Don't apologize. You didn't do anything wrong."

It was on the tip of Kate's tongue to say it again, but she caught herself.

Dropping her gaze to her lap, she bit the inside of her cheek. Recalling his past, loads of questions resurfaced, like how he'd severed ties with his dad or how he'd coped with the abuse. Her situation was emotional, not physical, but talking with him could help her feel less alone.

"How was the interview?" he asked. "I remember you mentioning it in your text."

Happy for a different topic, Kate beamed. "It went well. Much better than expected. It had nearly five thousand views in the first few hours after Ava and my sister shared it. It's not as popular as the wedding video, but it was seen, and people left very supportive comments."

The interview had been the highlight of her week. Kind wishes poured in from every corner of the world. They called her strong for enduring her hardship and having to see it over and over online.

Also, Kate was more optimistic about finding a job than a week ago. Now that her side of the story was out, perhaps employers wouldn't hold the video against her. She had to believe it would work out. Anything less was too bleak to consider.

"Do you feel better?" he asked as if reading her mind.

"Yes."

Her spirits lifted, and they rode the rest of the way in comfortable silence. When they parked next to a large building with a sign that read 'Skydive Phoenix,' Kate's heart skipped several beats, pumping adrenaline through her body. "We're skydiving?"

"Mm-hm. I thought we might try something different. Have you ever been?"

She shook her head, unable to form words. The farthest she'd ever been off the ground without walls was the roof of her house. As kids, she and her siblings climbed there to see the Fourth of July fireworks every year. With the exception of flying, the highest she'd ever been anywhere was The Space Needle, but she'd been inside the safe confines of the structure. There had been no threat of plummeting to her death, unlike skydiving.

It wasn't that she was afraid of heights, but anything could go wrong. What if the parachute malfunctioned or a bird hit her in midair?

Finally finding her voice, she asked, "No. Have you?"

"Yep. This will be my thirty-eighth jump. I got my Class A solo skydiving license when I was twenty-eight years old."

Holy moly, this man was crazy. Falling out of a plane once was enough to give Kate pause, and Ian was almost had forty under his belt. Did he have plans to become an action hero, or was he simply an adrenaline junkie?

"You all right, or do you want to skip it?" He'd opened his door but paused.

Well, he hadn't lied about going on an adventure. When he asked what her plans were, it never occurred to her to free-fall above the clouds. She'd been thinking a picnic or a hike. Oh, how wrong she'd been.

She gulped. "Nope. Let's do this."

An hour later, Kate didn't feel any more confident than before she watched the instructional video and signed the waivers. No matter how they reassured her that her tandem jump was with an experienced professional, her head buzzed with apprehension. She wasn't in the air yet, and her knees were already buckling.

Inside the hanger, Ian dressed in gear he'd brought for a solo dive. Kate's instructor helped her into a harness. Then she was given a set of goggles, which she slid over her wrist. She tied her hair into a messy ponytail with the hair tie Ian had given her.

Knowing her luck, her hair would get caught in the parachute lines. Ian and the instructors insisted she'd be fine, but her brain kept visualizing what would happen if she somehow got separated from her partner and fell to her death.

She followed Ian to a runway filled with small planes. As they waited for her jump partner, he took her hand and leaned in to whisper, "How do you feel?"

She chuckled and shook out her limbs. "Oh, nervous. I keep thinking the parachute won't deploy or I'll have a heart attack in mid-air."

"Relax. These instructors have tons of training and jump experience. There's nothing more liberating than being in the sky. You've flown before, right?"

"Yeah."

"It's not much different. A plane can malfunction just as easily, yet you fly anyway. The free fall is only sixty seconds before they pull the chute. The rest is smooth sailing. You'll love it."

She'd have to take his word for it. Dying was still dying, and she'd prefer to live a bit longer. Hugging her arms, she said, "I'm surprised you didn't offer to jump tandem with me."

His eyes glittered with mischief. "Are you saying you'd trust me with your life?"

She shrugged. "Well, I know you. Plus, if we died, at least it would be together. Then I could blame you in the afterlife."

"You're so morbid! But no, I don't have the right license or hours to do that kind of jump."

An instructor approached them, trailed by two men holding cameras, each of them dressed in red, white, and blue shirts with the American flag printed on the front. The first to approach them was a man who stood almost two heads taller than Kate.

He greeted them with a huge smile. "Welcome to Skydive Phoenix! My name is Darryl, and I'll be doing the tandem jump. Who do we have here today?"

Seeing the cameras recording, Kate's first instinct was to run. She reminded herself this was part of the skydiving package Ian purchased. It had nothing to do with her prior mishaps on social media.

She took a calming breath and reached for Ian's hand, squeezing it in a death grip. "Um, I'm Kate, and this is Ian."

"Welcome," Darryl said, pointing to each of them and bouncing on his feet. "We're gonna jump today, are you excited?"

Ian whooped and pumped his fist. "Yeah, let's do this!"

Vertigo threatened to send Kate into a swoon, and all she could manage was a warbling, "yeah," as she fought to keep her breakfast down.

"Aw, is this your first time skydiving?" Darryl asked, waving the cameraman closer.

She swallowed, trembling from head to toe. "Yes."

"No worries. It'll be fun! Are you two here on a date?"

Kate looked at Ian, and his lips turned into a broad grin. "I hope so," he said, lifting his eyebrows.

That was news. In the past, he acted like relationships were the worst thing in the world. Now he wanted to date her? This man was a mixed bag of signals.

Darryl cut off her thoughts with a whistle. "Ooh, that's what I call a hell of a first date!"

Kate snorted. "I'm still deciding."

Darryl grinned. "I guess you'll have to let me know your decision when we land."

"That depends on how much crying I do in the air," she said before dipping her head to hide the blush burning her cheeks.

"Then I'll have to make sure you have a good time. Let's do this!"

Darryl raised his palm for a high-five, and Kate slapped it weakly, too concerned with not fainting. She'd contemplate her dating status when she landed.

They boarded the small plane, with Darryl behind Kate and the cameramen in front of the cockpit, facing them. It wasn't long before they were in the air, leaving the ground behind. Miles of brown desert stretched across the distance, and soon, they were above the clouds.

Darryl clipped her shoulder straps to his harness, so her back was strapped to his front. Then he adjusted the straps on her legs, giving her no room to move.

Attached like this, everything she did, a shift in her seat or to turn, he had to do the same. It must have been harder for him, having each leg on either side of her as they waited for the plane to rise in altitude.

Soon, they'd be sliding toward the door, preparing to make their tandem jump. If the parachute somehow failed to eject, well…at least they'd go out together.

He yelled something, but the whistling wind muted his voice, making it difficult to hear.

"What?" she asked.

He cupped his mouth with his hands and shouted, "How do you feel?"

Glancing through the window, she released a squeal and laughed. "I can't believe I'm doing this!"

"You'll have fun. Remember, the most important thing is to smile."

"I thought I was supposed to survive so I can go on that next date."

Ian, who was sitting in the seat next to her, took her hand and brushed her knuckles with a kiss. "You've got this."

Warmth spread through her chest. She might have drawn him closer if she wasn't literally strapped to Darryl. Every time she and Ian touched, the spark was present. It left Kate wanting more, especially since he was dangling the possibility of them dating.

Her mind screamed it was too soon, but her heart resisted. Being with him was fun and exciting, something lacking in her previous relationship.

She beamed at him, and he winked. He released her hand and scooted forward until his legs hung outside. His videographer was already outside the plane and holding onto the ledge, waiting.

Ian gave her a small wave before he let go and dropped. The cameraman released the handle, disappearing from view.

"All right, we're next!" Darryl shouted, shifting them to the door.

Securing her goggles onto her face, Kate swung her legs over the edge and stared down. The ground below was a map of brown fields and farmland, and the structures were like ants on a hill. Even the mountains seemed small from where she sat.

She drew a deep breath to calm her racing heart. At the top of the world, less than a mile from God, she swayed. If not for the hooks holding her to her partner, she might have fainted. A red, white, and blue parachute unfurled in the distance. The jumper was too far away for Kate to determine who it was, and within seconds, another chute appeared, this one in a bright shade of blue.

A swath of clouds passed beneath her feet, concealing the other divers from view. Then, Darryl tilted her head back until it rested against his chest. He rocked back and forth three times, and Kate gripped her straps for something to hold. Then, pushing themselves forward, they left the floor behind, and it disappeared as they plummeted into the open sky.

A scream ripped from her throat, disappearing into the wind as they tumbled. At first, she was blinded by the sun. Then, Darryl turned, and his arms extended on each side of her. His hand closed around her wrists, tugging for her to let go of the strap. She uncurled her fingers, one at a time, and copied his movement, and soon, they were two birds in flight. Her heart slammed into her ribcage, but once her stomach settled, the drop was exhilarating.

The cameraman whizzed past them with a wave, then arched his back as Darryl moved to meet him, bringing the three of them within touching range. The cameraman reached for Kate, and she took his hands, laughing with abandon.

A moment later, he released her and gave them a double thumbs up. Her body jerked when the chute deployed, and she bounced before slowly continuing her descent. The ridges grew in size as they moved closer to Earth, and cars zoomed in the distance on the lone highway.

The fabric above them rustled, and Darryl whooped.

Adrenaline continued to surge through her veins, and it took a moment for her voice to return. Holding her straps again, she shouted, "Oh, my God, I can't believe I'm doing this!"

"And you didn't cry, so you'll have to tell your man this was a date."

"Maybe. You'll have to wait and see," she said, giggling as she splayed her arms akimbo.

"Until then, enjoy the view. I'm proud of you."

Even though he couldn't see her, she grinned, then did as he suggested, staring at the distant horizon where mountains rose above the city, and the desert stretched below them. Clouds drifted above them where they'd recently plowed through, giving way to a beautiful, clear blue sky.

The landing field came into view, and several people waited. Ian was easily discernable in his bright red shirt, waving and jumping as she approached. She lifted her legs until she was sitting in an invisible chair at a perpendicular angle, and Darryl brought her into a running stop.

When her bottom was firmly in the grass, she closed her eyes, sucking in several deep breaths. Her body trembled, and her pulse buzzed in excitement. The thrill of falling thousands of feet in the air with nothing but the sky between her and the rest of the world was liberating.

Someone's hand closed around hers, and she opened her eyes to find Ian standing over her. His hair looked like he'd stuck his finger in an electrical socket, and his wild eyes mirrored her excitement. Once Darryl unhooked himself, Ian helped her up, and she found herself pressed into his chest.

Darryl came around them and patted her on the back. "All right, moment of truth, Kate. Did you have fun?"

"Yes," she said breathlessly, nodding once.

"Would you do it again?"

She laughed. "Hell no! It was exciting, but once is enough."

"So? Does this mean today was a date?"

Ian dipped his head, watching her with a hopeful grin and a raised eyebrow. "Well?"

The urge to stand on her toes and kiss him was strong. She bit her bottom lip. They were moving fast, just like the jump, but she didn't care.

Snaking her arms around Ian's neck, she pulled him until his mouth connected with hers. Her eyes drifted shut again, and she sighed in contentment as he moved his mouth against hers.

When they broke apart, she remained in his embrace and grinned. "How's that for an answer?"

"I think I need to ask again," he said, moving in for another kiss.

Chapter Fifteen

"Where to, now?" Ian asked, tucking a lock of tangled hair behind Kate's ear. "I think you deserve to choose after willingly diving from a plane."

Kate didn't care what they did as long as the day didn't end early. She enjoyed his company, and she'd rather spend her time with him than at home. Everyone was there, and she'd be expected to socialize. She didn't have the energy to listen to her parents fight or count down the minutes until she could hide again. With Ian, she was free to enjoy herself any way she saw fit, without having to put on appearances.

"I'm down for anything, as long as it involves keeping my feet firmly planted on the ground," she said with a grin, sliding her hand into his, loving the scrape of his calloused fingertips.

"Do you have plans with your folks? I don't want to take you away from them if you do."

His eyes were wistful, but she couldn't tell if it was because he wanted her to himself or if he craved time with loved ones too. Kate wondered when he last spent a holiday with someone special.

"They will probably barbeque and swim, but I don't have to join them. I'm happy to spend today with you, whether we go to my place or watch fireworks on top of a mountain."

"I'm not ready to meet your family yet," he confessed, "but if you're okay with fireworks on that mountain, I wouldn't say no. I also have a cooler and a blanket in the back of the truck. We could have a picnic."

"Then let's go," she said.

Wasting no time, Ian grabbed her wrist and led her along, half running and half skipping the rest of the way to his vehicle. They drove until finding a small park. Families were gathered in full force. Groups of kids swarmed bouncy castles, families cooked at portable and park barbecue grills, and people fished at the manmade lake.

They chose a shaded patch of grass. The tree didn't stifle the summer heat, but the sun shining against the water provided the perfect backdrop for a restful holiday afternoon.

"What did you bring to eat?" she asked, reaching for the ice chest Ian had brought. "Anything as adventurous as skydiving or weird ice cream?"

He opened the cooler and passed her a beer. "Nope. Just Hasselback clubs and drinks. I didn't want anything that would melt."

She peeked inside, and her mouth watered at the clear containers. Inside were kebabs of fresh tomatoes, avocados, bacon, cheese, lettuce, and white meat. The preparation was tidy, like something she'd see on Instagram with a fancy background. "Did you make this?"

"As in prepare it verses takeout or something in a package from the store?"

Kate nodded, and Ian unlatched the container, holding it out to her. "I made it. I prefer to cook."

She prayed he would never ask her to or that it was on his list of deal-breakers for a girlfriend. Takeout was how she'd survived most of her adult life. Plucking a neatly stacked club on a stick from the pile, she took a bite and moaned. "Oh, this is good," she said after swallowing.

"I know it's not typical Fourth of July food, so I'm glad you like it. I don't usually celebrate the holiday with anyone, and I made it because I wasn't sure if you'd stay. If I'd been more confident, I'd have suggested we grill."

She scooted closer until their knees touched. Then she nudged his shoulder. "You can't get rid of me that easily."

"I wouldn't dream of it."

After they finished eating, they lay on the blanket, with their heads together and their hands resting on their chests. Big, fluffy clouds leisurely drifted overhead, and they searched for creatures in the different shapes.

Kate was curled in giggles, wheezing for breath as Ian pointed out a lobster claw squaring off against Godzilla. When she rubbed the moisture from her eyes, she noticed the sunlight illuminating a small scar across his left eyebrow. It was faded, half-hidden as it disappeared into his hair.

She squinted to get a better look, and she touched it before thinking better of it. "How did you get this?"

The laughter instantly died behind his eyes as he recoiled, shying away from her touch. Sitting, he drew in a rattled breath, keeping his gaze averted as his jaw twitched.

Kate sat too, crossing her legs and waiting for him to respond.

The longer the silence stretched between them, the more she worried she'd upset him. Ian avoided talking about the painful parts of his past, and if this scar was during that time, he might shut down.

"I'm sorry," she spluttered. "You don't need to talk about it."

He pressed a finger to her lips. Pain and fear warred behind his wide-eyed gaze until finally, he sighed. "It's okay. It was going to come up eventually anyway. I got this from my dad."

What could she say to that? *Hey, I'm sorry your dad was a piece of shit* seemed inadequate for what he must have gone through.

She rested her forehead against his. "I'll listen if you want to tell me, but I don't want to pressure you or make you relive bad memories."

His fingers curled behind her neck, and he drew her into him, closing his mouth over hers. His tongue teased her bottom lip, and he sucked on it before parting her mouth with a sigh. As the kiss deepened, his other hand glided down her back until it rested on her hip.

Warmth bloomed inside her chest, her body demanding more. Sitting on her knees, she shifted, matching the heat of his mouth with hers. His lips were soft and inviting, tasting of lingering beer. She didn't mind the taste and moved to run her fingers through his hair and stroke his face.

It was several moments before he broke contact, grazing her nose with his. "You're fine, I promise." With a peck on her lips, he sat across from her, fidgeting with a loose thread in his jeans. "My dad was backpacking through Colombia during his gap year in college when he met my mom. She never talked much about him, but from what I can tell, there were sparks right away. They were both young. Ma lived in poverty, taking jobs anywhere she could get them. She was serving at a local bar when he walked in."

Ian opened another beer and took a sip. He then set the can down and lay on his side, propping himself on his elbow as he picked at the grass. He plucked a dry blade and crushed it before he tossed it aside and continued, "Dad took Mom out for a night on the town, and in the beginning, he showered her with money and gifts. He even met her family and helped them around the house. Within six months, they were married in a Catholic Church in her village."

Kate tried to picture Ian's father. Was he tall with dark hair too? Did they bear a striking resemblance, or did he favor his mother? "What was he like?"

Grabbing another clump of grass, Ian shrugged. "He was charming. Mom used to tell me how he'd look at her, and she knew he loved her. She said his mouth would lift into a silly grin and that his eyes would twinkle. She took him to all the local places, and he proposed at her favorite waterfall."

It was easy to see how Ian's mother fell in love. This man was a stranger from another country, a place that represented freedom from poverty and danger. Ian made their story sound romantic. A classic tale of two young adults falling in love.

"What made your mom decide to come here? Was it hard for her to leave everything she knew behind?"

"She was poor. When she discovered she was pregnant, her parents told her to move to the U.S. The drug cartels were a huge problem where they lived, and they didn't want me to grow up around it. I guess Dad told them he wanted to join the Army. They told Ma to go with him. With safety and opportunities here, America offered sanctuary for her."

Living with the threat of violence would have been a compelling reason for her to leave. Just about anyone in her situation would have said yes.

Kate considered the story, wondering how a loving man could hurt his family. He seemed to have cared enough to bring his wife home and raise his son. Was he always angry, hiding it, or was it something that came on gradually? "You said your dad gave you that scar. Was he often violent?"

"If he had a nice side, I don't recall it. I spent my entire early childhood listening to him yell. He was never happy, and I remember being afraid of him. I used to hide under my bed and inside my closet because I didn't want him to hit me. He used to come home stumbling drunk. He'd see me or Ma, and start screaming. Ma would send me away, and they would argue. I was eight when he put her in the hospital. He took me aside and told me to lie to the police. He threatened to beat me if I didn't, and he said Ma would be deported if they got divorced. I wasn't old enough to understand what was going on, and I didn't want to lose her."

"I thought you said she took you and left."

He nodded, keeping his gaze on his lap, where he continued to fidget with the shredded grass. "She did, but it wasn't until later. I was ten, and she was pregnant. I woke in the middle of the night to go to the bathroom and heard something bang against the wall. I snuck into the hallway, and all I remember was Ma crumpled and crying on the floor."

Kate's blood ran cold, and she froze, covering her mouth. She couldn't imagine what it was like for him to live with such a horrible man. "Oh, my God. What kind of monster does that? What happened to the baby?"

Ian's jaw clenched, as did his fists in his lap. With a shuddering breath, he said, "She lost it during one of Dad's beatings. And he got away with it. I never understood how he wasn't arrested or charged with assault. The only thing I remember was Ma packing what she could carry and someone driving us from Indiana to Wyoming. I didn't see him again until she died."

Kate watched him in silence. Dozens of new questions emerged, but it felt insensitive to ask him to relive more than he'd already shared.

When their eyes met, ghosts haunted Ian's steel gaze. She brushed the loose earth and dead grass from his leg and linked her fingers through his. He grazed his lips against her knuckles and offered her a sad smile.

"My dad was remarried when the court ordered me to stay with him. My stepmother hated me, and she called me every derogatory slur she could think of. She used to threaten to dump me across the border, saying it was where I belonged. Once, she searched my room and destroyed any pictures she could find before stealing the little jewelry my mother had and sold it. My dad never stepped in. Hell, when he was around, he abused my half-sister and used me as a punching bag. He hit my stepmom too, but instead of leaving him, she self-medicated with prescription drugs and alcohol."

The way he described his past was as if it wasn't his own. That it had happened to someone else. It almost didn't feel real, and Kate couldn't believe Ian, a jovial and kind man, had lived with such monstrous parents. It was clear he'd never fully recovered.

"That's...wow, I'm sorry. I don't know what to say."

He brought her hand to his cheek, cradling it between his calloused fingers. "It was a long time ago." His eyes fluttered closed for a few seconds, and his breathing was husky. "After he slammed a broken whiskey bottle in my face, he panicked and locked me in the basement. I squeezed through the small window above the washing machine and ran to a neighbor's house. Dad went to jail. The man, George, initially helped me ended up adopting me. He's a psychologist who worked for the state. He'd never married or had kids. George took me in when I had nowhere else to go. I owe everything to him. He's been there through my dad's abuse, helping me come to terms with my mom's death, and my divorce. I wouldn't be here if it wasn't for him."

"God, your dad is awful. I'm glad you had someone to support you after all of that."

Ian curled a lock of Kate's hair around his index finger, wrapping and unwrapping it several times before responding. In a mild tone, he said, "George is the best."

Kate offered him a sad smile. "Sounds like it. My issues are nothing compared to what you've been through."

"It's not nothing," he assured her in a low voice. "You're hurting too, and I understand how hard it is to let people in. I wanted you to know I'm always here to listen, no matter how small you think your problems are."

Kate pressed her lips to his mouth and molded herself against him. Ian laid down again and pulled her with him, holding her tight. The afternoon sky had turned a deep orange with shades of pink and purple scattered across the clouds. The fireworks wouldn't start for at least another hour, giving them plenty of time to cuddle and talk. It would be a good opportunity to discuss boundaries.

Repositioning herself, she rested her head on his shoulder. Comfortable, she placed her palm on his chest and rubbed it in slow circles. "What changed your mind about dating? At Tempe Town Lake, you acted like it was the plague."

He chuckled and brought his hands behind his head. "Okay, maybe I got a bit carried away. I wasn't actively seeking a girlfriend, but I enjoy your company. You're fun and adventurous, and when I'm with you, I want to be spontaneous. I haven't felt that way in a long time, and it made me realize I'm cheating myself by refusing to see other people."

"And what are we? When you said you wanted more with me, did you mean you're looking for a girlfriend or a fling?"

"I don't like flings. How do you feel about a causal relationship? No labels, and we see where things go. I want to spend more time with you."

A swarm of butterflies exploded in Kate's stomach. She wanted the same. He was fun and spontaneous, and she enjoyed every minute they spent together. Each day together was an adventure.

Content, she stretched and then crossed her ankles. "I like being with you too."

The sky gradually turned darker. The sun was almost below the distant mountains, and the first stars appeared overhead. They twinkled, lighting back and forth like two friends talking.

It was so soon after ending her engagement with Matt. She was a little crazy for jumping into something with another man, but Ian provided a thrill she'd never experienced with Matt.

Her history with men was limited, and most had wounded her self-esteem, but this was different. There was no pressure to behave a certain way, and for once, she didn't worry about whether Ian settled for her. With him, she was only required to be herself, and he never made off-handed comments about her appearance or shortcomings.

Kate cuddled closer, happy to wait with him for the fireworks to begin.

Chapter Sixteen

When Kate arrived home, Mom's car was gone, and Maddie was nowhere in sight. Dad was sitting at the kitchen table with his head bowed and his hands wrapped around a glass. A bottle of bourbon sat in front of him, with the cap off and enough liquor left in the bottle for about two shots. His glass was half-full, and Kate was grateful. If both had been empty, there was no way he'd make it to his room.

Grabbing a beer from the refrigerator, Kate popped the tab and took a sip before taking a seat across from Dad, saying, "Hey."

He lifted his head. Dark circles lined his eyes as if he'd been awake for days. He should have been in bed. He had work in the morning and was going to be miserable without sleep.

When he smiled, he looked like someone shot his dog. "Hey, kiddo. What time did you get in?"

"Just now. What's wrong?"

He shrugged, dropping his gaze back to the glass in his hands. "It's nothing for you to worry about."

"Yeah, right," she huffed, pushing her beer aside. "What happened? Why aren't you asleep? Don't you have to work in the morning?"

He shook his head and ran his hands through his hair, sending curling, gray tufts into several directions. "Nancy filed for divorce. She gave me the papers after your brother took the girls home. Then she left to be with her boyfriend." Bitterness drenched his words as he clenched his cup.

Kate had never seen him so broken and defeated. "Oh, Dad, I'm sorry."

"It was a long time coming."

There was no denying it. She had grown up listening to her parents argue. Part of her was surprised they hadn't parted ways sooner. "Haven't you guys discussed divorce before?"

He shrugged. "She's threatened to leave for years. I guess she was waiting for the right man to come around. Before she left, she bragged about the things her boyfriend does for her and how happy he makes her. Good riddance."

Wow, that was a low blow. If Mom was unhappy, fine, but she didn't need to kick Dad while he was down. "I'm sorry. What's going to happen now?"

He drained his drink and emptied the rest of the bottle into the glass. Then he sighed, bringing the cup down with a bang. "I don't know. The house is in my name, but this is a shared property state. I'll have to hire a mediator and pray I don't go broke paying court fees."

Kate sighed. Dad didn't deserve this, and she wished she had the answers to make everything better. She couldn't tell him everything would be all right or that she was secretly relieved Mom wouldn't be around to terrorize everyone.

A tiny smile tugged at the corner of his mouth when their eyes met. "Maddie said you went out with a friend. Did you have a good time?"

"Yeah. I went skydiving."

Dad raised his eyebrows. "Seriously?"

"Yep."

He whistled. "Who did you go with?"

"Ah, a guy, I mean, well yeah. I'm sort of dating someone." She hadn't planned on announcing this yet, especially to her dad, but it was too late. She was a terrible liar, and she wasn't quick enough to make up a story about a friend.

The corners of Dad's mouth twitched. Swallowing as if holding back a laugh, he asked, "Do I need to have the safe sex talk with you?"

Heat flooded Kate's cheeks, and she covered her ears. "Oh my God, that's not necessary. I learned everything I needed to know in my Health and Life Development class in high school."

"Please tell me Nancy had this conversation with you girls. I might not have been around much, but I made sure David knew about the birds and the bees once he reached puberty."

Kate's entire face burned. This wasn't the talk she wanted to have with him or Mom, *ever*. He didn't need to hear that neither of them were around enough to have the important discussions with their children. Kate had to learn on her own before educating her little sister.

Drawing in a slow breath and releasing it, she said, "I promise, I'm a big girl. I can live without the traumatizing questions."

Dad chortled. "Eh, you've heard worse growing up." He paused, staring across the room in space before directing his gaze back at her. "I remember David coming home on his first day of school and asking me what a brothel was."

"What did you tell him?"

"I told him it was a special bar where men go to meet women. I didn't tell him it involved prostitution."

Laughter bubbled inside Kate's chest. "Why am I not surprised? David always did have a foul mouth and a way of learning inappropriate words. If they haven't already, the girls are going to ask something crazy, like 'Mommy, what's a testicle?' Tracy would be appalled if their kids asked them that."

Kate loved her sister-in-law, but she couldn't picture the quiet, soft-spoken woman uttering anything that wasn't a clean substitute. She was the exact opposite of David, who learned all the bad words by the time he was eight.

Dad smiled again, this time with genuine mirth. "You never gave me the name of the man you're dating. Is he important to you?"

Keeping her gaze on the beads of condensation sliding down the beer can, she picked at the tab. "He's nice."

He snorted. "So, who was he? How long have you been seeing him?"

"Oh, I'm not ready to talk about him yet. We're having fun and getting to know each other."

"Can't I make sure you're not setting yourself up to get hurt?"

"What's that supposed to mean?" she demanded.

Raising his hands as if in surrender, Dad shifted in his seat and lowered his voice. "You're a smart girl, but don't you think you're moving a bit fast? You and Matt ended your engagement a month ago."

She pinched her lips and exhaled through her nose before speaking. She didn't want to shout at him, not when Mom had trampled his heart. "I like him. We have fun together, and he doesn't judge me."

"That's great, but I'm worried about the repercussions of a rebound." Dad scrubbed his hands over his face before lowering them to the table with a thud. "Your mother was a rebound, okay? My college sweetheart had dumped me, and I was looking to have a little fun, when I met Nancy. Things were great for a while too. I mean, obviously, I married her, and the first few years of our marriage were good. It wasn't until she wanted to go back to work that things soured for us."

Holy crap, why was he telling her this? "Does Mom know?"

Dad grimaced. "Hell no. You don't tell someone they're a rebound."

Kate massaged her temples and groaned. "Wow, Dad. Did you love her at all or is this where you tell me you fell out of love or something? Because that's really crappy."

"I'm not saying I'm proud of myself," he said, sounding defensive. "I'm telling you this so you don't make the same mistake. What if you have a change of heart and realize it's too soon? Will he be okay with that? Better yet, what if you develop serious feelings he doesn't reciprocate? You need to be careful. I don't want to see you get hurt."

Hadn't she just been asking herself this a few hours ago? She didn't want to admit it, but Dad had a valid point. She and Ian both could get hurt, but she didn't want to dwell on the what-ifs. "We've agreed to see where things go. He knows about Matt, and I'm not sure if he's looking for anything serious."

Which suited her, she wasn't ready for a relationship so soon after her breakup. Casual was fine with her.

"Okay," Dad said, standing and taking his cup to the sink. He washed and dried it before setting it in the rack and turning around. "I won't tell you how to live but keep my words in mind. I wouldn't say these things if I didn't care. I love you."

"I love you too, Dad."

He squeezed her shoulder before heading out of the kitchen. "I need to shower and find a lawyer."

"Is there anything I can do for you?"

He shook his head. "No. As I said, this was a long time coming. I'm the one who's been prolonging the inevitable, and now I'm paying the price. No matter how ugly things get between your mom and me, I want you to promise you won't be too harsh. She's crazy, but she does love you."

Kate had mixed feelings about that last part, but she didn't argue. Mom had said some unforgivable things, and no amount of apologies could excuse her behavior. It could be a long time before Kate was ready to reconcile.

Alone in the kitchen, she drained the rest of her lukewarm beer. Dad's conversation replayed itself, nagging her with her earlier fear. She could imagine moving on to something more meaningful with Ian, and the thought thrilled her. He might be a rebound, but that didn't mean they were doomed like her parents. Only time would tell if their feelings waned or deepened.

Chapter Seventeen

The rest of the week passed without any drama. Mom had come over on Saturday to pack some of her things. Dad took his car keys and left without a word while Maddie hid in her room. Kate didn't seek her mother's attention, but she didn't avoid it either. She sat in the living room, applying for more jobs.

She had a date with Ian later, but that wasn't for another few hours. Until then, she hoped to make use of her time and search the daily postings.

An email pinged, alerting her to available jobs. She opened it and laughed. There was no way she'd consider being a phone sex operator. She moved it to her trash folder and started on another application.

Her mother strode downstairs, bringing a large suitcase with her. When she reached the foyer, she stopped to adjust her ponytail. When she finished, her gaze traveled to Kate.

"Hey," she said.

Kate closed her laptop. "Hi."

"I saw your interview on YouTube. It was good."

Coming from Mom, that was almost a declaration of excellence. She strove for perfection and dismissed anything that didn't meet those standards.

"Thanks." Not knowing what else to say, Kate rubbed her thighs and stared at the floor. Mom cleared her throat, prompting her to glance up again.

"Have you had any luck finding a job?" she asked.

"No."

"I can make some calls and see if anyone is hiring. You don't need to stay in teaching, do you?"

"I'd like something related to Geology, if possible," Kate said slowly.

She loved her job at the university, but she was amenable to trying other things. At this point, she'd take anything, provided it paid more than minimum wage and didn't involve removing her clothes.

"I'll text you when I get settled in with Rob. Keep your phone turned on."

Kate cringed. Rob must have been Mom's new beaux. "You're officially leaving Dad?"

She couldn't fault her mom for wanting to be happy. Her marriage was a mess, Dad didn't seem to love her, and Mom had gone looking somewhere else for it.

"I am." She smoothed the front of her blouse. "You and your siblings are grown, and I'm tired of being trapped with your father."

"I understand," Kate said, meaning it. "I hope this works out for you."

Mom's eyebrows lifted as if she were surprised. Then a warm smile graced her lips, making her appear younger as her sharp features softened. "Thank you. I appreciate your support."

It was ironic that they both wanted the same thing, yet Mom didn't give it to her kids. All Kate had ever wanted was her approval, a kind word to validate her achievements and hard work.

However, she was trying in her own way, and Kate decided not to mention her shortcomings. Even if she could still hear the nagging voice in the back of her mind, criticizing her every fault. Her mother would never change, and this side of her was better than the woman who hurled insults at her family.

After that brief conversation, they didn't exchange more than a handful of words before Mom left. Maddie soon appeared, leaning over the upstairs banister. "Is she gone?"

"Yeah, she left a few minutes ago." Kate stood and stretched, holding her arms above her head until her back popped. Then she picked up her laptop and made her way to the stairs.

Maddie watched her, resting her foot on the bottom rail. "Do you want to go out tonight? I was thinking we could go mini-golfing or window shopping on Mill Avenue."

"Can I get a rain check? I've got a date with Ian."

Maddie smirked. "Oh really? Last I checked, you insisted you two were just friends. What changed?"

"He took me skydiving."

"Woah! That's bold. What if you hated heights?"

"He wouldn't have made me go. Before going, he asked if I wanted to skip." She waved a dismissive hand. "He's definitely adventurous. I thought he was crazy when he told me what we were doing."

Kate reached the top step and moved to go around Maddie, who blocked her way to her bedroom. "Aren't you going to tell me how it went?"

"I'm going on another date, aren't I?"

"But I need details," she whined. "A girl wants to know these things."

Kate stifled a giggle and ducked under her sister's arm. "Then I suggest you find your own boyfriend. My lips are sealed."

Entering her room, she closed the door behind her and set her laptop down on the desk. Then she searched for a pair of clothes that didn't look like they'd been dragged through the mud. She and Ian weren't doing anything fancy. They were having dinner at his house and maybe a movie. July was the hottest month of the year, and it was difficult to go on dates outside when the air felt like an oven blasting.

She dressed in a blue tank top and denim shorts, fixing her hair into a side ponytail. On her way to the bathroom to apply makeup, Maddie approached with a sly grin.

Kate placed her hands on her hips. "What are you up to?"

"Me, up to something?" Maddie's hand fluttered to her chest, and she blinked innocently.

"You've been pestering me non-stop since I stayed the night at Ian's house last month."

Maddie's smile widened before she held out her hand. "Oh, I'll bug you again when you come home, but right now I wanted to give you these."

Heat spread from Kate's cheeks to her neck and ears as her sister shoved a box of condoms at her. "Oh my God! Ian and I haven't even talked about sex."

"And you won't be talking when you two are writhing in bed together. You'll thank me later when you're giving me all the juicy details."

That was doubtful. Kate had never been one to kiss and tell, much less gossip about sex. Loads of women discussed details with their friends. She simply wasn't one of them.

She gave the box back to her sister and moved toward the bathroom. Leaving the door ajar, she rummaged through the cabinet for her cosmetic bag.

Maddie squeezed past and took a seat on the edge of the tub. She opened her mouth to say something, but Kate cut her off. "I think I'll keep my love life to myself. But thanks anyway,"

Her sister raised her hands as if in surrender. "Fine, but take the condoms. Even if it doesn't happen tonight, it doesn't hurt to be prepared. Have you two discussed anything serious yet?"

"Like what?" she asked while massaging primer into her skin.

"Oh, if you plan on being casual or having something more. Whether your relationship is monogamous or non-exclusive. That sort of thing."

"We aren't having a fling, if that's what you mean," Kate said, glancing at Maddie from the corner of her eye. "Ian said he wants to get to know me better. Aside from that, we're still in the early stages of our relationship. Anything more serious will be off the table for a while."

"You don't have to be engaged or even exclusive to have sex." She splayed her hands defensively when Kate shot her a dirty look. "I'm not saying to be a ho about it. I'm emphasizing that sex happens, sometimes faster than we plan."

"What makes you think it's going to happen right away? Isn't that jumping the gun a bit?"

Maddie shrugged. "Maybe, but you were never this excited with anyone so soon, not even Matt. You were with him for two years, and you took everything slow. There's nothing wrong with rapid progression if he's the right man."

She wasn't wrong. Kate had hesitated to move in with Matt until she was certain he was committed. Even though, recent transgressions aside, there weren't any major red flags to stop her.

It had been Matt to propose when she'd been content to remain as they were. Any time they took the next step, it had been Matt to suggest it. Kate had gone along because it had been the logical thing to do and not because she'd been inclined.

She'd never wanted to move quickly, and wasn't sure why she'd hesitated. Perhaps it had been a gut feeling on a subconscious level, telling her the relationship wasn't right. That, and she wasn't confident enough to believe anyone else would show interest in her. Matt had been safe; someone to come home to each night and cuddle with as they watched TV. The passion was non-existent and stale, and more than once, she wondered what was wrong with her when he craved sex and she didn't.

However, with Ian, she found herself daydreaming about their future. She didn't imagine wedding bells anytime soon but pictured different locales they could visit or things she wanted to do with him. She wondered if he had similar fantasies.

Whether he was Mr. Right, that was something she would learn in time. If not, she'd add it to her list as another life experience and move on to someone else.

Placing her palms on the counter, Kate studied her reflection in the mirror, working her bottom lip through her teeth. Suddenly, the idea of being with anyone else seemed impossible. The moment she'd met him, they clicked.

Dad told her to take it slow, but her heart rejected that notion, swelling with sunshine and rainbows every time they were together. Perhaps Maddie was on to something after all.

Kate's lips curved into a slow smile as she turned to face her sister. "I think you're right. I guess I'm used to being cautious, and this is a bit new to me."

It was also exciting, and she was already impatient to finish getting ready. Reaching for her foundation and sponge, she directed her gaze to the mirror again, humming an upbeat tune as she worked.

~ * ~

As she parked in Ian's driveway, a warning for an impending dust storm blared on Kate's phone. Dust kicked up by the wind, blotting out the sun, replacing the clear day with an ugly shade of brown. In the distance, a giant wall of sand stretched from the ground to the sky, swallowing everything in sight. The system would be huge, and she thanked the heavens she wasn't stuck on the road.

The front door to Ian's house opened, and he waved for her to come inside. Kate exited the car and ran to the porch. The air was heavy with sand, tickling her nose and making her throat itch. She hung her purse on the rack to the side and undid her ponytail, running her fingers through her hair. "Thanks. I was afraid I wasn't going to make it in time."

"I'm glad you made it too," he said, meeting her lips in a kiss. His hands slid down her arms to her waist, and he brought her closer.

She caught the scent of his cologne and inhaled. It was woodsy and masculine, a smell that stirred her more sensitive areas.

He touched her like a man who knew how to show affection to a woman. He was self-assured in the way he held her. One hand rested firmly on her waist while the other caressed her cheek with his knuckles. It left Kate wanting more, to explore his body on a very intimate level.

Damn Maddie for putting that idea into her head. Kate was going to be thinking about it all night.

They kissed again, and she had to resist the compulsion to cup his ass. She didn't know how he'd respond, and she'd rather not make things awkward if he wasn't ready.

The smell of food distracted her from her dangerous thoughts. "Something smells good."

"I'm making arroz con pollo, my mother's recipe."

Wow. For him to make such a personal dish must be a good sign.

Her tummy did a little flip, and her heart skipped half a beat. "That's your favorite, right?"

He nodded. "You remembered. I wanted to share a little piece of home with you."

Her heart thumped faster. "That's really sweet. I don't know why I deserve such an honor."

For a third time, he kissed her, this time sweeping her hair away from her neck and moving his mouth along the curve until he ended with her shoulder. He chuckled softly. "I don't make a habit of allowing people to get close like this, but it's easy with you. You're fun and willing to try new things. I love your intelligence and passion. And I hate to sound cliché, but you're freaking gorgeous."

Her? What planet did she suddenly find herself on where she was paid such a generous compliment?

"I bet you say that to all the girls," she breathed, arching her back when his fingertips grazed the base of her spine beneath her shirt.

"Nope. I only have eyes for you. Forgive me for saying this, but your ex was a douche for cheating and blackmailing you."

"Yes, he was, but I'm not here to discuss him." She rose on her tiptoes and met his mouth again. "I'm more interested in your company."

"Good, because we're going to be inside for a while," he said, glancing at the door, where the wind was howling outside.

"I'm fine with that. What do you want to do tonight?"

"While we wait for the food to finish simmering, would you like to hear a song I've been working on?"

"Sure."

He led her into the living room, where she sat on the couch. Ian disappeared for a moment before returning with his guitar. Bringing a chair into the middle of the room, he took a seat and tuned the strings, strumming one at a time, occasionally twisting the knobs and plucking the wires. Then he played all six notes again before strumming a full chord.

"Okay, this is kind of a work in progress, so bear with me if it's not perfect."

"I'm sure it'll be great." Kate never learned to play, and she admired anyone who studied music as a hobby or professionally.

Her remark was met with a grin, and he dipped his gaze to his guitar, picking at the notes with ease while he sang. The song was cheerful and upbeat, about a serendipitous relationship and the joys of being together. The words touched Kate's heart. It was as if the song was written for her, regardless if that were true.

She tapped her foot in time with the melody, swaying to the

catchy lyrics. When he finished, he watched her with guarded eyes and a shy smile.

"Well?" he asked.

"I love it. When did you write it?"

His cheeks turned pink, and he looked away, inserting a finger into the collar of his shirt and fanning himself with the fabric. "Oh, um, after our last date. Is that weird?"

Kate jumped to her feet and crossed the space between them. Cupping his face, she rewarded him with a sound kiss. "No. It's the nicest thing anyone's ever done for me."

Ian unslung his guitar and propped it against the couch. Then he brought her onto his lap, so she was straddling him. His arms encircled her as she gripped his neck. Their lips met again, and his soft mouth caressed hers. Beard stubble scratched her chin as he deepened the kiss, and his callused fingertips traveled beneath her shirt, exploring her torso until they stopped below her bare breasts. He sucked in a sharp breath, and Kate felt him harden beneath her.

"Is this okay?" he rasped.

Heart pounding, she leaned back and slowly lifted her shirt. Bit by bit, it rose, and his bulge grew larger. The corners of her lips twitched, and her hands trembled as she removed her top, baring her breasts and leaving herself utterly exposed. She sat in his lap, shivering from nerves and the fan twirling overhead.

In a shaking voice, she turned his question around. "You tell me. Is this too bold?"

He gaped, lowering his gaze to her chest. He rubbed small circles over her nipples, scraping his rough thumbpads on her sensitive flesh. "Holy mother of…" He swallowed before speaking again. "Your breasts are exquisite."

A giggle burst from her throat. "Okay, now I know you're lying. My boobs are tiny."

His eyes darkened to a deep shade of gray. "I would never disrespect a woman by paying her a false compliment. When I say you're beautiful, I *mean* it."

Panic surged through her veins at the admonition, and she instinctively pulled away, afraid she'd made him angry. He caught her, stopping her from sliding off his lap and pressing her against him. With one hand firmly against her back, he cupped her neck with the other. His mouth clashed with hers, hot with need, as he deepened the kiss and swept his tongue inside.

When he stopped, he fisted her hair and tugged, bringing her head back. Breathing deeply, he spoke again, this time in a gentle tone.

"If I didn't find you attractive, I wouldn't be tempted to take you to my bed. I adore your freckles, that quirk you do with your lips when you smile, and your soft skin."

He kissed the inside of her palm, her wrist, and the rest of her arm until he landed on her collarbone. Then he worked his way down to her breast and sucked on it, lightly grazing his teeth against her skin. When he stopped, he cupped her face with both hands. "Your eyes are so expressive. I can read every emotion behind them, and I love that you have nothing to hide. And when you smile, it actually reaches your eyes, and they sparkle."

"Really?" The declaration took her breath away, and she blinked several times.

The words were genuine and romantic, chipping away at her self-doubt. No one ever praised her appearance unless she dressed up, and even then, people made fun of her flat chest, her height, and the freckles dotting her arms. Yet, these were things he called out, as if he were reading Kate's mind and reaffirming that there was nothing wrong with her.

When Ian looked at her, it was with desire. He made her *feel* beautiful. "The only reason I haven't done it sooner is because I want you to be ready. Everything we do is at your pace. If you say no, then we'll stop."

"And if I do this?" She unclasped his belt buckle, popping the button on his pants and tugging the zipper down.

His chest heaved, and he rose, lifting her with him. His jeans slid to the floor, pooling at his feet, and he kicked them away. Kate locked her legs around his waist, and Ian carried her to his room, laying her on the bed.

He sank down beside her, bringing her ankle to his mouth, kissing upward inch by tantalizing inch until he stopped at her inner thigh. He repeated the process with the other leg and moved to her stomach, removing her shorts and his boxers without missing a beat.

Kate trembled with each kiss, each touch until she was wet with anticipation. By the time he finished, only her lace panties remained. Ian pinned her hands above her head when she tried to take them off.

"Not yet," he rasped, moving to her wet center.

He sucked on the flimsy fabric. She pulsed and ached for him, squirming when his tongue connected with her sensitive area beneath the lace.

Arching her back, she clawed at his shoulders, his back, any part of him she could reach. "Please," she gasped, unable to withstand the erotic torture inflicted by his tongue.

He hooked his thumbs in the sides of her underwear and took them off, leaving her completely vulnerable and exposed. Their eyes clashed for a split second, and lust, desire, and affection passed between them.

"Are you sure you're ready for this?"

Yes, yes, a thousand times, yes. She'd never wanted anyone as much as she wanted him.

Pulsing in anticipation, she released a small whimper. "I'm a hundred percent sure."

He rolled over and opened the drawer on his nightstand, where he produced a box of condoms and ripped the top off the packaging. He then tore the wrapper with his teeth and tossed it aside, pulling the rubber over his length. When his tip met her center, he slowly brought himself down until he filled her completely, then he thrust, hitting her special spot.

"More," she panted, "Faster."

He increased the pace, and she moved with him, rocking her hips against his as he drove deeper. Words, thoughts, and reason abandoned her when her body exploded with heat and pleasure, leaving her breathless as the universe danced across her eyes. Ian's climax followed hers.

His breath, his skin against hers, was intoxicating, and when she could finally see him again, feral yearning burned behind his gaze.

"That was incredible." He sighed, dropping beside her. Resting on one elbow, he brushed her hair aside and stroked her face. "I could see myself falling for you."

She bit her lip. She felt the same. Whatever reasons his ex-wife had for leaving him were stupid. Ian was the most loving, affectionate, and tender-hearted man Kate had ever met, and any woman would be a fool for not holding onto him.

She wouldn't let him go if she could help it. Everything she wanted was in front of her, and she'd never been this happy in her life.

Entwining their fingers together, she smiled wide. "Me too."

Chapter Eighteen

Whatever reservations Kate had about Ian melted away after their night together. By the end of July, her things started finding themselves at his place, and she spent less time at hers. Every day was fun and unpredictable. An afternoon lunch progressed to a night on the town. Or a quiet evening in would transform into raucous sex.

Within weeks, Kate already had a key to his place. They weren't necessarily living together, but close enough.

While Ian was at work or otherwise engaged in his volunteer activities, she continued her job search in vain until the second week of August approached, leaving her in a mental and emotional rut. School had started for most of the state, and she was still without a job.

Mom pulled strings to ensure Kate received a decent severance package. Despite a wrongful termination lawsuit having the potential to fail, the university settled out of court, giving her six months of pay.

Mom hadn't texted or called since moving in with her boyfriend, but the gesture was a start. Kate didn't want false platitudes. Her mother would berate her again the moment she was angry.

This act was her way of showing love. It didn't atone for the pain she'd caused, but Kate was happy to accept her mother tried in her own way.

With the media frenzy forgotten and her interview broadcasted to every corner of the internet, Kate had initially hoped it would help with her job hunt. However, after several hundred applications, she'd only received a couple of polite form rejection letters.

Months of heartache, drama, and turmoil passed, leaving her in a rut. She'd done everything right to dig herself out, yet no one seemed interested in hiring her.

Exhaustion weighed her down, and she was more than ready to see the light at the end of the tunnel. With each day that passed, she repeated the mantra that things would improve.

She reminded herself that she had a boyfriend who respected her and siblings who'd stood by her through it all. However, after checking this morning and seeing her last submission showed the posting had been closed, she was worn down and defeated. No amount of positive thinking could raise her spirits.

Tired of Kate's moping, Maddie dragged her outside to swim. She'd resisted at first but finally gave in, just so her sister would stop hounding her.

Kate had taken an inflatable lounger and lied belly-first on it, skimming her fingers through the water. Maddie lounged nearby, soaking in the afternoon's rays with her perfectly tanned legs, shielding her face with a wide-brimmed hat and sunglasses large enough to befit a movie star. The only things visible beneath were her lips and nose, both pink from the sun.

After gliding in her eighth lazy circle, Maddie splashed Kate from her side of the pool. "Okay, sis, I'm getting depressed watching you sulk. What's wrong?"

"Nothing," she grumbled, fixing her gaze on the rippling water.

"Liar. I thought you were happy. What happened to your hot boyfriend?"

Kate smirked. Ian was a fine specimen of masculinity. He was one of the few things she was happy to celebrate in her life. "He's working."

"Is he withholding sex?" Maddie asked. "Because I know some ways that'll definitely get his attention."

Kate laughed at the randomness of the question. Rolling over, she rose into a sitting position and straddled the float so she could look at her sister. "We're fine in that department."

Maddie perched her sunglasses onto the edge of her nose and peeked above the rim with raised brows. "Oh? Are you two serious yet?"

Yeah, right. They hadn't established anything other than that they were exclusive. There was no serious discussion of whether there was a future beyond, 'let's see where this goes.'

Kate wasn't in a rush, nor did she want to pressure him, but she hoped they'd eventually have the conversation. She liked him a lot, but she didn't want to seem clingy.

They'd only been together for a month, and it was crazy, but she wanted more. She wasn't sure what 'more' entailed, just that when she was with Ian, her heart wanted to sing with joy. Everything about him felt *right*.

"Nope."

"Are you going to bring him here soon?" Maddie pried, sitting up and folding her arms across her chest.

"I will if you and David promise not to swarm on him like a pack of vultures."

Kate scratched her nose to hide her grin as Maddie flung water in her direction, saying, "We're not that bad. Besides, I'm dying to meet him."

"I'm sure you are, and I might trust you, but we both know what David is like. He'll start acting like the protective big brother and threaten Ian to not break my heart."

"To be fair, that's every brother's right. Plus, you can count on Dad being worse."

"All the more reason not to invite him. If we make it through the summer, I'll ask him to meet the family. Until then, I want to take it easy."

She paddled to the edge of the pool and took a sip from her diet soda before setting it down again. Then she plopped her sunglasses on her face and leaned back.

"You haven't mentioned your friend you used to work with in a while. What's going on with him?" Maddie asked.

"He ended our friendship," she snapped.

It had been two months without a word from Carlos. Kate preferred to shove him to the darkest recess of her mind, lock him away behind a vault, and throw away the key. If he didn't want to speak to her, that was fine, but she wouldn't waste one more minute pining over someone who'd abandoned her.

A tense silence hung between them, and Kate was about to apologize for being snippy when her phone rang. Curious, she slid off the float, exiting the in-ground pool. She wiped her hands on a nearby towel before answering halfway through the chorus of *Just What I Needed*. "Hello?"

"Hi, may I speak with Doctor Katherine Miller please?"

"Speaking."

Was it too farfetched to hope this was the call she'd been waiting for since the beginning of June? She squeezed her eyes shut and held her breath, waiting for the woman on the other end to respond.

"I'm Doctor LaShonda Gipson with Northern Arizona University's Geology department, and I was wondering if you'd be interested in interviewing for a teaching position for the Spring semester."

Kate's knees buckled, and she tumbled into a nearby chair, scraping her toes against the hot pavement. Stunned, she grinned as she processed Dr. Gipson's words. Teaching. University. Job interview.

She'd all but abandoned her search, and now an opportunity was falling in her lap with the force of a meteor.

"Doctor Miller, are you there?"

Kate shook her head and forced her vocal cords to work. If she weren't on the phone, she'd have squealed. Dancing in her seat, she said, "Yes, sorry. Thank you for calling me back. Of course, I'm interested."

"Can you come to the university next Monday for an interview at two o'clock?"

Oh god, this was really happening. "Absolutely." Her voice sounded far away. It was like she wasn't in her own body.

"Wonderful. I'd like you to bring four copies of your resume for the committee and a slideshow for the teaching demonstration. You'll be meeting with President Varton, as well as the dean, myself, and one other. In addition to the interview, we'd like to see how well you perform in front of a panel."

It was the standard hiring process. Kate continued to dance in her seat, saying, "Yes, I can do that. Thank you again."

"Okay, we'll see you Monday. Enjoy the rest of your week."

"You too."

Hanging up, she turned when Maddie asked, "Who was it?"

Kate cannon-balled into the pool with a squeal, splashing her sister from head to toe. Then she dragged Maddie into the water and wrapping her in a crushing hug.

"It was the Geology department at NAU," Kate said. "She called me for an interview!"

Maddie jumped, taking Kate's hands and joining in the shriek-fest. "Oh my god, that's great! You're going to do it, right?"

Duh. It was the only place to call her back, and she needed a job. She didn't want to live with her dad forever.

The only problem was that the location sucked. She'd have to move halfway across the state.

She stopped her happy dance and frowned. "Yeah, totally, but it's in Flagstaff."

If they hired her, she'd be two and a half hours away. She and Ian never discussed what they wanted from their relationship. The distance would probably kill any chance they had at a meaningful connection. However, if she didn't take this position, and their affair ended, where would she be?

Her heart went from soaring to deflating in less than three seconds. How had she become emotionally attached in such a short span of time? Dad warned her to be careful, and she'd brushed him off, only to fall into the trap.

She needed to be by herself and reflect on the news. This opportunity was a good thing, and she wanted to celebrate, but she couldn't do that with anxiety twisting in her stomach.

"You look upset," Maddie said, touching Kate's shoulder.

She pasted on a cheerful smile and deflected the comment, saying, "I'm fine. It's a lot to take in, that's all."

It wasn't a lie, but it wasn't the entire truth either.

Maddie frowned but didn't pursue the topic. Instead, she said, "Okay. Do you need anything? A few shots of rum?"

An entire bottle would be amazing, but Kate had too much to do. "Later. I have an interview to prep for."

She climbed out of the pool again and hastily wrapped her towel around her waist. Taking Maddie's phone and unlocking the screen, she dialed fast, not giving herself time to talk herself out of what she was about to do.

The caller answered. "Doctor Hernandez."

"Carlos, don't hang up," she said in a rush, prepared to call as many times as needed.

"Kate, I don't think it's a good id—"

"If you wanna ghost me again after this, fine, but I have a job interview with NAU, and I could use your help with the presentation."

The line was quiet for a moment, and Kate was afraid he'd ended the call. She checked, and he was still there.

After a moment of silence, he asked, "Really?"

"Yes." Her breath hitched. She was angry with him for ditching her, but she missed him. Despite his short answer, her chest inflated with delight at hearing him.

"I can email my teaching materials and some old slideshows this afternoon. Do you need a character reference too?"

Moisture filled her eyes at his offer. His voice was guarded, and there was no offer to celebrate, yet he was willing to help when it mattered.

"Yes, please," she whispered, fighting the urge to cry.

"Of course. Hey, I have a student in my office, so I need to go, but good luck with everything. You deserve this opportunity. Take care."

He ended the call without saying goodbye, and Kate let the tears fall. Yes, she was grateful for his assistance, but she wanted his friendship more.

She prayed he'd feel the same again someday. He was a good guy, and guilt weighed on her. She couldn't have answered him any other way, no matter how much she wanted to spare his feelings. She'd hurt him, and maybe she needed to accept that things between them were over.

Wiping her cheeks, she texted Ian next. *'Hey, I have some big news to share. Can I come by after you leave work?'*

Ian's text was almost immediate. *'Everything okay?'*

No. How was she supposed to tell him that she was crying because of another man and that she might be moving almost three hours away? Her stomach churned at the thought. With shaking fingers, she texted, *'I'd rather talk about it in person.'*

'Sure. I'll see you then.'

Chapter Nineteen

Kate was in the lobby of Northern Arizona University, waiting for the committee to greet her. She tried to keep her nervousness in check. At least she had her sister to keep her company.

The day before the interview, she and Maddie drove to Flagstaff, where they'd rented a cabin for three days.

The rental was in a secluded, wooded area, giving Kate a much-needed break from city noise. Being there also gave her a chance to ponder her feelings for Ian. When she told him, it hadn't gone well. She sighed, recalling the conversation.

When she first told him the news, he'd been excited. He'd cheered and kissed her, offering his congratulations. However, when she told him it was for a job in Flagstaff, he'd become quiet, drawing the shutters behind his eyes.

"Please say something," she begged, chewing on her bottom lip. Not knowing what he was thinking made her fear the worst.

Ian leaned forward from his spot on the couch and rested his hands on his knees, releasing a heavy sigh. "This is a wonderful opportunity for you."

His flat tone hurt, and Kate felt like she'd been slapped. Was that all he had to say? Was it possible he didn't care as much for her as she did for him?

"But what about us?" she asked.

He shrugged. "We'll see what happens when the time comes. You should go for the job opportunity. You love teaching."

Her lower lip trembled, and she drew in a shuddering breath, struggling to keep her voice steady. "It's not so far that we can't drive out on weekends or do video calls. I'm sure we could find a way to make this work."

Ian cupped her face and kissed her on the forehead. "Go to the interview. When you get home, we'll go from there."

It wasn't a dismissal or a breakup, but she couldn't help the ache in her heart, telling her to prepare for the worst. The inflection in his tone was resigned, as if he'd already decided a long-distance relationship wouldn't work. If she stayed, it could, but it would be foolish to turn down a good career prospect for a man.

Since that discussion, they'd barely spoken and had said nothing about their relationship.

Kate's time was spent on putting together a slideshow and rehearsing for her demonstration. Ian worked longer hours, sometimes texting to say he was too tired to see her. By the time she left for her interview, the emotional distance separating them had expanded to the size of an ocean.

Maddie lightly tapped Kate's bouncing leg, asking, "Why are you nervous? You've been teaching for five years. This should be a cinch."

Kate expelled a loud breath and tucked her hair behind her ear. "Sorry. I keep worrying I'll find a way to mess this up."

Maddie scooted her chair closer and rested her head on Kate's shoulder. "You'll be great."

"I'll take your word for it."

ASU had been Kate's first job, and despite standing in front of hundreds of students each semester, anxiety twisted her stomach into knots. She could botch the interview in a whole multitude of ways, from using profanities to something as simple as not connecting with the panel of interviewers.

She could recite her presentation in her sleep. It was her nerves that were the problem.

When she rehearsed the practice questions with her sister the night before, every reasonable answer left Kate's mind. She sat on the bed, stammering and swearing her way through the responses. It had been a disaster, ending with Maddie tossing the paper into the air and Kate taking a walk. After that, they didn't try again.

As she waited to be called, she fidgeted with the hem of her blazer, twisting a loose string around her finger. When the door opened across from her, an older man in a sharp, gray suit entered the room.

Directing his sea-green gaze on them, he asked, "Doctor Miller?"

After wiping her palms on her jacket, Kate rose to her feet and took his extended hand.

"I'm President Varton, and I will be conducting your interview. Are you ready?"

"Yes."

She followed him into the conference room, casting a final glance over her shoulder. Maddie gave her an encouraging smile before mouthing the words 'good luck.'

Cold air blasted overhead, and goosebumps erupted along Kate's bare legs. Several pairs of eyes met hers, and she offered them a polite smile as she assessed the group. Including President Varton, the delegation consisted of four people. Only one of them was a woman, and she was also the sole person to offer a genuine smile.

"Hello, Doctor Miller. My name is Doctor LaShonda Gipson. How are you?"

Kate beamed back as she took her seat, placing her resumes in front of her. "I'm good. Thank you for interviewing me."

Taking the documents, Doctor Gipson handed them to the men seated around her, introducing them with a nod. "This is Dean Nelson and Doctor Rivera."

The men shook Kate's hand, but none of their gazes held any warmth. Varton sat beside Nelson, who whispered in the president's ear while casting a disdainful scowl her way.

The odds didn't look good. Kate tried not to shift in her chair. The last thing she needed was to show weakness.

Varton cleared his throat and folded his hands in front of him. Despite his rigid posture and ancient creases lining his saggy face, his lips were turned up, and his eyes sparkled with professional curiosity.

"Welcome," he said. "Why don't you tell us about your past employment and education?"

Rubbing her thighs beneath the table, Kate dove straight in. "I'm a Phoenix native, born and raised, I'm a Summa Cum Laude graduate from ASU with a four-point-two GPA, and I taught Geology there for three years. When I'm not teaching, I study structural geology for research in the field. I've published eight articles on the subject and extended to riverbed study and oceanography two years ago."

The dean mumbled something along the lines of her writing being sufficient. Gipson smiled, radiating nothing but positivity and encouragement.

Varton continued, asking, "What are your biggest publishing achievements?"

"*National Geographic* and the *Smithsonian*. I also co-wrote last year's article on Yellowstone for *Science Today*."

The room fell into silence as everyone seemed to be taking in her accomplishments. Nelson, who'd minimalized her literary successes, tapped a few buttons on his phone before whistling and putting it away. She assumed he googled the articles.

Her first few research pieces had been small, but her and Carlos's paper on the Yellowstone Caldera was a big deal.

Gipson spoke next, starting where Varton left off. "You have quite an impressive resume. Why did you become a teacher?"

"Because I love seeing my students achieve success," she answered easily. "Whether they pursue Geology or move on to a different degree, they leave my class with the important skillset I've taught them."

"What skill set is that?" Nelson asked, eying her with derision.

"To work hard in everything they do," she said in a firm voice, daring him to challenge her. "To learn that the important things in life, such as respect and success, are earned through merit rather than handed to them."

Her response was followed by the staccato noise of the committee members typing on their laptops. Kate bounced her foot beneath the desk, hoping she hadn't botched her answer. Regardless, she felt confident as she straightened her shoulders and lifted her chin.

Gipson raised her head and met her gaze. "How do you make Geology fun for your students?"

"I offer occasional extra credit on weekends by taking class trips to places where we can identify what we've studied. I also ask them to take pictures of rocks they find and to tell me what they've learned. Sometimes I'll bring in my collection and let them study them. The students love a hands-on approach."

"How do you utilize higher-ended thinking in the classroom?" Nelson asked.

"I ask open-ended questions, especially on tests. It's not enough to have the answer. It's how you get to it that matters."

The dean eyed her skeptically. "That sounds a lot like common core teaching."

Kate resisted the urge to scoff. "With all due respect, I'm not asking my students to tell me why one plus one equals five when everyone knows it's two. I'm encouraging my students to express themselves freely and tell me how they arrived at their conclusion, even if it's incorrect. I can then ask more questions to redirect their thoughts to find the correct answer, but I won't hand it to them."

Gipson placed her fingertips on her mouth, a grin peeking behind her hand. Clearing her throat she asked, "What do you consider to be your most important value in the workplace?"

"Honesty and integrity," Kate answered, aware she'd just listed two. "Honesty because there's no trust without it and integrity because you should always strive to do the right thing."

Everyone nodded, adding more notes to their laptops.

"And finally," Gipson said, "why should we hire you?"

Kate swallowed, hoping her answer wouldn't cost her the job, but needing to be honest with what she learned since leaving Matt. "As I'm sure you're all aware, I was dismissed from ASU because of my wedding video that went viral. It wasn't my best moment, but what makes me valuable to NAU is owning my honest reaction and refusing to hide from it. I can stand in front of these students and lead by example. When I make a mistake, I admit it and move on, determined to do better next time. One bad choice doesn't define me."

A broad smile filled President Varton's face. He then lifted his hand in a sweeping motion. "This concludes our questions. Are you ready to give us your teaching demonstration?"

"Absolutely."

This part of the interview was a cakewalk compared to the Q and A. In the fifteen minutes allotted to her, she breezed through it, reciting her points from memory as she took questions from the hiring panel.

When she finished, the committee took turns shaking her hand. The president informed her she'd hear back soon. It didn't inspire confidence, but at least Kate had made it through the interview.

She followed Gipson into the lobby where her sister waited, attached to her phone. Maddie lifted her head, and a wide grin crossed her features. "Doctor Gipson," she called.

The professor's eyes twinkled, and the women gravitated to each other like a pair of magnets. The doctor wrapped Maddie in a tight hug. "If it isn't my little M&M!"

Of course, Maddie would know her. NAU was her alma mater. As the committee filed out of the room, President Varton's eyes rested on Maddie, and he laughed. "Madeline Miller. I should have known you two were related."

Kate wasn't sure if she should be nervous. Was Maddie infamous during her tenure as a student? She was a free spirit who landed in all sorts of trouble but had the charisma and skill to smooth things over.

Maddie flashed him a brilliant smile, like a child caught with a half-eaten cake. "Did you think you could get rid of me?"

"I hope your art career is keeping you far away from the sciences," Gipson said with a laugh.

Kate cast a questioning glance at Maddie, who giggled. "I failed Geology and Chemistry. I spent a lot of time in Doctor Gipson's office. Science was the only thing holding me back from my degree."

Why on earth would she consider Chemistry? Geology made

sense because it was the class people took for an easy A. However, Maddie with dangerous chemicals was more frightening than Kate in the kitchen.

Varton patted her on the shoulder before bidding them farewell. Everyone trailed behind him except for Doctor Gipson, who turned to Kate and squeezed her arm. "I'm glad you interviewed with us. When do you return to Phoenix?"

"We're going home on Wednesday."

"Hopefully, we'll be in touch with you by then. I shouldn't tell you this, but I had the president consider you because I saw your interview with Ava Montenegro. Keep an ear out for my phone call."

Chapter Twenty

The next day, Kate walked onto the deck overlooking endless rows of trees. Instead of being deafening, the silence was peaceful, with sporadic bird chirps and the wind rustling through the flora.

As much as Kate loved Phoenix, she could imagine living in Flagstaff. The temperature was significantly cooler, dipping into single digits during the winter. The city offered everything Phoenix did, but in a picturesque setting, surrounded by green trees instead of brown rock.

She sat on a nearby Adirondack chair and opened the camera on her phone, snapping a picture of a mountain in the distance. She was about to upload it to Instagram when Maddie strolled onto the deck in a pair of bright Hello Kitty fleece pants with a shock of tangled hair.

"Do you thrash around in your sleep?" Kate teased.

Maddie dropped into the vacant seat beside Kate and yawned loudly. "Screw you. There's no one here to care."

She chuckled, leaning back in her chair. The view was gorgeous, and the temperature agreeable. She could get used to this, if not for what she'd be leaving behind.

Maddie snapped her fingers. "Hey, are you listening to me?"

Kate blinked and glanced at her sister. "Hm? I'm sorry, what where you saying?"

Pursing her lips, Maddie shook her head. "I was asking you about the interview. I assumed it had gone well, since Doctor Gipson spoke with you afterward."

"Oh, it went fine," Kate said, lifting her shoulder in a shrug.

It had been easier than she expected, once her nerves had calmed. She did wonder if she'd gone a tad overboard in challenging the dean, but she couldn't recall saying anything that would ruin her chances.

"What's bothering you then?"

Kate sighed. "I guess I'm not prepared to leave Phoenix if I get this job. I'm not sure if Ian will commit to a long-distance relationship."

She didn't mention the part where he'd been distancing himself. They hadn't talked once since this trip, and every time she texted, he replied with short responses. Although he hadn't said he wanted to stop seeing her, she could feel it in her gut, a nagging instinct that told her they wouldn't be together much longer.

"But aren't you two like official?" Maddie prodded. "Have you asked him?"

Why couldn't her sister drop it? Kate straightened in her chair and crossed her legs. "No. He told me to wait and see where it goes. He didn't seem very keen on discussing us, and I haven't had a chance to mention it again. With our current status, there's no telling if he'd want a long-distance relationship."

"Do you think he's worried you'll drift apart?"

"I have no idea what's going through his mind," she snapped. When Maddie's eyes widened, Kate blew out a breath and softened her voice. "I'm sorry. I really don't want to talk about it."

Her sister began to say something when Kate's cell rang, providing a welcome interruption. Snatching the phone, she unlocked the screen and answered.

Doctor Gipson's cheerful voice came across the line. "Hi, Doctor Miller. This is Doctor Gipson at NAU. How are you?"

Kate hadn't expected to hear from the university so soon. She'd anticipated waiting at least a week. Weren't there other candidates the committee needed to interview?

She cleared her throat. "I'm good, thank you. How are you?"

"I'm great. I'm calling to ask if you're still interested in teaching next semester."

Her heart leaping in her chest, Kate jumped to her feet and gasped. "You mean I got it?"

"President Varton was very impressed with your demonstration. After watching you teach, it didn't take long to decide you were a great fit for our department."

A breathless laugh escaped Kate's throat. After an entire summer of dismal luck with finding a job, she'd almost given up, then NAU called. "I don't know what to say. Thank you."

"I'd like to offer you the position, if you're still interested," Gipson replied.

"Absolutely." Kate nodded emphatically, bouncing on her feet. Maddie was right next to her, watching her with an amused expression.

"Great!" Gipson said in a cheerful voice. "I'll email your welcome packet, and we'll go from there. Welcome to NAU."

When the call ended, Kate ran her fingers through her hair. Then she paced the wooden deck, processing the information.

She officially had a job teaching at a good school, but it meant leaving Phoenix. More importantly, she was leaving Ian. He shouldn't matter, not when they'd only known each other since June. Two months was not enough time to fall in love, let alone ask him to commit to a long-distance relationship.

When she and Maddie arrived home, Dad took them to Kate's favorite steak house to celebrate. She hadn't argued when Maddie insisted Kate wear a nice dress or when her sister did her hair and makeup.

Out of habit, Kate ordered her favorite cut. Her food sat mostly untouched as she pushed it around on her plate, her mind buzzing about Ian.

She'd succeeded in finding a job. It was what she wanted, as well as a chance to redeem herself in the eyes of the public. Her victory was achieved, but it would be nicer to share it with Ian. Yet, she couldn't reasonably ask him to drop everything to go with her. Nor could she expect him to maintain a relationship if he was unwilling.

Maddie cleared her throat before sipping her water, asking with her eyes if Kate was okay.

She chanced a glance at Dad, who was cutting into his steak. Then, she looked back to her sister and mouthed, 'not now.'

Maddie nodded and mimed eating, tilting her head toward their dad. Not wanting to upset him, Kate forced herself to chew and swallow her food.

In the parking lot, Maddie took Kate's hand and led her to the car. "Kate, are you okay?"

She shook her head, working her jaw. "No. I'm worried Ian is going to tell me we're through."

Maddie wrapped her arms around Kate, rubbing her back. "Because of the distance? It would be difficult, but it's not impossible."

Kate held her sister close and swayed in place with her. "That's on him to decide."

"The only way to know is to talk to him."

"I don't want to lose him." She shrugged in defeat. "Still, if he doesn't want to stick around, then it's best to let him go, right?"

Maddie stroked Kate's hair. "Everyone thinks there aren't deep emotions when the relationship is new, but sometimes, two people just connect."

There was an air of experience in her somber tone, and Kate wondered who broke her heart. Then she considered different ways to make him suffer. Only a prick would hurt someone so precious.

She kissed Maddie's forehead and sighed. "I guess I'll find out soon. No matter what happens, I will be okay."

The worst part of Kate's life was over. She'd weathered the video and found a job. Now she needed to build walls around her heart and protect it.

~ * ~

Ian stepped onto the porch to his house and brought Kate in for a slow, sensual kiss before nuzzling her neck. It was the first time all week he'd shown her any affection.

He'd been so emotionally distant, and it made her question whether his feelings were genuine or if he'd been caught in the moment of their whirlwind relationship.

He whispered, "I've missed you."

Her fears were both assuaged and confirmed. Kate did believe he cared but couldn't determine whether it was enough for him to commit to a long-distance relationship.

For now, she let her worries fall away. Snaking her arms around his neck, she molded herself against him, desperate to convey everything she felt for him. She wanted to memorize everything about him before they parted ways.

His mouth moved against hers with fiery intensity as he trailed his hands down her arms and then slipped them beneath her shirt to massage her breasts. He pulled her shirt off and unhooked her bra before dropping them to the floor. Then he kissed her neck, collarbone, and shoulders.

Her body responded, sending every rational thought from her mind. Her nipples hardened, and wet heat gathered between her thighs. She wanted him, and soon her shorts and panties followed the rest of her clothes.

Ian's shirt and pants went next. Naked, he pressed her against the wall in the foyer. Dropping to his knees, he closed his mouth over her center, inserting two fingers.

She clenched around him and tossed her head back, grabbing him by the hair. "Ian—"

He stopped sucking, sat on his heels, and met her gaze with wild eyes. "I know you want to talk first, but I need you."

This was her chance to say no and tell him they needed to discuss their relationship, but she couldn't. She craved this as much as he did, and if there was a possibility they were done, she wanted one more night with him.

He returned his mouth to her. Pressure built in her spine when he flicked her clit and touched her g-spot. Gasping, she arched her back.

When her orgasm struck, pleasure crashed upon her in waves, and his name left her lips.

Her body shuddered when he got to his feet, and he nuzzled her neck. "My room," he demanded in a husky voice.

Trembling from her climax, she stumbled after him and fell onto the bed. Ian put on a condom and climbed above her, bracing his arms on each side of her. He closed his eyes, thrusting in a deep, steady rhythm.

Kate gripped his shoulders and rocked her hips, matching his pace. This time when she came, he orgasmed with her.

Arms shaking and breathing heavily, he pulled out. Then he fell to his back and brought her into an embrace, planting a kiss on top of her head.

"Thank you," he whispered.

She cuddled close and tangled her leg with his. The sex had been mind-blowing, love on its most primal level. Studying the pale moonlight through the blinds, she trailed her fingers through his chest hair.

Ian craned his neck and kissed her temple. His voice hitched like he was going to say something. Instead, he turned his gaze to the ceiling.

Kate sighed. The time to talk had come, but she wasn't ready.

The longer you wait, the worse it will be.

Her inner voice was a pain in the ass, but it was right. She needed to say something.

With a fortifying breath, she put some distance between them and propped herself on her elbow. "What's bothering you? You've been quiet all week."

Ian twisted onto his side as well, and in the moonlight, she could see the storm clouds behind his eyes. "I'm not sure how to express what I'm feeling."

"Can you try?"

"What we have has never been only about sex. I haven't been this happy with another woman since I was married, and there are times I imagine what it would be like to share a life with you. There's so much I want to give you—a home, a ring, kids, but I can't. As much as I want to have a future with you, it isn't possible." A long pause ensued, and almost a minute passed before he declared, "I think it's best for both of us if we break up."

His words slammed into her with the force of a freight train. He mentioned kids, the one thing he wanted more than anything but couldn't have naturally. She knew there were other options, but nothing was guaranteed.

Being with him meant accepting it might not happen for them. She was willing to gamble on the possibility, but he seemed to have given up.

Tears splashed onto her cheeks, and she turned away. Seeing her cry would make him feel guilty, and the last thing she wanted was for him to comfort her because he felt obligated.

His hand came around her waist, drawing her close. "Kate?"

She drew in a shuddering breath and shook her head. Her heart cracked, releasing a floodgate of anguish as tremors rocked her body.

Since June, she'd lost a fiancé, a good friend, and her job. Then Ian had entered her life, becoming her rock, keeping her grounded as she pieced her life back together. Now he was abandoning her.

"I care about you," he whispered in a tight voice. "I just don't know how we'd work with you all the way out there while I'm here."

"Please don't," she choked, fighting to reign in her emotions. No matter how much he tried to soften the blow, he was tearing out her heart and stomping on it.

He planted a rough kiss on her shoulder. "I'm sorry."

She shoved his hand away and sat up, drawing her knees into her chest. "You can't break up with me and tell me a minute later you care."

"I have very intense feelings for you, but long-distance relationships almost never work. People promise to try all the time, and before they realize it, they've drifted apart. Who's to say you won't meet someone else who turns your head?"

Unbelievable. After everything she'd been through, Ian was afraid she'd leave him for another man?

"I am not some wishy-washy floozy who can't make up my mind," she croaked, half-tempted to smack him for being so damn flaky. She also wanted to kick herself for allowing him to become her whole world. As much as she didn't want to admit it, the fault lied with her too, knowing he never promised anything long-term.

She continued to sob, gulping for air every few seconds in a futile attempt to compose herself.

It wasn't until Ian tried to kiss her that she jolted away, wrapping the sheet around her. She swung her feet over the edge of the bed and launched herself forward, putting as much space between them as she could.

In a daze, she searched for her clothes. Then she remembered they were in the living room, and she rushed through the dark house to find them.

He followed. "Where are you going?"

She couldn't answer. She needed to get dressed and put this

behind her as fast as possible. The longer they prolonged this, the more her heart would ache.

Dropping the sheet, Kate haphazardly stepped into her clothes. Ian did the same, hopping into a set of jeans.

"Kate, look at me."

She shook her head, refusing to look at him as she slipped into her flip-flops. "I can't."

Ian firmly gripped her shoulders and spun her around to face him. "I'm sorry, but I can't do the long-distance thing," he said, regarding her with broken, moisture-filled eyes. "It doesn't work. Plus, I can't have kids. You should be with someone who's closer and can give you a family."

"That's bullshit, and you know it," she shouted. Sucking in a deep breath, she lowered her voice, fighting to keep calm. "We haven't discussed children, but if you'd asked, I would have been willing to try other avenues. Sex isn't the only way to have a family. You're inventing excuses because you're afraid."

He cleared his throat. "Forgive me for being insecure, but I've been through a divorce already. It's easy for you to say you'll stay when you're here and living in the moment. I don't want to wait and see if you'll leave me too."

Kate wanted to scream at him. To shake some sense into him, call him a dumbass. Not that it would do any good. Ian had already made his decision.

"For the last time, I am not her. Also, in case you forgot, Matt cheated on me. I remember how it feels to give my trust and heart to the wrong person. I'm not someone who would leave for the next man because a situation got hard."

She broke free and stumbled through the front door, making a beeline for her vehicle. She couldn't let him say anything else, lest she lose her resolve and start begging.

Once inside her car, she looked toward the house. Ian watched her, making no effort to go after her.

Buckling her seatbelt, she backed out of the driveway, stopping twice when her tears obstructed her vision. When she got home, she ran upstairs and barged into Maddie's room. Her sister mumbled incoherently, and Kate dropped onto the bed, sobbing loudly.

Without a word, Maddie hugged Kate until she fell asleep.

Chapter Twenty-One

The passing of summer and fall dragged. Time should have flown with so much to do, but there were moments between packing and putting together lesson plans for the spring semester where she'd think of Ian.

Their first day apart, she'd cried, replaying everything that had gone wrong. In the end, all she could determine was that Ian had insecurities he needed to move past. She couldn't put her life on hold to be with him when there was no guarantee they'd last.

Still, the initial three weeks after their breakup had been difficult. Every little thing reminded her of him, whether it was a TV show or Spanish rice. Each had her recalling the fun they had together.

She'd fallen fast for Ian, drawn in by his adventurous nature and charm. He was easy to be with, and she never felt like she had to be on guard around him. They shared a multitude of common interests, making him almost ideal boyfriend material. Well, if not for his self-doubt.

The passage of time dulled the heartache of her loss. It also helped that by mid-December, her life had finally calmed as most of her preparations to move were settled. She'd be in her apartment the day after Christmas, leaving Phoenix and everything she knew behind.

Money would be tight, but she'd make it work. Struggle was nothing new to her.

However, thanks to Maddie, Kate had her first month's rent and the security deposit.

At least one good thing about her life nearly going up in flames was that she'd managed to repair her relationship with Maddie. Kate never wanted to lose her sister to jealousy or distance again. She'd miss her and promised herself to stay in touch.

Now it was the Wednesday before Christmas, and she'd finished packing her last boxes. With her things neatly arranged in mini-towers, stacked and labeled by function, all that remained of her things was basic furniture and a small duffle bag with essentials for the next few days.

With a glance at the bare surroundings, her heart swelled at the memories she'd be leaving behind.

She'd become accustomed to the purple walls she and Maddie had painted together, and the blinds she constantly fixed because Dodger would devise new ways to knock them down or break the slats.

This bedroom had been her sanctuary since she came home, and to her surprise she was sad to say goodbye.

She settled onto the bed, where Dodger had hooked his claws on one end of the mattress, sprawled out so his legs stretched to the other end as he snored. He reminded her of a giant, noisy speedbump, and she chuckled at the sight.

Stroking his fur, he stirred, detaching himself from her comforter and snuggling in her lap. When he arched his back and began to purr, Kate wrapped her arms around him.

"So what do you think, buddy? Are you ready to start a new life?"

He didn't acknowledge her except to knead his paws against her legs before plopping down and resting his chin on her thighs.

A soft knock on her door brought her out of her musings. "Come in."

Maddie stepped inside, dressed in polar bear fleece pants and a pink camisole. Her fuzzy socks were striped in shades of mint and white to match her pajama bottoms. "Hey. David and I were wondering if you wanted to join us for game night downstairs."

Kate narrowed her eyes. "What game are we playing?"

"Dirty Minds."

"We already know David will lose," Kate said with a laugh. "Do you have enough energy to handle his rants?"

Maddie breezed across the room and took Kate's hand, dragging her to her feet. Dodger jumped with a yelp and left the room hissing.

Linking their arms, Maddie tugged and guided Kate to the hallway. "That's the fun of it. Besides, David will be laughing at the questions like a ten-year-old. He can't be mad if he's on the floor in hysterics. Besides, if he complains, we can gang up and tickle him."

"David *hates* that."

A wicked gleam flashed through Maddie's eyes, and she smirked. "I know."

Godspeed. "You can do that at your own risk. I know better than to taunt him."

Though he was a man with advanced degrees in medicine, he turned into a big child the moment games were brought out. It never ceased to entertain the sisters, and they teased him mercilessly when given the opportunity.

"Well, that's no fun," Maddie said with a pout.

They walked downstairs, where David was in the living room, setting up a board on the coffee table. Behind him was the Christmas tree, decorated in metallic red and silver garland and cheery lights. The top almost scraped the ceiling, and ornaments they'd crafted as kids hung from the branches. Dozens of brightly colored boxes littered the floor.

Kate's gaze traveled from the tree to David, taking in his snowman pants and socked feet. Folding her arms, she smirked. "Nice pjs."

Her brother glanced up from the game with a grin. "Since you're leaving, Maddie and I thought it would be fun to sleep out here tonight. It'll be just like when we were kids and used to wait for Santa."

They'd set up sleeping bags before placing a glass of milk and cookies for Santa, with Maddie adding carrots for the reindeer. Then they'd play games as they watched feel-good movies, arguing over whether Santa was real.

"You mean when *you* waited for Santa," Kate corrected with a snort. "I never saw the point."

For as long as she could remember, she never believed, much to her siblings' ire. She couldn't wrap her mind around someone who traveled the world on magic reindeer and dropped into chimneys. David and Maddie had no problem clinging to the myth while she'd stuck to science and logic.

"Can you play along this one time?" David asked in an exasperated tone, slapping his palms against his legs. "Where's your Christmas spirit?"

"The Grinch stole it," she deadpanned.

Indicating the game on the table, she asked, "We're not playing in the kitchen? I don't know about you, but my legs will fall asleep if I sit too long."

"Nope," he replied, grabbing, then tossing three couch pillows on the floor. He pursed his lips when his eyes landed on her. "Don't tell me you're not planning to change into your holiday sleep clothes. Maddie was supposed to tell you this is a themed game night."

"I had to make sure she'd come out of her room first," Maddie defended, planting her hands on her hips. "Baby steps. Get Kate downstairs then mention pjs once we have her cornered."

Kate laughed. "You're out of luck. I don't like fleece, so I can't change into something I don't have."

Maddie crossed the room to retrieve a small shopping bag. Then she held it out to Kate. "It's a good thing we anticipated this, because you're wearing 'em."

She took it. Inside were sleep bottoms with Snoopy, Woodstock, and various Christmas items, along with a pair of matching 'Peanuts' socks. The nostalgia transported her to a simpler time when family shows were wholesome and silly.

Since this would be their last time together before she moved and everything changed, she decided to humor them. "All right. Let me get dressed. Don't start without me."

She left to change, and once decked in her holiday finest, she joined her siblings, dropping a purple encased pillow onto the pile. Once their handiwork was complete, Dave and Kate sat in a circle around the table to claim their pieces and deal the cards.

Maddie returned from the kitchen with a bottle of Baileys and three cups. "You can't have game night without drinks."

"What about food?" Kate asked, her stomach rumbling.

"Relax, I have pizza on the way," David replied, stretching his legs under the table. "I ordered extra cheese, just the way you like it, with onion and jalapeño. I also got pepperoni for Maddie and me because unlike you, we're normal and don't like to punish ourselves the next day."

Kate stuck her tongue out. "Don't knock spicy until you try it." She eyed the bottle of Baileys and wrinkled her nose. "Isn't this more of a dessert drink? That won't mix well with pizza."

"This is all I have, and David didn't bring beer," Maddie answered with a shrug.

"Alright, so who goes first?" David asked, changing the subject as he placed a set of dice on the board and drew cards.

Maddie sat and scooped the small cubes into one hand while she took her booklet. "Me, since I own the game. Then it goes clockwise."

She rolled, and her piece landed on a Dirty Minds tile. She turned to Kate. "Okay, you get to read a clue from the book. I get three guesses, first one is free."

"Yeah, yeah," Kate muttered, flipping to the page. She scanned them for a moment before settling on one, barely able to contain the giggle threatening to erupt. Clearing her throat, she read. "I assist an erection."

David cackled and Maddie bit her lip, looking away as pink tinged her cheeks. "Oh lord. Next hint."

"Oh, come on," Kate whined, "the first answer if free anyway. Give it a guess."

The blood soon moved to the rest of Maddie's face until her ears were the color of a lobster. "I can't think of anything that isn't Viagra!"

They weren't even a minute into the game, and David was laughing so hard he had his face buried into a pillow and his shoulders were shaking with the force of an earthquake. Not that she blamed him; hers was beneath the surface, dying to explode.

In a shaking voice, she recited the next clue. "Sometimes big balls hang from me."

"Kate," Dad yelped behind her.

The three of them turned to see him standing in the foyer and watching her with a gaping mouth and wide eyes. David's pillow did little to muffle his hoots, and Maddie's curtain of hair barely concealed her flaming skin. That left Kate, with the booklet still in her hands, fighting to meet Dad's eyes with a straight face.

She coughed, resisting the urge to hide. "I swear the answer is clean."

Dad pinched his nose and closed his eyes. "You know what? I don't want to know. Have fun."

He retreated upstairs, as if he couldn't leave fast enough.

Clutching the answers in her hand, she turned to her brother and sister in indignation. "Oh, my God, why didn't you tell me he was right there?"

"Because it's more fun that way," David replied, wiping away tears. He blew out a sharp breath and pressed his lips together as his shoulders continued to bob. Then he nudged Maddie. "You still have to answer, or lose a card."

Maddie's eyes blazed, and Kate scooted back. She knew that look and braced herself. Her sister's competitive side was coming out, and she was going to annihilate David if she got the chance. "Fine. Just wait 'til I pick a question. I'll make sure you can't answer it."

"Now, now, children," Kate chided in her best teacher voice. "Don't make me separate you two. Maddie, pass or play?"

Maddie sighed. "Uh... is it something to do with architecture?"

Kate glanced at the answer before holding the booklet to her chest. "Can you be more specific?"

"Ugh, this game is so stupid. Is it an architect?"

"How is it stupid? It's *your* game." David demanded, dodging when Maddie tried to flick his nose.

"No," Kate cut in. "Put back a card."

Maddie slipped a card under the deck and huffed. "Okay, last hint."

"I'm called a big swinger."

Her eyes lit up and her arms flapped like a panicked bird as she bounced in place. "Oh! It's uh, one of those wrecking ball thingies! A crane!"

They played several more rounds, giggling between questions and pausing long enough to grab the pizza when it arrived. When they'd finished, Maddie won while David finished last and glowered.

Kate watched them pull faces at each other, amused by their rivalry while also appreciating the distraction. They helped to take her mind off her uncertain future.

She was happy with the job waiting for her but couldn't help dreading being all alone. She'd visit often, but it wouldn't be the same as living in Phoenix, where she could see her family all the time.

Her thoughts drifted to Ian. No matter how much she tried to push him out of her mind, she missed him and wished they could have spent the holidays together.

What would her Christmas have been like if they were still together? Would he have met her family by now?

Burying her melancholy thoughts, she returned her attention to her siblings. It was best not to dwell on what-ifs.

"Wanna play again?" Maddie asked.

David fixed her with a pointed glare and dropped his cards to the table. "No."

"Let's watch a movie instead," Kate suggested, climbing to her feet. She crossed the room to where the old DVDs were kept and thumbed through the selection. The Christmas movies were all in the back, arranged in alphabetical order. She ticked off the titles aloud, "Okay, we can watch *A Charlie Brown Christmas*, *It's a Wonderful Life*, *Rudolph*, or *The Santa Clause*."

"Definitely *The Santa Clause*. I love Tim Allen," David answered.

"I'm down for that." Maddie put the game away, then tossed out an empty pizza box. When she returned, she twisted the cap on the Baileys bottle and poured the flavored liquid into each cup. She passed them out, then took her seat again.

Raising to toast, she said, "Here's to Christmas."

"And new beginnings," Kate added.

"To the best siblings anyone could ask for." David clinked his drink against theirs.

"Cheers."

They sipped before turning off the lights and settling onto the couch together as the movie credits began. Maddie and David each claimed a corner while Kate sat between them.

A few minutes into the movie, Maddie rested her head on Kate's shoulder. "I'm going to miss you when you leave."

Kate slid her arm around her sister's waist in a side hug. "It's only two and a half hours away. I'll make sure I visit on holiday."

"It's not the same," she said in a sad voice. "Do you want me to stay with you in Flagstaff?"

Gratitude filled Kate's chest, and she broke away, overwhelmed by Maddie's offer. She took her sister's hand and squeezed. "Didn't you say you wanted to move to Europe?"

She shrugged. "I do, but I want to make sure you get on your feet first. I can go later."

God, that was sweet. Maddie had such a great capacity for love, so much that it was enough to melt the chilliest heart.

"Thanks, but you belong here," Kate replied, stroking her sister's hair.

Maddie had only ever known the comfort of her childhood home. Kate's one-bedroom apartment wasn't much bigger than a matchbox. She didn't want to take her sister away from her luxuries.

David flopped onto his sisters, squashing them beneath his large frame. "Hey, I want to be part of this sibling love-fest."

"Get off!" Kate squealed, pressed into Maddie's bony shoulder.

He offered her a smirk but shifted so the women could breathe again. "Couldn't let you go without being a little obnoxious."

"Well, your obnoxious self can sit in that corner." Kate pointed to the other end, where David scooted. Then she settled on the middle cushion, giving Maddie space to breathe.

As the movie progressed, they giggled at Tim Allen's antics.

Draining the rest of his drink, David smacked his lips and set the cup down. Then he nudged Kate. She turned to face him, and he took one of her hands in his. Ignoring the TV, he said. "I know this isn't the best timing, but I want to ask before you leave. Are you doing okay?"

She folded her arms and stared at her lap, considering her words. She hadn't talked about the breakup, except for when she spilled everything to Maddie right after it happened.

At first, she'd been in a state of constant tears, but with a few months gone and more time to think about her breakup with Ian, she'd describe herself as disappointed more than broken. It still hurt and she wished things could have turned out differently, but she was no longer a mess. Even as a small part of her held out hope he'd change his mind.

With a sigh, she met David's eyes and offered him half a smile. "I'll be fine. I can't say I didn't hope Ian and I would go somewhere with our relationship, but I've accepted it. It was my fault for expecting too much, and it's for the best if he can't move past his insecurities."

David hugged her without crushing her this time and patted her back. "It's his loss." He released her and crossed his legs, bumping his knee against hers. "You're a great person, and I know you'll find someone when the time is right. Any man would be lucky to have you."

Kate snorted. "Well, that's not inclusive. What if I wanted a woman?"

His eyes widened, and his cheeks flushed red. Clearing his throat, he stammered, "I mean, if you want to swing the other way, that's cool. I'm just saying you're a great person. Don't make it weird."

"Who's making it weird? I think it's important to not assume, no matter how well you think you know someone. Not just with me, but with anyone."

He shifted and cleared his throat. "Okay, fine. Love is love, okay? Will you just take my compliment already?"

She grinned and patted him on the shoulder. "Thank you."

"Have you talked to Ian since you two split?" Maddie asked, redirecting them back to the original subject.

"No, unless you count the awkward hello when he brought my stuff back. I didn't see the point in rehashing anything if we're still going in separate directions."

She patted Kate's knee. "I'm sorry."

"Not your fault," Kate mumbled, suddenly not in the mood to continue watching their movie. When she rose, she grabbed her pillow. "I think I'm going to go to bed. I had fun though."

"Wait." Maddie snatched Kate's hand and clung to it as if it were a lifeline. "We have something for you."

"It can't wait until Christmas?"

David jumped to his feet and turned on the overhead light. Then he walked to the tree, saying, "This is something Maddie and I wanted to give you tonight, when it's just the three of us." He returned to the couch and sat, handing Kate a small box. "Open it."

Kate took the brightly wrapped gift and traced the delicate blue ribbon. Untying it, she let the fabric fall as she tore off the paper. Then she lifted the lid to find a heart-shaped pendant on a silver chain, with three small gemstones in the middle—amethyst, diamond, and emerald. The stones shimmered in the light, creating a kaleidoscope of rainbow hues. The quality was perfect.

"It's beautiful," Kate whispered, tracing the metal jewelry mounts. Love filled her chest. "Are they our birthstones?"

"Yep," Maddie chirped, beaming. "Amethyst for you, diamond for David, and emerald for me. Even though you'll be in Flagstaff, we wanted you to feel close to us."

"And you love rocks," David added.

Kate laughed as she unfastened the chain and donned the necklace. "These are gemstones, you goof, not rocks."

"Same field of study," he defended. "The point is that it's a combination of your passion with a personal touch from the people who love you most. No matter how far apart we are, we're family, and if you need anything, Maddie and I will be there."

Moisture welled in Kate's eyes as she beamed at them. The gift was so thoughtful, and her heart expanded until she thought it might burst.

"You guys are the best." Kate sniffled. "If you keep this up, I won't want to leave."

"Nonsense," David said. "You have a bright future ahead of you. Now it's up to you to seize it with both hands and enjoy your life. All I ask is that you call once in a while."

"I will," she promised.

Yes, her summer had been rough, and despite hitting an all-time low, her prospects and outlook never seemed brighter.

Chapter Twenty-Two

Five Months Later

Finished with her last class of her first semester, Kate walked into her office.

Someone had shoved her folders, papers, and rocks to the side of her desk to make room for an arrangement of premium roses. Sitting next to them and grinning was her friend, Doctor LaShonda Gipson.

Kate returned a distracted smile, eyeing the flowers. "This had better not be another attempt to set me up."

"I was about to ask who they were from," LaShonda answered with a pout. She hopped down and adjusted her skirt. "You haven't been seeing someone and not telling me, have you?"

"Yeah, right." Kate laughed, gathering a stack of papers precariously teetering atop one of the makeshift piles, and placing them on her keyboard. Whoever made the effort to woo her was wasting their time. "You know I'm not interested."

About a month into their friendship, LaShonda tried to set her up with a friend. He'd brought a bouquet of daisies, paid for the meal, and taken her for a romantic walk beneath the stars. The evening had been nice, but her heart wasn't into it. He wasn't Ian, and she didn't want to lead the poor guy on.

So, she'd thanked him for his time before heading to her apartment and collapsing on the sofa, mentally and emotionally exhausted. In some ways, she was past nursing her wounds. She didn't cry anymore, but she couldn't flip off her lingering emotions like a switch.

"I know Ian broke your heart, but it couldn't hurt to test the waters again. It's been what, eight months?" her friend pressed.

"Nine," Kate corrected, then sighed. Sooner or later, she'd have to move on, but she wasn't ready to go down that rabbit hole.

If not for LaShonda's warm welcome, the transition from

Phoenix to Flagstaff would have been unbearable. Kate hadn't known anyone, nor did she make an effort to meet people. If it had been up to her, she'd have stayed home in her pajamas, living as a hermit. Instead, they went out together or stayed in, enjoying wine, ice cream, and any horrible disaster movie they could get their hands on, always having a great time.

"Did you want to go out tonight? I think some of the girls are going for drinks," Kate said, wanting to change the subject and pretend the flowers weren't invading her space.

LaShonda waggled her finger and scowled. "Ah-ah-ah. I want to know who these are from."

Kate shook her head and examined the roses. There were so many, she almost had enough to open a small flower shop. The petals were crisp as if the stems had been freshly cut, and a strong floral scent permeated the air. The bouquets must have cost a small fortune.

"Is there a card?" Kate asked.

LaShonda motioned at a slim, square package on the desk, wedged between the flowers. Taking it, she handed it to Kate. "No, but this was delivered thirty minutes ago with the flowers. I've been dying to see what's inside and who it's from."

Kate rolled her eyes, thinking of tossing the flowers from her secret admirer into the trash. "Does it matter? As sweet as the gesture is, I'm not up for any emotional attachments."

LaShonda huffed in exasperation. "Oh my god, would you open the gift already?"

Curious, Kate carefully unwrapped the paper, her lips curved into an amused smirk at the toy parachute attached. Inside was a vinyl of *The Cars*. She laughed as her heart soared.

She clutched the record to her chest briefly before setting it between the flowers and the wall.

Gripping LaShonda by the shoulders, she demanded, "Did you see who delivered these?"

"No, I came in here to ask if you wanted to go out and found them on your desk. Do you know who it is from?"

"Me," a soft tenor voice said from behind them.

Kate whirled around with a gasp. Ian stood in the doorway, dressed in dark pants and a deep blue button-up shirt with his sleeves folded and the top button undone.

He appeared the same as the night she'd met him almost a year ago. His dark hair was freshly cut, and a day's worth of stubble speckled his jaw.

Kate ran into his embrace, throwing her arms around his neck.

LaShonda cleared her throat. Kate reluctantly broke away.

Ian reached around and extended his hand. "Sorry. I'm Doctor Anderson."

"As in Ian Anderson, the man who broke Kate's heart?"

Heat scorched Kate's face. "LaShonda!"

Watching him with pinched lips and a single raised eyebrow, she said, "Don't even think about hurting her. She's been through enough."

Kate scrubbed her face and groaned. Then she mumbled, "It's fine, LaShonda. Please go."

Her friend uttered a soft 'harumph' and strode toward the exit, pausing at the threshold. "All right. I'll leave you two alone, but I expect details later."

"Some details are for the bedroom's eyes only," Ian muttered, closing the door as LaShonda disappeared into the hallway. Then he drew Kate into a slow, seductive kiss.

She couldn't believe what was happening. Her head spun with elation, and her heart thumped faster than a rabbit on steroids.

Please don't let me be dreaming. When she arrived in Flagstaff, she'd accepted never seeing Ian again. After all this time, his presence didn't seem real.

Ian brushed her cheekbones with the tips of his thumbs. "Can you forgive me?"

She cleared her throat, swallowing several times before she could answer. "What changed? You were convinced we couldn't make things work."

"I was stupid," he confessed, dipping his chin to his chest. "I was insecure and terrified our feelings would dissolve over time, and I thought if I ended it, I could walk away and move on."

He watched her with wide, glossy eyes and scratched the back of his neck. "No matter what I did to take my mind away from you, I couldn't stop thinking about you. I screwed everything up. I don't deserve it, but I'm asking for another chance anyway. I love you."

She bit her lip, afraid to echo the sentiment and hope for too much. And though he'd hurt her, she understood why he chose to end things. He was here now, and that was what mattered.

"You love me?" she echoed.

He pressed his forehead against hers and cupped her cheek. "I do," he whispered. "I'm so sorry."

She swallowed, taking several shallow breaths. Then she took a step back and bobbed her head in a jerky nod. "I love you too." Taking the record from the desk, she held it up. "You remembered my favorite band."

"I hoped it would get your attention. You deserve an apology along with your comfort music." His hands settled around her waist. "Is it too much to start over and ask for an exclusive relationship? It's a lot to ask, but I've never been more sure of anything in my life." He paused, then added, "I understand if you don't want to though."

She rewarded him with a sound kiss. "I'd like that," she murmured against his mouth."

"I can't guarantee children. You know this."

"I don't care," she assured him. "All I need is you." Then she paused, remembering one of his reasons for breaking up with her. "What about the distance? You were convinced it wouldn't work, and I'm contracted to teach for another semester."

"I sold my practice," he said with a broad smile. "I finalized it a month ago so I could be closer to you."

"That was a big leap of faith," she teased. "What if I'd said no?"

His eyes sparkled. "But you didn't."

Returning to his embrace, she inhaled his sandalwood cologne. "Okay, you got me, but you have to promise me something."

"Anything."

"No matter what we do together, our lives stay off social media."

He pressed his forehead to hers and rubbed their noses together in an Eskimo kiss. "That I can promise."

Acknowledgements

First and foremost, I'd like to thank everyone who believed in my dream, even when I didn't. I wouldn't be where I am without your encouragement to continue and keep writing.

My uncle was my biggest cheerleader while he was alive, always optimistic in my skills. I am deeply saddened that he will never see this published, but I know wherever he is, he's cheering me on from the sidelines.

Stephanie, I wouldn't be here without you. You've put in so many hours of feedback and critiques, and it is my greatest dream to see you published as well. Your thoughts and kind words have meant everything to me, and I couldn't ask for a better best friend.

Finally, thank you to everyone who has read this story and loved it. Without your love and support, I'd be dreaming instead of doing.

Love always,

Kristi

About the Author

Kristi Elliot is an American author born in Germany to U. S. Air Force parents and spent her childhood all over the country. After serving eight years in the U. S. Army Reserve, she actively pursued her lifelong interest in writing—incorporating life experience into her work while telling stories about topics close to her heart, particularly social anxiety, autism, and PTSD.

A romance writer at her core, Kristi writes across several genres while seasoning her tales with the belief that love comes in many varieties across each wake of life. Kristi resides in Phoenix with her husband, two kids, and an energetic ferret.

Kristi loves to hear from her readers. You can find and connect with her at the links below.

Website/Blog: https://kristielliot.wixsite.com/mysite
Facebook: https://www.facebook.com/kristi.elliot.71
Instagram: https://www.instagram.com/kaiddance/
Pinterest: https://www.pinterest.com/kaiddance/
Twitter: https://twitter.com/kaiddance

~ * ~

Thank you for taking the time to read *The Social Media Bride*. We hope you enjoyed this as much as we did. If you did, please tell your friends, and leave a review. Reviews support authors and ensure they continue to bring readers books to love and enjoy.

Turn the page for a peek inside *Some Assembly Required*, where Ro Andrews, an overworked, undersexed, exasperated single mom, learns whether she can find love with Sam, a man allergic to chaos and crumbs, and make it stick, not sticky.

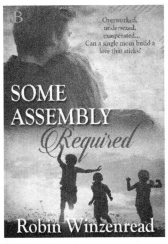

When new divorcee Ro Andrews moves her pack of semi-feral children to a run-down farmhouse, helping her brother restore the moldering homestead and living an authentic life—per the dictates of Instagram and lifestyle blogs everywhere—tops her to-do list. But romance? Hell, no. Between hiding from her children in baskets of dirty laundry, mentally eviscerating her cheating ex, and finding a job, Ro has a full plate.

Until she meets Sam Whittaker, a hunky Texas transplant with abs of steel and a nameplate that reads Boss. Clad in cowboy boots and surfer curls, this child-free stud has Ro on edge—and rethinking her defective Y chromosome ban. Somehow, this overworked, undersexed, exasperated single mom needs to find time to fall in love with a man allergic to chaos and crumbs and make it stick, not sticky.

CHAPTER ONE

As my young son's cries echo through this diner, I'm reminded again why some animals eat their young.

It's because they want to.

"Hey, Mom! Nick farted, and he didn't say excuse me!"

Normally when Aaron, my spunky six-year-old, announces something so crudely, we're at home, and his booming voice is muted by the artfully arranged basket of dirty laundry I've shoved my head into in hopes of hiding like an ostrich from a tiny, tenacious predator.

This time, however, Aaron yells it in the middle of a crowded diner in the small, stranger-adverse, southern Illinois town we're about to call home and, frankly, we don't need any more attention. Thanks to my semi-feral pack of three lippy offspring, we've already lit this place on fire, and not in a good way.

Despite our involuntary efforts to unhinge the locals with our strangers-in-a-strange-land antics, this dumpy, dingy diner, minus its frosty clientele, has a real comfortable feel, not unlike the ratty, stretched-out yoga pants I love but no longer wear because a) they don't fit any more and b) I burned them—along with a voodoo doll I crafted of my ex-husband (see my Pinterest board for patterns), after I forced it to have sex with my son's GI Joe action figure (see downward-facing dog for position).

Crap. I should have put the pictures on Instagram. Wait, I think they're still on my phone.

"Mom!" Aaron bellows again.

Right now, I'd kill for a pile of sweaty socks to dive into, but there's nary a basket of tighty-whities in sight, and that kid loves an audience, even a primarily rural, all-white-bread, mouth-gaping, wary one.

Frowning, I point at his chair. "Sit."

More than a bit self-conscious, I scan the room, hoping for signs of defrost from the gawking audience and pray my attempt to sound parental falls on nearby ears, earning me scant mom points. Of course, a giant burp which may have contained three of the six vowel sounds just erupted from my faux angelic four-year-old daughter, Madison, so I'll kiss that goodwill goodbye. I hand her a napkin and execute my go-to look, a serious I-mean-it-this-time scowl. "Maddy, say excuse me."

"Excuse me."

belch

Good lord, I'm doomed.

"Listen to me, Mom. Nick farted."

I fork my chef salad with ranch dressing on the side and raise an eyebrow at my youngest son. "Knock it off, kiddo."

"You said when we fart, we have to say excuse me, and he didn't." Finally, Aaron sits, unaware I've been stealing his fries, also on the side.

Kids, so clueless.

Nick, my angelic eight-year-old, is hot on his brother's heels and equally loud, "We don't have to say it when we're on the toilet. You can fart on the toilet and not say excuse me. It's allowed. Ask Mom."

Aaron picks up a water glass and holds it to his mouth. "It sounded like a raptor." He blows across the top, filling the air with a wet, revolting sound, once again alarming the nearby locals. "See?" He laughs. "Just like a raptor."

I point at his plate and scrutinize the last of his hamburger. "Thank you for that lovely demonstration, now finish your lunch."

Naturally, as we discuss fart etiquette, the locals are still gawking, and I can't blame them. We're strangers in a county where I'm betting everyone knows each other somehow and, here's the real shocker, we're not merely passing through. We're staying. On purpose.

We're not alone, either. My brother, Justin, his wife, Olivia, and their bubbly toddler twins kickstarted this adventure—moving to the sticks—so we're eight in total. Admittedly, this all sounded better a month ago when we adults hashed it out over too much wine and a little bit of vodka. Okay, maybe a lot of vodka. Back then, Justin had been headhunted for a construction manager job here in town, and I was in a post-divorce, downward-spiral bind, so they invited the kiddies and me to join them.

For me, I hope it's temporary until I can get settled somewhere, as in land a job, land a purpose, land a life. When they offered, I immediately saw the appeal—the more distance between me and the ex and his younger, sluttier girlfriend the better—and I decided to move south too.

Now I can't back out. I've already sold my house which buys me time, but I've got nowhere else to go. Where would I land? I've got three kids and limited skills. Plus, I don't even have a career to use as an excuse to change my mind or to even point me in another direction.

In other words, I'm stuck. Whether I want to or not, I'm relocating to a run-down farmhouse in the middle of nowhere Illinois to help Justin and Olivia with their grandiose plans of fixing it up and living "authentic" lives since, according to Instagram, Pinterest, and lifestyle blogs everywhere, manicured suburbs with cookie-cutter houses, working utilities and paved sidewalks don't count. Unless you're stinking rich, which, unfortunately, we, most definitely, are not.

Let's see, Justin has a new career opportunity, Olivia is going to restore, repaint, repurpose, and blog her way to a book deal, and me…and me…

Nope. I got nothing. No plans, no dreams, no job, nada. Here I am, the not-so-proud owner of a cheap polyester wardrobe with three kids rapidly outgrowing their own. I better come up with something, and quick.

Where's cheesecake when you need it? I stab a cherry tomato, pluck it from my fork, and chew. The world is full of people living their dreams, while mine consists of an unbroken night's sleep and a day without something gooey in my shoes. I take aim at a cucumber slice, pop it in my mouth, and pretend it's a donut. At least I don't have to wash these dishes.

Across from me, Olivia, my sometimes-vegan sister-in-law is unaware I'm questioning my life's purpose while she questions her lunch choice. Unsatisfied, she drops her mushroom melt onto her plate and frowns. I knew it wouldn't pass inspection. She may have lowered her standards to marry my brother, but she'd never do so for food. This is why she and I get along so well.

Olivia rocks back in her chair and smacks her lips, dissatisfied. "There's no way this was cooked on a meat-free grill. I swear I can taste bacon. Maybe sausage too." Her tongue swirls around in her mouth, searching for more hints of offending pork. "Definitely sausage."

Frankly, I enjoy finding pork in my mouth. Then again, I have food issues. Though, if I liked munching tube steak more often, perhaps my ex wouldn't have wandered. The bastard.

Justin watches his wife's tongue roll around, and I don't blame him. She's beautiful—dark, luminous eyes, full lips flushed a natural pink glow, cascading dark curls, radiant brown skin, a toned physique despite two-year-old twins. She's everything I am not.

She tells me I'm cute. Of course, the Pillsbury Dough Boy is cute too. Screw that. I want to be hot.

Regardless, I expect something crude to erupt from my brother's mouth as he stares at his lovely bride, so I'm pleasantly surprised when it doesn't. Instead, he shakes his head and works on his stack of onion rings. "What do you expect when you order off menu in a place like this, babe? Be glad they had portobellos."

Across from me, she frowns. Model tall and fashionably lean, she's casually elegant in a turquoise and brown print maxi dress, glittery dangle earrings, silky black curls, and daring red kitten heels that hug her slender feet. How does she do it? She exudes an easy glamour even as she peels a corner of toasted bun away from her sandwich, revealing a congealed mass of something.

"This isn't a portobello. It's a light dove gray, not a soft, deep, charcoal gray. I'm telling you this is a bad sandwich. I'm not eating it." She extracts her fingers from the offending fungus and crosses her bangle bracelet encased arms.

Foodies. Go figure. No Instagram picture for you, sandwich from hell.

Fortunately their twins, Jaylen and Jayden, adorable in matching Swedish-inspired sweater dress ensembles and print tights, are less picky. Clearly, it comes from my chunky side of the family. They may be dressed to impress, but the ketchup slathered over their precious toddler faces says, "We have Auntie Ro's DNA in us somewhere."

I love that.

Justin cuts up the last half of a cold chicken strip and shares it with his daughters, who are constrained by plastic highchairs—which I can't do with my kids any more, darn the luck—and, in addition to having no idea how to imitate raptors with half-empty water glasses like my boys or identify mushrooms by basis of color like their mother, they are still quite cute.

Love them as I do, my boys haven't been cute for a while. Such a long while. Maddy, well, she's cute on a day-to-day basis. Yet, they are my world. My phlegm covered, obnoxious, arguing world.

Justin wipes Jaylen's cheek and checks his phone. "We need to get the bill. It's getting late."

I survey the room, hunting for our waitress. Despite the near constant stranger stares, this place intrigues me. It feels a hundred years old in a good, cozy way. The diner's creaky, wood floor is well worn and the walls are exposed brick, which is quaint in restaurants even if it detracts from the value in Midwestern homes, including the giant moldering one Justin and Olivia bought northeast of town. Old tin advertising posters depict blue ribbon vegetables and old-time tractors in shades of red and green and yellow on the walls, and they may be the real antique deal.

They're really into primary colors, these farm folks. Perhaps the best way to spice up a quiet life is to sprinkle it with something bright and shiny. As for me, I've been living in dull shades of beige for at least half a marriage now, if not longer. Should I try bright and shiny? Couldn't hurt.

Red-pleather booths line the wall of windows to the left, and a row of tables divides the room, including the two tables we've shoved together which my children have destroyed with crumbs, blobs of ketchup, and snot. Of course, the twins helped too, but they're toddlers so you can't point a finger at them especially since all the customers are too busy pointing fingers at mine.

Bar stools belly up to a Formica counter to the right, and it's all very old school and quaint, although I would hate to have to clean the place, partly because Maddy sneezed, and her mouth was open and full of fries.

Kids. So gross.

Three portly gentlemen in caps, flannel, and overalls overflow from the booth closest to our table and, clearly, they're regulars. They're polishing off burgers and chips, though no one is sneezing with his mouth open, most likely because his teeth will fly out in the process. I imagine the pleather booths are permanently imprinted with the marks of old asses from a decade's worth of lunches. Sometimes it's good to make an impression. The one we're currently making, however? Probably not.

Nearly every table, booth, and stool are taken. Must be a popular place. Or it may be the only place in this itty, bitty town. It's the type of place where everyone knows your name, meaning they all stared the minute we walked in because they don't know ours, it's a brisk Tuesday in early November, and we sure aren't local.

Yet.

Several men of various ages in blue jeans and farm hats sit in a row upon the counter stools, munching their lunches. A smattering of conversations on hog feed, soybean yields, and tractor parts fills the air. They all talk at once, the way guys tend to do, with none of them listening except to the sound of his own voice, the way guys also tend to do, like stray dogs in a pound when strangers check them out and they're hoping to impress.

Except for one of them, the one I noticed the minute we walked in and have kept tabs on ever since. Unlike the others, this man is quiet and, better yet, he doesn't have the typical middle-aged, dad-bod build. While most of the other men are stocky and round, square and cubed, pear shaped and apple dumpling-esque, like bad geometry gone rogue, he isn't. He's tall with a rather broad triangular back and, given the way it's stretching the confines of his faded, dark red, button-down shirt, it's a well-muscled isosceles triangle at that. Brown cowboy boots with a Texas flag burned on the side of the wooden heel peek from beneath seasoned blue jeans, and those jeans cling to a pair of muscular thighs that could squeeze apples for juice.

God, I have a hankering for hot cider. With a great big, thick, rock-hard cinnamon stick swirling around too. Hmmm, spicy.

This Midwestern cowboy's dark-brown hair is thick with a slight wave that would go a tad bit wild if he let it, and he needs to let it. Who doesn't love surfer curls, and his are perfect. They're the kind I could run my fingers through forever or hang onto hard in the sack, if need be. Trust me, there's a need be.

His body is lean, yet strong, and beneath his rolled-up sleeves, there's a swell of ample biceps and the sinewy lines of strong, tan forearms. It's a tan I'm betting goes a lot further than his elbows. His face is sun-kissed too, and well-defined with high cheekbones and a sturdy chin. A hint of fine lines fan out from the corners of his chocolate-brown eyes and, while not many, there're enough to catch any drool should my lips happen to ravage his face.

Facial lines on guys are so damn sexy. They hint at wisdom, experience, strength. Lines on women should be sexy too, even the stretchy white, hip-dwelling ones from multiple, boob-sucking babies, but men don't think that way, which is why I only objectify them these days. Since getting literally screwed over by my ex, I'm the permanent mascot for Team Anti-Relationship. I blame those defective Y chromosomes myself. Stupid Y chromosomes.

Regardless, it's difficult not to watch as this well-built triangle of a man wipes his mouth with a napkin. I wouldn't mind being that white crumpled paper in that strong tan hand, even if I, too, end up spent on the counter afterward. At any rate, he stands, claps the guy to his left on the back, and I may have peed myself.

The sexy boot-clad stranger pulls cash from his wallet and sets it on the lucky napkin. "I've got to get back to the elevator, Phil. Busy day."

Sweet, a Texas accent. How very Matthew McConaughey. Mama like.

A pear-shaped man next to him raises his glass. "See ya, Sam. You headed to George's this afternoon?"

"I hope so. I need to get with Edmund first, plus we have a couple of trailers coming in, and I've got to do a moisture check on at least two of them." His voice is low, but soft, the way you hope a new vibrator will sound, but never does until the batteries die which defeats the purpose, proving once again irony can be cruel.

And what the hell is a moisture check?

I zero in on the open button of his shirt, drawn to his chest like flies to honey, because that's what I do now that I'm divorced and have no husband and no purpose—I ogle strange men for the raw meat they are. Nothing's going to happen anyway. Truth be told, I haven't dated in an eternity and have no real plans to start, partly because I've forgotten how; just another unfortunate aspect of my life on permanent hold. I've been invited to the singles' buffet, but I'm too afraid to grab a plate. At this point in my recently wrecked, random life, I would rather vomit. Hell, I barely smell the entrees. I'm only interested in licking a hunk of two-legged meatloaf for the sauce anyway. There's no harm in that, right?

Where was I? Right, his chest, and it's a good chest, with the "oood" dragged out like a child's Benadryl-laced nap on a hot afternoon. It's that goood.

Of course, as I mentally drag out the "oood," my lips involuntarily form the word in the air imitating a goldfish in a bowl. While I ogle this particular cut of prime rib, I realize he's noticed my stare not to mention my "oood" inspired fish lips, which is not an attractive look, despite what selfie-addicted college girls think. Our eyes lock. An avalanche of goosebumps crawls its way up my back and down my arms and, I swear, I vibrate. Not like one of those little lipstick vibrators that can go off in your purse at the airport, thank you very much, but something more substantial with a silly name like Rabbit or Butterfly or Bone Master.

That, my friends, is the closest I've come to real sex in two and half years. Excuse me, but we need a moisture check at table two, please. Not to mention a mop. Okay...definitely a mop.

For a moment, we hold our stare—me with my fish lips frozen into place, vibrating silently in my long-sleeved, heather green T-shirt and jeans, surrounded by my small tribe of ketchup-covered children, and him all hot, tan, buff, and beefy, staring at us the way one gawks at a bloody, ten-car pile-up. All too soon, he blinks, the deer-in-the-headlights look fades, and he drops his gaze.

C'mon, stud, look again. I'm not wearing a push-up bra for nothing.

Big, dark, brown eyes pop up again and find mine. All too soon, they flit away to the floor.

Score.

Damn, he's fine. Someone smoke me a cigarette, I'm spent.

I scan the table, imagining my children are radiating cuteness. No dice. Aaron imitates walrus tusks with the last of his French-fries, Nick is trying to de-fang him with a straw full of root beer, and Maddy's two-knuckles deep into a nostril. And I'm sitting next to Justin.

Figures. My big, burly, ginger-headed, lug of a wedding-ring-wearing brother is beside me. Does this hunk of burning stud think he's my husband? Should I pick my own nose with my naked, ring-less finger? Invest in a face tattoo that reads "divorced and horny?" Why do I even care? He's only man meat. After all, was he really even looking at me? Or Olivia? Sexy, sultry, damn-sure-married-to-my-brother Olivia? I whip back to the stud prepared to blink "I'm easy" in Morse code.

blink *blink* *bliiiink*

With a spin on his star-studded boots, Hotty McHot heads toward the hallway at the back of the diner, oblivious that my gaze is rivetted to his ass and equally clueless to the fact that I have questions needing immediate answers, not to mention an overwhelming need to scream, "I'm single and put out, no strings attached" in his general direction.

Olivia pulls me back to reality with her own questions. "I mean, is it that difficult to scrape the grill before you cook someone's meal?"

She's still honked off about her sandwich, unaware I'm over here having mental sex with the hunky cowboy while sending my kids off to a good boarding school for the better part of the winter.

"I didn't have many options here," she rattles on, "even their salads have meat and egg in them. Instead of a writing a book, I should open a vegan restaurant. I was going to give them a good review for the ambiance, but not now. Wait until I post this on Yelp."

Eyeballing the room, Justin polishes off the last of his double-cheese burger. "Sweetie, we're moving to the land of pork and beef. Vegan won't fly here, and I doubt the help cares about Yelp. Did you notice our waitress? She's got a flip phone. Time to put away your inner princess and stick with the book idea."

Long fingers with bronze gel manicured nails rat-a-tat-tat on the tabletop. She locks onto him with dark, intelligent, laser-beam eyes. "Would it kill you to be supportive, honey bunch? You might as well say, uck-fay u-vay."

Apparently channeling some weird, inner death wish, Justin picks up an onion ring, takes a bite, then pulls a string of overcooked translucent slime free from its breaded coating. He snaps it free with his teeth, then offers it to her. "Your book is going to be great, babe, and it will appeal to a larger audience than here. Remember the goal, Liv. As for me, I'm trying to keep you humble. No one likes high maintenance."

The limp, greasy onion hangs in the air. She ignores it, but not him. "Okay, this time, sweetie, I'll say it. Uck-fay u-vay with an ig-bay ick-day."

Jaylen looks up from her highchair and munches a chicken strip. "Uck-fay?" she repeats through fried poultry. "Ick-day?"

Behind her an older woman, also fluent in pig Latin, does a coffee-laced spit-take in her window booth. I hope she's not a new neighbor.

Justin chuckles and polishes off the offending string of onion. Olivia stews. Time to implement an offense. Clearly, we need an exit strategy.

Out Now!

What's next on your reading list?

Champagne Book Group promises to bring to readers fiction at its finest.

Discover your next
fine read!
http://www.champagnebooks.com/

~~~

We are delighted to invite you to receive exclusive rewards. Join our Facebook group for VIP savings, bonus content, early access to new ideas we've cooked up, learn about special events for our readers, and sneak peeks at our fabulous titles.

https://www.facebook.com/groups/ChampagneBookClub/
Join now.

Printed in Great Britain
by Amazon

78338152R00119